THE HEART TEACHES BEST

M.J. Schiller

PROLOGUE

The call had come in the night before—murder at Phat Jack's, the newest club in downtown L.A. When Cooper got there, several squad cars already occupied the parking lot, slanted haphazardly across the entrance. Their lights cast blasts of colors onto the surrounding buildings, reminding him of the laser lights bouncing around the dance floor inside. He scooted under the yellow tape, flashing his badge at the uniforms who were trying to keep the curious onlookers back. The body of Sydney Essex, the famous author, had been found on the pavement next to her car, her deep blue eyes wide and unseeing, ligature marks prominent on her slender neck, head tipped at an odd angle.

Cooper was getting the details from the first to arrive on the scene when the blonde broke through the crowd, ducking under the tape and running, screaming, toward the car. Two uniforms caught her up by the waist, though she struggled against them, hysterically calling out, "Syd. Syd! Oh, my God! No. No!" She collapsed in their arms, a puddle of tears melting onto them as they stood, emotionless, not allowing themselves to be affected by her pain as they had been trained to do.

"Who's that?" he asked.

"Must be the sister," the officer he was talking to responded, shrugging. "Looks like the vic."

Cooper tuned out the rest of the conversation as he looked at the crumpled form of the crying girl on the sidewalk. They hadn't reached the next of kin yet, so how did she know to come to Phat Jack's? Then it dawned on him, she must have been meeting her sister here. So she was looking forward to drinks with her sister one minute, viewing her broken body the next. He knew they were supposed to distance themselves from the victims, but during times like these, it was nearly impossible.

CHAPTER ONE

Cooper Sullivan nursed his scotch, letting his eyes roam over the crowded bar. He didn't know what he was doing there, but he always found himself returning to the scene of the crime.

He found it helpful to immerse himself in the environment. He wanted to figure out the players and the playing field. From what he could tell so far, the new club was about the most pretentious place he'd ever been in. Definite haven for the young and rich. He stuck out like a sore thumb; his suit was not as pressed, his shoes not as expensive or polished, even his posture was too loose. He felt completely out of place, and glad of it.

He swiveled on his stool and admired the bar set up. At least that was interesting. Multicolored bottles of every alcohol known to man were sitting on a glowing, translucent polymer shelving, backlit against the mirrored wall which ran the length of the deep, dark mahogany bar, giving the place a sort of sci-fi feel. A black leather bumper covered the edges of the bar, complimented by a white tube of lighting, adding another futuristic touch. The bartenders wore black tuxedo vests, males with tight, short-sleeved shirts, females with no shirts at all, red bow ties around their necks, giving them an elegance that allowed them free reign to overcharge their customers.

As he soaked everything in, Cooper's eyes landed on the reflection of a young woman in the mirror. Her long, straight, blond hair was twisted up in a clip, and she wore an elegant, short black dress which v-ed down temptingly across her chest. On her right shoulder hung a black evening bag from its long, rhinestone strap, sparkling bold against the black, silky fabric of her dress. He studied her face. It looked so familiar, somehow. She had a long graceful neck rising to a sculpted chin, and big, blue, doe eyes with long lashes. He turned his head so he could get a look at her straight on. She tapped her foot up and down as she sat with legs crossed, the fabric of her dress pulled beguilingly above the knee. Her elbow was on the bar, chin on her fist. Was she waiting for someone?

As Cooper watched, she looked up and caught his eye. He smiled, and she gave a nervous half-smile before dropping her gaze and looking away. He was not the only one who felt out of place in this environment; he was sure of it. He found the woman's reaction to him so charming he began to wonder why someone like her was there in the first place. A large, African-American man approached her, blocking his view, and he turned away.

He took another drink of the scotch, letting it roll around on his tongue before swallowing it. A loud trill of feminine laughter, accompanied with the low hum of male posturing, drew his attention in the other direction. Three beefy-looking guys in shirts and ties were entertaining a black-haired siren in a red dress to his right. She was the opposite of the girl to his left, totally at home in the bar scene. Her dress was short and tight, with fringes at the bottom like a 1920's flapper. It sparkled all over, and her breasts all but flowed out of the top, pressed up as if someone took a rolling pin to her midsection to form the mounds above it. She ran a long, painted fingernail under the chin of one of the members of her male entourage, making all three take in a breath and adjust their stances hopefully. Cooper wondered if they had any idea how foolish they looked as she played them like a conductor commanding his orchestra's well-tuned string section. He chuckled to himself and shook his head. Poor slobs. More than likely none of them even stood a chance. His bet was on the bartender the girl kept flitting her gaze toward.

He leaned back against the bar, and caught sight of the blonde again, this time as she was being led out onto the dance floor. The large man with her, his skin a dark-chocolate brown, moved his hand from her elbow to the skin of the small of her back, where the dress gave way to silky flesh. Cooper saw the girl flinch at the man's touch, and instinctively sat straighter, his body on alert. He didn't know why his jaw became tight and his stomach knotted; he just knew he didn't like the way the man was touching her.

The two began to slow dance to a sultry song, swaying on the floor amidst the others. When another couple blocked his view, Cooper shifted over a seat so he could still see her.

The man now put his colossal paw under the girl's chin and lifted her face. She was shaking her head and not looking him in the eye, her face flushed but, he guessed, not from the dancing. The man pulled her closer, but her body language was clear, as she was leaning her upper body as far away from him as possible. His hand slid down from where it was holding hers to grip her wrist. She seemed to be struggling with him now as he leaned in as if to kiss her. Cooper took a step forward, but she abruptly pulled out of her partner's grip and rushed toward the bar, her jaw set. The big man trailed after her.

"Come on, baby. Don't be like that, now." He grabbed the blonde around the waist and spun her toward him.

"Get your hands off me!" she hissed, passion, and perhaps fear, heating her words as she pushed him.

Maybe seeing the fire in her eyes, he released his hold, backing away. "All right. All right." He chuckled at her reaction, watching her butt like she was a piece of meat and he was the world's hungriest carnivore. "I'll take it slow."

"Just 'take it' someplace else," she said with finality, but he didn't appear to get the message.

Cooper tried to act preoccupied as the girl returned to the stool one seat over. He tilted his glass back and she raised her hand to order another drink. Her former dance partner again stepped between them. When he spoke, she jumped, seeming surprised to hear his voice so close.

"Come on, baby," he begged, his voice velvety smooth. He slipped his arms around her waist. "You know you want to."

"Stop. Please. I'm *not interested*." The desperateness in her voice had Cooper setting his drink down. As he turned, he saw the man's hands come up from her waist. He couldn't tell for sure, but he thought the man had touched her breasts. His suspicion was confirmed a few seconds later when he felt a few drops hit him as the girl whooshed the man with her drink and turned to leave.

"Listen, bitch. Nobody throws a drink in my face." The man grabbed the girl roughly by the arms.

"Let her go." Cooper's voice was a low growl.

The big man's back stiffen. With as little effort as it took to pop a beer cap, the man tossed the girl aside. She crashed into the bar and fell against the stool, sliding down even as she attempted to right herself. Her attacker turned around slowly and Cooper stepped up until they were chest-to-chest.

The dark-skinned man stared down his somewhat flattened nose at him. He was a good deal taller than Cooper's six-two, and weighed maybe seventy-five pounds more. Cooper noticed now how truly massive the man's arms were, but it only made him madder. Why the hell did a guy like that need to push a woman around? "You gonna do something about it?" his opponent snarled.

"Yeah. I'm going to do something about it." Cooper shook his blond hair out of his eyes, ready to get a couple of shots in before the brute pummeled him. The bartender reached across the bar just as a couple of bouncers made their way over to the fray.

"No one's pushing a woman around in here," the bartender snapped. The distraction allowed the bouncers time to reach them. They clasped their hands on the big man's shoulders and grabbed a hold of the back of his pants. "Get out of here, and don't show your face in here ever again," the bartender added, brave from his position behind the bar. The troublemaker shook off the bouncers and took a swing at Cooper who ducked and came up, landing a punch in the man's ribs. The bouncers seized the man once more and started pulling him away.

"Okay, okay. Damn." The big man shrugged them off again, but seeming to measure the aggressive stares he was getting from every man in the room now, he cut his losses. Straightening his suit coat, he turned and strode out of the room, the bouncers following in his wake.

Cooper bent and offered the girl his hand. She had been watching, wide-eyed and stunned, from her position on the floor. "Are you okay?" he asked, concerned by the way her hand was shaking in his.

She found her voice. "Y-yes. Yes. Thank you." She looked confused and he wondered for a moment if she hit her head. "I...I...this was all wrong. I shouldn't have come here. I'm sorry." She looked at him, tears in her eyes, and then turned and rushed away.

"Wait. Wait!" He hurriedly pulled out his wallet and plopped some bills on the bar. He just recognized her. She was the sister of the victim.

CHAPTER TWO

Laney Essex pushed through the crowd inside Phat Jack's, blinded by her tears, angry at herself for causing a scene. When she hit the doorway to the parking lot, she stumbled, hearing a crack as her heel separated from her shoe. "Dammit." Her voice reverberated off the nearby buildings as she entered the empty parking lot. She felt like such a fool. What had she hoped to accomplish by coming back here tonight? It made her ill to look at the parking spot where her sister's car had been, occupied now by a red convertible. How could this have happened to Sydney?

The night before, Sidney had called and asked Laney to meet her for drinks, telling her, cryptically, she had something to discuss. Laney, happy to set aside her night of grading papers, scrambled out of her PJs and into her bar-hopping outfit, snug jeans and a sheer black and white blouse over a lacy, black cami.

As she approached the new club, she saw a crowd gathered outside. Unsure about what was going on behind the yellow police tape, she scanned the curious faces for her sister, excited about a chance to spend some time together, complaining about their domineering mother, or hearing about Sydney's newest book; it really didn't matter what they discussed. Sydney had teased her when she found out she was already in her pajamas at seven-thirty, telling her she was becoming an old maid at twenty-three. Laney planned on ordering a pair of shots when she arrived, to prove to her older sister she was no stick-in-the-mud, but she was having trouble making her way to the door. She heard the voices around her, coming from all directions.

"They're not letting anyone in or out."

"...strangled right in the parking lot..."

"I can't believe it. We must have walked right by."

As she worked her way through the mass of bystanders, looking at every blonde, and realizing, when each one turned to talk to someone, that it wasn't her sister, a sick feeling stole over her.

She's probably inside, she told herself, to stem the panic that was now rising to choke her. *Or she's late. She's always late.* Laney moved to the front of the crowd, trying to steal glimpses over people's shoulders at the police officers gathered around the car. *That's not her car. That's NOT her car.* But as she nudged past the last person blocking her view, she saw it was. Her knees buckled, but she made it under the tape, between two policemen who had become complacent with the well-behaved crowd.

"Syd. Syd!" She saw her blond hair, and—the shoes. They were Laney's shoes. The shoes Sydney had borrowed before her trip. "Oh, my God! No. No!" Her mind collapsed inward with the final horrified scream. The men grabbed her, and she stared in utter shock at the scene before her, overcome with grief.

NOW SHE STOOD, THE next night, reliving the agony. Things shouldn't go on as normal. There shouldn't be a car in that place. A woman had taken her last breath here while people were dancing and drinking inside. Laney had come back to try to make sense of it all, to find some clue to explain why someone would want her sister dead, and instead, she'd almost started a fight. She hobbled on the broken shoe to her car, leaning against it, and staring, uncomprehendingly at the heel she had picked up. It was torn, and broken, like Sydney had been.

COOPER BURST THROUGH the door, the cooler air a relief on his warm skin. He looked around for the blonde, not seeing her at first, then caught movement out of the corner of his eye. He turned to see her sliding down the side of a car, exactly as she slid down the stool inside. As he moved in that direction, she grabbed her legs, put her forehead down on her knees, and sobbed uncontrollably. He knew, as a cop, he was supposed to remain impassive, being the calm source of strength for the victim. But he hadn't quite learned how to manage that yet, hadn't built up the layer of callousness needed to turn away from another's tears.

"Hey. Are you okay?" He squatted and put a hand on her shoulder. *That's a stupid question. Of course she's not okay. She's sitting yards from where her sister was brutally murdered.*

She jumped at his touch and tried to rise, swallowing her sobs. "Y-yes, I-I'm okay." She stood, lopsided, which would have been comical in another situation, and he could see now she held a damaged shoe in her hand. She followed his gaze. "It's broken," she explained in a childlike way, still in a daze, wiping at her tears with the back of a hand.

"I see." She stared at it with a befuddled expression. "Why don't you let me drive you home?"

"No, no. That's okay." She shrunk away from him, perhaps afraid, after what had happened inside, of his having bad intentions. Cooper reached into his suit coat for his badge, glancing around. "I'm a police officer. You're in no shape to drive. Why don't you let me take you home? You shouldn't be here."

She hung her head and paused for a few breaths before she said, her voice small, "Okay."

"If you want, I'll drive your car home, and have another policeman meet me there and drive me back here to get my car." She nodded without saying anything and removed her other shoe. He helped her around to the passenger's side, tried the handle, but it was locked. She stood by his side, still looking at her hands wordlessly. "Ms. Essex?" he prompted. "The keys?"

She peered up at him, seeming curious for a second about how he knew her name, searching his face for an answer to a question she couldn't articulate. Then she rummaged around in her purse for the keys. After several moments he offered to find them for her, reached in, and pulled them right out. He opened her door and she slid in, staring straight forward. He shook his head, making sure she was all in before closing the door. He returned to the driver's side, climbing in awkwardly and moving the seat back to accommodate his longer legs. The engine of her racy two-seater roared to life, and Cooper backed out of the parking space. He got her to mumble an address and shifted into drive.

CHAPTER THREE

Laney stared out the window, the speed and her tears blurring the street-lights to long streaks of white as they drove. The police officer had turned the radio on low, to some music he no doubt believed would soothe her, but there was no soothing her now. Sydney was gone. Gone in a flash of light. Gone in the twinkling of a star. Gone forever. She couldn't comprehend it. How could someone who was so full of life—so bright and vibrant—be snuffed out without a sound? Without the world even blinking?

She started sobbing again, too lost and exhausted to be embarrassed anymore. The policeman reached over and rubbed her back. She felt bad for almost getting him into a fight. If that jerk had hurt him...she didn't even want to think about it. She realized, suddenly, they were no longer moving, but she didn't know how long they had been at a stop. She raised her head from her hands and could see the familiar parking lot of her condo.

"I'm sorry. I'm sorry," she blubbered. "I should go." She tried to open her door but it wouldn't open. She continued to pull on the handle and slam her shoulder into the door over and over again, becoming mad. He reached over and put a hand on her nearest shoulder. His touch made the anger melt away. She fell against the door, overwhelmed by a new bout of tears.

COOPER LET HIS PASSENGER cry, wanting to pull her into his arms, but unsure of how she would take that, and whether it would be appropriate at all, as an officer of the law, for him to do such a thing. But he wasn't thinking as a police officer right now, he was only thinking of comforting her. She was incredibly good-looking, even as she was now, eyes swollen, hair disheveled, body drooping like one of the plants on his front stoop. He tried to put that out of his mind.

After a time, she became still. "I'm sorry," she said again, somewhat more controlled this time. "Thank you so much for everything you did tonight. It was irresponsible of me to..." She trailed off, staring out the front window at the tree trunk of a huge elm. After a few seconds she twisted her body to him, concern showing in those immeasurably deep blue eyes of hers. "You're okay, aren't you? He didn't hurt you?" She laid one of her soft hands on his arm.

Finding his voice was a struggle as he was unnerved by her closeness. "Not a scratch." He gave her a smile to reassure her, but she dropped her eyes, so he couldn't tell what she was thinking.

"Thank you for driving me home." She turned to her door again, and he saw her shaking hand fumble with the lock then get it open.

He hopped out and raced around to her side of the car. "I want to see you safely in." She nodded her assent and he loped along beside her, hands stuck inside his jacket pockets. The wind had picked up and she shivered. The light was on outside her door. It was a nice place, a two-story townhouse with a balcony on the second level. She unlocked the door and turned to him. "Thank you, Officer...?"

He stuck out his hand. "Cooper Sullivan."

"Officer Sullivan. My name's Laney."

"Cooper, please. My dad's Officer Sullivan."

"He's on the force, too?"

He nodded, glad to see she seemed to be regaining her equilibrium.

"Won't you come in to wait for your ride? It's cold tonight."

He wasn't the least bit cold, but he followed her inside. When the lights came on, he was surprised by the palatial space in front of him. He was standing on a wide, marble semi-circular landing, with steps leading down to a luxurious living room. A classy-looking wet bar stood on the left and a large, U-shaped couch had been placed in front of a massive fireplace. A gilded mirror hung over it. A long staircase with an elaborate banister that ended in a swirl ran along the wall at the right. Above, a hallway was open to the floor below, hemmed in by wrought-iron railings.

Cooper bit off the low whistle rising in his throat. "Nice place," he commented, trying to look nonplussed. "What do you do for a living?"

"Huh?" she said, preoccupied. "Oh. I teach high school English."

He couldn't hide his surprise this time. "Wow. They must be paying English teachers a lot these days."

"Hmm...oh, no. My mother bought me this place for my birthday. She refused to visit me at my other place," she added, without explaining why.

He looked around some more, taking in the crystal chandelier and what he guessed were some pretty expensive paintings on the wall. At the far side of the room, a dark, tigerwood bar separated the living area from a spacious kitchen. Three lights hung over it, suspended several feet from the ceiling, and covered with frosted amber-colored shades. Beyond that, he could make out black cabinetry with several glass-fronted doors. Pretty nice birthday present.

A small glass and wrought iron table stood to the right of the door, and as the girl turned to put her keys down on it he noticed a huge bruise beginning to form in a line across her back. He touched her shoulder so he could bend and get a better look. "Ooh. Is that from hitting the bar?"

"Umm...I think it was the stool, actually."

"That son-of-a-bitch should have never laid a hand on you. I should have arrested him for assault."

Her eyes widened at his outburst. "No. I'm okay." She squinted up at him, changing the subject. "You were working undercover, weren't you?" Cooper nodded.

"And I almost blew it for you." Her voice was remorseful. "I was being stupid."

"Out of curiosity, just what were you doing there?"

She stepped into the living room. He still winced at the sight of her back, and something about her being barefoot made her seem vulnerable, touching him as well. He followed her.

"I don't know. I thought somehow..." She sighed and shook her head.

He put his hands on her shoulders and turned her to face him. "You thought what?"

She dropped her eyes. "I thought...maybe I could discover something. I don't know, something that would maybe—somehow—help it all make sense."

He placed his hand gently under Laney's chin and lifted her face. Her eyes were misty and her lips trembled. His mouth was dry. "Are you going to be okay, Laney?"

She nodded and a piece of hair fell into her eyes. Without thinking, he brushed it back. Lights beamed in through the narrow windows on either side of her door, announcing the arrival of the police cruiser he had called for.

"I should go," he murmured, more to himself than to her. She didn't move. "Good night, then." He stepped back. She didn't say anything as he turned to walk away, closing the door behind him. He paused outside her door, breathing a heavy sigh. He shrugged into his jacket more, feeling the chilly night air now, and headed down the steps.

"HEY, COOP." AIDAN MCCONNAHY, his roommate and partner, pulled in just as he was getting out of his 'Vette at their apartment.

"Late night?" Cooper raised an eyebrow with a grin. Aidan had been out on his third date with a cute brunette, a former EMT who had recently joined the department's Victim's Services area.

Aidan folded his arms on the roof of his sedan and put his chin down on them with a goofy grin. "I think this is the one, Coop."

Cooper chuckled and shook his head. "Mmm-hmm." He shut his car door. "That's what you say every time."

"Yeah. But this time I mean it. Jenna's really—"

"Special?" Cooper finished, having heard it before. "Just like Ali was special, and Karen was special, and—"

"Okay, okay. Shut up, will ya? You sure know how to ruin a guy's mood." Aidan shut his own door and met him on the sidewalk.

"Sorry, man." He slapped Aidan on the back and then let him pass. He was feeling a bit moody himself, and he didn't know why. Something was irritating him. He decided a cold brew would go a long ways toward mellowing him out. "You wanna have a beer before we hit the sack?"

"Thought you'd never ask." Aidan flashed his neon white smile and turned the knob he'd just unlocked to let the door open. He was as tall as

Cooper, but that's where the resemblance ended. He had dark, thick hair to Cooper's blond, and was lanky, where Cooper was muscular.

As the door opened, Cooper surveyed the room with a fresh eye, unconsciously comparing it to Laney's place. It was a standard bachelor pad, complete with pizza boxes still on the coffee table—left over from the night before, when they'd been watching the fight—sports pages unfolded on the chair, beer bottles here and there as accent pieces, and dirty laundry of varying degrees of uncleanliness throughout. He stepped in with a frown.

"So," Aidan quizzed, heading for the fridge while Cooper stopped to fold the newspapers, "how was the stakeout? Did you learn anything new at Phat Jack's?"

"No, not really." What should he tackle next? The pizza boxes or the clothes?

Aidan returned. "What's with your hand?"

"Huh?" He looked down. He hadn't even realized he'd been clenching and unclenching his fist. "Oh, got in a fight."

"What?" Aidan laughed, handing him a bottle of beer. "With who?"

"Oh, some asshole who thought it was fun to push a woman around." He gave up and flopped down in a worn, tweed chair, which had been beige once, but now was a sort of muted grey.

"Man." His roommate plopped down in the chair on the opposite end of the coffee table, putting his feet on the table to mimic him. "I wish I could have been there for that one." He gritted his teeth. Cooper knew his partner had a special hatred for men who hit women because of his sister's abusive relationship with her ex-husband. "Did you at least score a couple?" Aidan pantomimed throwing a few punches.

"Not really, Rocky," he retorted. "The guy was huge. I gave him my best to the rib cage and he didn't even flinch." He rubbed his sore knuckles. "Speaking of Rocky, now I know what it feels like to hit a side of beef."

"Wish I'da been there. I'd have laid him out cold."

"Yeah, sure you would have, A-hole." Cooper picked up a stale piece of pizza crust from the end table and whipped it at him.

Aidan laughed, dodging it easily. They both took a drink of their beers.

"Was she hurt?"

"Yeah. Guy tossed her like...like she was pizza dough," Cooper stated, finding inspiration at his fingertips. "Only, he didn't catch her. She had a nice bruise on her back." He got hot again just thinking about it.

Aidan sat up, perhaps catching something in his tone. He raised an eyebrow. "You saw her back?"

He glanced away, then, looked him in the eye. "She had on a backless dress, you moron."

"Umm." Aidan leaned into the cushions again but his gaze never left Cooper's face as he took a long pull on his beer.

"And get this." Cooper leaned forward. "She's the victim's sister."

"What victim?"

"What victim? Sydney Essex. The author."

"Oh." Another long pause filled the air. "Is the sister as hot as the author?"

Before he could think better of it, Cooper's mouth spoke for him, "Oh, yeah." He glanced over at Aidan, but he seemed to be busy messing with his bottle label.

Just when he thought he had gotten off the hook, Aidan asked, "Any chance she could be...'special'?" His brown eyes danced with suppressed laughter.

Time will tell, Cooper thought speculatively, but he shut his mouth, noting how his partner was examining him. He rose from his chair, stretching. "Thanks for the beer." He clinked his bottle against Aidan's as he passed him on the way to the kitchen. "I'm going to bed."

"Good night, then..." Aidan's voice trailed off, but Cooper could feel his eyes following him out of the room. The pair had lived together since their days at the police academy. It was a rarity for Cooper to talk about a girl. In all that time, he had never brought a girl home, never even dated anyone, besides the few girls Aidan had pressed him into taking out on a double date. He kept his nose to the paperwork grindstone, so to speak. He was always finishing up their collars, allowing Aidan to go out. He dated a lot in high school, had been involved in one longer relationship senior year. The girl dumped him right after he entered the academy, and his dating life had suffered since.

Once alone in his room, Cooper removed shirt and pants and sat on the end of the bed to take off his socks. He rubbed his chest. His blond hair, which he wore short in the back and long on the top, fell into his face. Maybe it was time for him to be seeing someone. Certainly, he was over the whole Carrie breakup, and this girl seemed to invoke some strange response in him. But he discovered long ago, physical attraction wasn't enough to make a relationship work. And, if his dad found out, he would kill him. He could hear the old man now, *Coop, if there's one thing I know for certain, it's reputation is as important to a cop as his gun is.* He drilled that into Cooper time and time again. And getting involved with a victim's sister—that was taboo. He whipped off his socks, throwing them carelessly on the floor. He bounced his way up to the top of the bed. He couldn't shake a feeling of disappointment, though.

He lay awake for hours.

CHAPTER FOUR

Laney paced around her living room. She had tried tackling the stack of papers she was grading when Sydney called, but stopped on her thirteenth perusal of the same student's essay. She hadn't slept a wink, and now the thought of lunch with her mother, the jetsetter, Camille Essex, was making her ill. She didn't know if she could face "The Baroness de Dragon", as they liked to call her, without Sydney around to help her let off steam afterward. Nobody else knew how expertly their mother could trigger emotions with just a half-sigh. But, because of what her sister meant to her, she'd do it for Syd. She'd sit through lunch while her mom prattled on about Paris, or Istanbul, or wherever the hell her City d' Jour was. Or, if she was in one of her foul moods, Laney would listen to her mother rattle off her faults like a child's Christmas list. Or, perhaps it would be one of those stiff, stilted meals, when she wasn't sure what she would say to set her mother off on a tirade. The thought sent a chill down her spine.

She sighed and continued her lap around the room, though slower this time. She picked up a tear-shaped lead-crystal paperweight her mother had selected for her in Ireland. It was the one thing in the room she liked. She held it up to catch the sun like a prism and saw the reflected jewels of color dance over her wall. Syd had been like that. She'd taken the cold, hard crystal, which was her mother, and splintered her into the myriad of colors that was the laughter they shared after an encounter with The Baroness. Laney would be down, or aggravated, and Syd would schedule dinner and greet her with an uncanny imitation of their mother, one time going so far as to don a white feathered boa like their mother sometimes wore.

After today, she was sure it would take her weeks to pull herself up out of the hole her mother created for her. *I let her create for me*, she corrected. She knew her mom would not have that power if she didn't hand it to her.

But as yet, she had not discovered the trick to not turning back into a child when her mother was around. Sydney had. Although there were times when their mother cracked through her armor, for the most part, Sydney was able to laugh her off, sometimes to her face, Laney recalled with a smile.

"Oh, Syd. How I wish you were here," she said aloud to the empty room. How ironic it was that it was now Syd's death which had her mother flying halfway around the world to make her life even more miserable. In a sudden burst of temper, Laney raised the crystal as if to throw it in the fireplace, but thinking better of it, she returned it to its spot on the table. She straightened the cream-colored pantsuit she had chosen as her armor today and headed for the door, grabbing her purse off a chair along the way. She would get to the restaurant early so she could collect herself and have a drink, before her mother arrived.

Cooper sat at his desk, drumming his nails. What to tackle next? He'd talked to Sydney Essex's agent yesterday and found out nothing. Yes, Sydney was working on a new book. No, she didn't know what it was about, but she couldn't imagine anyone trying to kill Sydney over one of her romance novels.

He knew he needed to talk to Laney, but for some reason he kept putting it off. The mother, Camille Essex, had been a real case, inviting him to lunch to discuss details. She "didn't want to be bothered with talking over the phone." Never mind it was an inconvenience for him to drive halfway across town to some hoity-toity restaurant to talk to her.

Aidan had pulled up Sydney's financials, and nothing out of the ordinary had shown up there. The nightclub was another story. Red flags were popping up all over the place when it came to Phat Jack's. Apparently, some high-end drugs were being run out of the establishment and the place was already under investigation. The narcs agreed to pull out though, for the time being, so they could get a handle on the murder case. Murder trumps drug running, at least in this case, where the victim was a prominent citizen. Cooper read through the narcotics unit's file though, and it seemed like all they had was a lot of suspicion and no real hard evidence yet. But what if Sydney Essex had seen or heard something that night she shouldn't have? Could it have led to her murder? It was something they would have to investigate.

By the time he had read through the file, and talked to the Narcotics detectives, it was rolling on twelve-thirty and he had to break to go downtown to meet up with Camille Essex. Aidan and Cooper agreed only one of them would go, no need to double team the grieving mother, and neither wanted to shell out that kind of money for lunch in the first place. Cooper was almost certain they would have no real food anyway and he'd be searching down the menu in vain, but he lost the coin toss.

COOPER PULLED A TIE out of the glove box of his car and put it on, straightening it in the rearview mirror. But when he entered the restaurant, for the second time in as many days, Cooper felt underdressed. His suit cost much less than the designer suits the businessmen surrounding him wore. He was casting looks around uncomfortably when the maitre de led him to the table tucked away from the others, so he didn't even notice her sitting there, at first.

Camille Essex was what he expected. Her snowy-white hair was meticulously coifed, her teal blue suit impeccable. But what caught him off guard was the pretty blonde sitting next to her in the large circular booth. Camille shook his hand and then introduced her daughter.

"Nice to meet you," Laney hurried to say after the introduction, looking him intensely in the eyes.

Cooper caught on. "And you, Miss Essex. I'm sorry, what was your first name again?" He fought the smirk twitching his lips.

"Laney." She appeared annoyed, much to his amusement. It was obvious she didn't want her mother to know about her nocturnal visit to the club and the ensuing incident.

"Yes, it's a dreadful name, I know. But her father let me name Sydney, so he insisted on naming her Laney, of all things."

Laney stared down at the tablecloth, her cheeks becoming flushed.

"Well, I think it's a pretty name."

She glanced up, smiling at him gratefully.

"Yes, well..." Camille sniffed, as if his opinion was beside the point. "You had some questions, Detective?"

"Ahh. A lady who comes straight to the point. I like that." He smiled at her broadly, trying to charm his way into her good graces, but she would have none of it.

"Well, I don't know what you expect to find out from me. I don't even know what Sydney was doing at such an appalling establishment in the first place."

"She was going to meet me," Laney murmured.

"What is that, Laney? Speak up, dear, I can't hear you," Camille sniped, seeming irritated.

"She was going to meet me there, Mother. All right?"

"Well, you needn't yell. I'm not that hard of hearing yet."

Laney sighed. "I'm sorry, Mother. I guess I'm just sort of unnerved—"

"Well, really, Laney. Can you imagine how I must feel? To receive a call when you're halfway across the globe, telling you your daughter has been strangled?"

One of Laney's hands lay on the table, clenching a napkin. She looked down and relaxed her grip. "Yes, Mother, of course." Cooper's eyes slid from mother to daughter during the exchange, incredulous. Didn't Camille Essex realize Laney had stumbled right into the murder scene? What could be more difficult than that?

He cleared his throat, unsure for a moment how to proceed. "Mrs. Essex, I'd appreciate any information you could give me which might help in the investigation. For instance, besides her writing, what type of things was your daughter into?"

"For heaven's sakes. I have no idea. Do you have any children, Detective? No, of course you don't," she answered herself. "You're far too young to have grown children, anyway. But let me tell you, they leave and go about doing whatever it is they damn well please, and you don't have the foggiest idea what that is, and don't really want to know."

The waiter arrived then and took their orders. Cooper looked over the top of his menu at Laney while Camille went into an in-depth description of how her order was to vary from the item she was choosing printed on the menu. Laney's face looked pinched and tired, jaw stiff, eyes tense. She slipped two fingers to her temple and rubbed briefly. She must have a tremendous headache to match the one sitting next to her. He tried to figure out a way to continue his questioning without causing her any more pain, but for the life of him, he wasn't sure which way to approach the old goat who'd given birth to Laney and Sydney.

After he gave his order and the waiter left, Cooper leaned forward, crossing his hands on the table in front of him, and began again. "Mrs. Essex, perhaps if you could describe Sydney for me, it might help me to get a better handle on things."

For the first time, he thought he saw a glimpse of pain on the older lady's face. "Sydney was...beautiful, stunning, really. You would have found her attractive, all the men did. She was vivacious, creative, not like Laney." She reached over and patted Laney's hand on the tablecloth as if sympathetic to her. "She's my quiet one." Camille smiled at her condescendingly, "My little Plain Jane."

He studied Laney. Her hands were squeezed together now on the table and her jaw set but she remained silent. Why wasn't she sticking up for herself?

"Of course," Camille continued, "having a flamboyant daughter like Sydney does have its drawbacks. She could be a source of embarrassment at times."

Laney's head snapped up, her eyes flashing. It seemed she'd found something she would fight for. "Sydney was not a source of embarrassment. She was just different from you, Mother." She addressed him now. "Syd was full of life, she was always there when I needed her—" Her voice broke, but she recovered it. "She was a good friend to everyone, funny...she could walk into a party, and suddenly everyone would want to be near her, to listen to her stories, to...just watch her face as she talked..."

Cooper could not imagine anyone's face being more beautiful than Laney's was at the moment. Her deep blue eyes were warm and sincere, her face open and honest. Her admiration for her sister colored every word she spoke, and the pain laced through them was palpable. His heart went out to her. Camille Essex looked at her daughter in horror, shocked she would contradict her. Laney stopped, self-conscious.

"Is this the kind of rudeness you learn from those snotty-nosed kids you teach?"

"I teach high school students, Mother. They pretty much know how to blow their nose by that age."

"Well, then, they spend their time doing other disgusting things...probably fornicating and—"

"Oh, Mother. As if you weren't ever a teen in the back seat of a car—"

Without warning, Laney's mother reached across the table and slapped her, hard, across the face. In the stunned silence which followed she said, her voice low and steely, "Don't you ever talk to me that way again, Laney Cassandra Essex." The waiter chose that very moment to show up with their food.

"Excuse me," Laney whispered hoarsely, and rose to leave the table.

Camille seemed further appalled by her daughter's departure. She turned to him. "I must apologize for my daughter's—"

"No, Mrs. Essex," Cooper said, sliding out of the booth. "You don't need to apologize for Laney. With all due respect, however, you should apologize to her." The waiter raised an eyebrow at him. "I've lost my appetite," he said in reply, peeling off bills from his pocket and laying them on the table.

"I don't want your money," Camille Essex screamed after him, apparently scandalized he would think she would not take care of the bill herself. "Well, I never."

CHAPTER FIVE

"Laney? Laney? Wait!"

Cooper was running after her. She was so mortified. How could her mother have done such a thing? She quickened her steps, pretending not to hear, but when she reached for her door handle, his hand came down to cover hers.

"Laney," he panted. "Please, wait."

She stood still, not looking at him while he caught his breath. Her hands were shaking.

"It occurs to me, you've been physically accosted twice in the past twenty-four hours."

She raised her head a little to look at him. It was sort of an odd statement to make, but she shook it off. "Yeah, well. Maybe my behavior was out of line, in both cases." She tried to yank on the door handle again, but he gently resisted.

"Laney, no. There's no way with that creep last night. And, no offense, I know she's your mother and all, but she was way out of line." He gestured with his thumb back toward the restaurant.

She exhaled, frustrated with everything. "Yeah, maybe. But, I shouldn't have said what I did."

He reached up and ran the back of his hand down the side of her face where the slap still burned. "Laney, give yourself a break. You've been through hell. The fact you were able to roll out of bed this morning is a testimony to your will."

"I don't know."

"And the fact you've been attacked twice, now that's plain bad luck." He grinned at her.

She looked at him sideways, and a smile spread across her face. She hesitated for a minute, but then turned to him, asking tentatively. "Detective, it seems one of the Essex women owes you lunch. Would you like to join me?"

His smile widened. "It would be my pleasure." He nodded his head down the sidewalk. "There's a place a few blocks south. Not much in the way of atmosphere, but they have fantastic pizza."

"Sounds terrific." She smiled and her shoulders relaxed. They walked side-by-side down the street.

"So, you teach high school English. I think that's pretty incredible."

She grimaced, looking straight ahead. "My mother obviously doesn't." She sighed, looking down and shaking her head. "I'm sorry. Bad habit. I've spent so much of my life trying to please that woman and always falling far short. But I don't need to let it ruin my day. Or yours," she added, looking up at him and smiling wryly. "I'm so sorry you had to witness our little dysfunctional family scene."

"No biggie. Someday you can come over and see one at my family's."

She studied him for a second, not sure of how to take that comment, and then laughed. Gosh, he was good-looking. That easy, surfer-boy charm, blond hair shining in the sun, which had decided to peek out from behind the clouds, and built. Man, was he built. Lean and trim, but with a muscular chest and arms. Not to mention having the whole cop thing going for him. He may not be in uniform, but he still projected that tough, in-command mystique. She looked away, embarrassed to be ogling him when he glanced in her direction.

She tried to recover. "So, do you have a big family?"

"No. Just me and my two sisters and a brother. Oh, shoot. That reminds me. Do you mind if I call my mom really fast? I need to find out what to bring for dinner tomorrow, and if I don't do it now, I'm liable to forget."

"Sure, go right ahead."

He flipped open his phone and dialed, leaning against the old building that appeared to house the pizzeria they were going to. "Hey, Mom. What's going on? Oh? Are you sure?" Hearing the worry in his voice, Laney tried to read his face, concerned. "Yeah. I think that's a good idea. Do you want me to come over and take you?" He glanced up and caught Laney's eye and smiled. He reached out and ran a finger under the lapel of her suit while he talked, holding up a finger on his opposite hand to indicate he would only be a minute more. His blue-green eyes danced over her face.

She wondered if he could tell how much her heart raced whenever he brushed a finger over her face or casually handled her, as he was doing now. She was not used to having someone touch her like that, but she was thinking she could get used to it. He finished his conversation and hung up the phone.

"Anything wrong?"

"Cat's sick."

"Oh. That's too bad. Do you need to go take her to the vet?"

"No." He opened the door for her. "Mom said she'd take care of it."

Laney entered a quaint bar inside the older brick building resting on the corner of the street. Tables were squished in between the bar and the wall, leaving barely enough room to squeeze through. The room was dark and the bar old and nicked, but it had a homey feel to it.

The bartender, spying Cooper, grinned, lifting his chin in greeting as he stood behind the bar drying a mug. "Hey, Coop."

"Hey, Mike." He wove through the narrow aisle, leading her to a table up front near a big window, which did let some light into the deep room. He pulled out a chair for her. Mike, who had followed them over, reached out to shake Cooper's hand. "Long time no see, buddy." He was barrel-chested with dark, curly hair in need of a trim, coming to just above his collar.

"Yeah. It has been a while." Mike's curious eyes had turned to her, so Cooper made introductions. "Mike Zimmerman, meet Laney Essex. Laney, this is Mike."

She shook the hand he offered. "Nice to meet you."

"No, the pleasure's all mine," Mike responded suavely, his eyes lighting up as they trailed over her. Cooper's smile dimmed.

"Cooper tells me you make a mean pizza."

"Cooper has good taste." Mike shifted his gaze to Cooper. "Can I get you guys something to drink?"

Cooper raised an eyebrow at Laney.

"I'll have a beer."

His eyes widened. "Make it two." He sat next to her, tilting his head. "What? Did I do something wrong?"

"No. No." She continued to scrutinize him. "It's just…I hadn't pegged you as a beer kind of girl, is all."

"Just what is that supposed to mean?" She was quick to challenge.

"Nothing, nothing." He laughed, holding his hands up innocently. "I just saw you more as a fruity drink or, maybe, wine drinker."

"Hmm." She studied him, her lips turning up as she began to feel playful. "Spoiled little rich girl, eh?" She leaned toward him and he reached up to loosen his tie.

He was saved from answering by Mike arriving with the brews. "He giving you trouble?" Mike asked with a faux frown.

Laney hesitated, not taking her eyes from Cooper's. She was enjoying making him squirm. The moment stretched out, Mike waiting expectantly for an answer. She reached for her mug. "No, he's okay, I guess."

Cooper looked up at the bartender, seeming unduly happy with his mini-victory, wearing a "Na-na-na-nana" expression on his face.

"Well, you let me know, Laney—" Mike seemed to emphasize the fact that he remembered her name, "if this guy gets out of hand, and I'll come put him in his place."

She smiled up at him. "I'll do that, Mike."

This time it was Mike whose face registered triumph. "Are you ready to order, Coop?"

"You want to try the pizza?" he asked Laney.

"Sure."

"What do you want on it?"

"Anything. I usually get pepperoni and sausage, but I can pick off anything I don't like."

He handed the menus back to Mike. "One large pepperoni and sausage."

Mike looked at Laney with a smile. "Coming right up."

They waited until Mike walked away. "I thought I liked that guy," Cooper muttered.

"What?" Laney blinked. "He seemed very nice to me."

"Yeah. Too nice." He turned toward Laney, giving her his full attention. "So, what school do you teach at?"

"Walter Davis."

Cooper whistled. "Wow, that's a pretty rough crowd over there."

"Yeah. It can be. But a lot of them are really good kids. They just sometimes lack…guidance."

"Well, that's a nice way to put it."

"I did have a student threaten me last year, though," she said thoughtfully, taking a sip of her beer. It felt cool and comforting as it slid down her throat.

"You're kidding?"

She shook her head. "He said, 'I know where you live, and I know what kind of car you drive', and then he recited my make and model and license plate number," she said, with a shiver. "He said, 'I won't get you now because we're on school property, but I'll get you.'" She shrugged it off. "Then he called me several colorful names."

"What did the dean do?"

"The dean, who was a woman, had it in for me for some reason, maybe because of the family name. So she accused me of bringing it on."

"You're joking?"

"Nope." She took another drink of her beer, wondering over how relaxed she felt in Cooper's company. Normally, eating lunch with a man she didn't know would make her nervous. Not to mention eating lunch with someone as attractive as Cooper.

"Why was the kid upset with you?"

"I gave him a zero on a paper."

"Why?"

"Because he didn't turn it in."

"Man, you are a hardass," he said sarcastically. "He threatened you because he didn't turn in a paper, and the dean thought you were to blame?"

She nodded.

"That takes the cake," he sputtered. "So, what did you do?"

"Nothing. Lucky for me he was picked up for breaking and entering that same night and I never had to see him again."

Cooper sat there, stunned. "And you went back there?"

She shrugged. "I like to teach. And there are a few kids who make it all worthwhile." She smiled, thinking of several.

COOPER WATCHED HER eyes. They displayed her emotions so clearly. "Tell me about one of them," he said, his voice soft.

Laney paused. "There was this girl, J.J.—J.J. Jenkins. She came in after school one day and told me she was pregnant. She told me I was the only one she had talked to about it. That's when you realize there are kids out there you are reaching. When they feel they can trust you with more than grading their essays." She stared off into space.

He put his hand over hers on the table. "I bet you're a great teacher." She looked up into his eyes, and he saw dozens of emotions swimming there, hope, gratitude, and fear, but chiefly fear. She became guarded, her body stiff, she removed her hand, but they were saved any awkwardness by the arrival of the pizza.

"All right, Gorgeous." Mike scooted things around on the table so he could place the pizza down. He lifted a piece and held it to her mouth. "Try me."

Cooper about choked. What a stupid come-on.

She dutifully took a bite. Her eyes grew wide. "Mmm...this is delicious."

"What did I tell ya?" he responded with a wink.

"Hey, Mike." A loud, heavyset man in a velour jogging suit strode across the restaurant toward him.

"Sorry. Gotta go. This guy's a food critic."

Laney glanced in his direction. "Oh. Good luck."

Mike headed off, giving the newcomer an enthusiastic greeting.

"I'm beginning to think I should have never brought you here."

"Why?"

Before Cooper could tell her he didn't appreciate the attention Mike was giving her, another male voice spoke from behind her.

"Ms. Essex?"

She turned to a young, lanky man with the pizzeria's t-shirt on standing beside her chair. He looked like he had a little Latino in him with dark hair and pimpled skin. "Jimmy Johansson!" She leapt out of her chair and threw her arms around him. Cooper rolled his eyes and set his napkin on the table; this was not going to be his day. "How are you?"

"Good, good." He ducked his head for a moment, seeming uncomfortable. "I'm really sorry about your sister, Ms. Essex. I read about it in the paper this morning."

"Thank you, Jimmy. That's nice of you to say." She paused. "So, you work here?"

"Yeah. But I'm going to school, too," he added. "I even took a Shakespeare class, thanks to you."

"Shakespeare? Well, how did you do in it?"

"I got a 'B'." He grinned, looking proud of himself.

"That's awesome!" Laney shouted, but then she glanced around and reeled her enthusiasm in. "Oh, Cooper. I'm sorry to be so rude. I'm just so excited to see this guy." She slung her arm around his waist. "Cooper Sullivan, this is Jimmy Johansson. He was a student of mine."

"No kidding? Nice to meet you, Jimmy."

"You, too, sir." He looked back at Laney. "Well, I better get back to work. I just wanted to say hi."

"Well, I'm glad you did. You made my day. How's your mom, by the way?"

"Better. The second round of chemo seems to have taken care of things."

"Fantastic. Tell her I said 'hi,' would you?"

"Sure thing, Ms. Essex. Good seeing you again."

She gave him one more squeeze. "You, too. And keep up the good work at school." She sighed contentedly as she sat. "Good kid," she commented to Cooper.

"Seemed like it." He observed her flushed face and distracted but satisfied expression. "Things like that make it all worth it, don't they? I mean, putting up with all the bullshit and heartache."

She looked at him, seeming surprised by the statement. "Yes," she murmured.

"It's like that with police work, too. When things work out right—which, grant it, they seldom do— it's all worth it."

LANEY NODDED, CHEWING on the pizza that had suddenly become tasteless. She found it hard to swallow. He reminded her of why they were here. She had been able to forget for a few happy minutes, but now she remembered. This wasn't some kind of fun..."date," for lack of a better word. He was here as a police officer. He was only being kind because he felt sorry for her.

She didn't look up. "You need to talk to me about Sydney." It came out as more of a statement than a question.

"Yes." He again placed his hand over hers and this time she didn't withdraw it, seeing it strictly as an act of comfort, as she was certain it was intended, instead of something more. "Whenever you're ready."

She nodded, looking up and taking a deep breath. "What do you need to know?"

He hesitated. "You said you were meeting her at Phat Jack's that night."

She nodded again, tearing a piece of pizza crust into little pieces as she talked. "She called and asked me to come out. Told me she had something to tell me."

"Do you have any idea what it was?"

"No. She was being very secretive."

"Did you have a sense about whether it was a good thing or a bad thing?"

"I don't know. I was just so glad to hear from her. She'd been gone for a couple of weeks."

Cooper took a notebook out and started jotting down notes. "Where had she been?"

"I'm not sure. She said she was doing research, so I went over to her place to bring in the mail, water the plants, take care of the pool..."

"Do you still have a key to her place?"

She nodded. "I never had the chance to give it back to her."

He closed his notebook. "It would be very helpful to look around her place."

"I'll take you there now."

He looked surprised. "Let me call my partner, Aidan, and let him know. You have sauce on the side of your mouth, by the way." Before she could react, he reached over and touched her lip, rubbing the sauce off with his thumb.

She froze for a minute, her heart pounding and her cheeks warm. "I'll settle up with Mike. Be right back."

"Oh, no. It's my treat, remember?"

"No. It's on the precinct." He hopped up before she could argue.

Cooper approached the bar where the young pub owner was trying to be unobtrusive as he watched the food critic eat. His focus changed as Cooper approached. "Hey."

"Can I get the tab?"

"No charge, Officer." Mike looked pointedly over his shoulder back to the table and Cooper turned, too. The sun was haloing Laney's hair as it poured through the window. She was reaching under the table for her purse and her curtain of hair shimmered down her arm. "Thank you for introducing me to Laney. She's something."

Cooper leaned back against the bar, his body sighing in response. He shook his head and spoke out of the corner of his mouth. "You're out of your league, Zimmerman."

"And you're not?" he countered.

Perhaps feeling their eyes on her, Laney turned to look in their direction. Both men waved at her. She waved back, a look of confusion on her face.

"She's crazy about me," Cooper said easily.

"Yeah, right."

Cooper turned back to him with a grin. "See ya, Mike."

He sauntered over and pulled Laney's chair out for her. As they turned to leave, he placed a proprietary hand on the small of her back, winking at Mike, who shook his head with a smile.

CHAPTER SIX

Cooper was behind the wheel of Laney's sports car again as she gave him directions to Sydney's house up in the hills. He tried to draw Laney out, but she was quiet. As they pulled up the long, curved driveway, he whistled. The house was a white, adobe-like complex with a red-tile roof, and it was huge.

Laney smiled. "Syd's taste was a little...ostentatious, don't you think?"

He switched the engine off. "Maybe a little."

He and Laney got out and crossed to the house. She unlocked the door, but hesitated before opening it. "This feels sort of strange."

"We could come back at another time. Or I could do this myself."

"No. I should do this." She took a deep breath and opened the door.

If he was impressed with the outside, he was astounded by the inside. The room went on forever to a wall of windows overlooking the Pacific. It was decorated tastefully in a Santa Fe theme, with luxurious white carpeting giving way to red accent rugs and Indian statuary. Awed, he crossed the room to look out the window. The back of the house was terraced with multiple decks and a pool with an infinity edge, seeming to fall off the cliff into the ocean below. A straight bridge crossed the pool to an island entertainment area with couches and a massive grill set-up. A tiled fire pit was surrounded by comfortable furniture and he spied a bar on the far side of the pool. *Man, I could really enjoy myself here.*

"Maybe I should write a romance novel," he said out loud. He looked at Laney. *And I know right where I'd start.*

Laney laid the keys on the coffee table. "I hate to burst your bubble, but Syd bought this place before she published her first book, with money she inherited from my father's estate."

"Ahh. It's tough when you're not the firstborn."

"No. I inherited as much as she did," Laney said, running her hand over the back of a hand-painted horse statue. "I just chose to spend it in a different way." Cooper was curious about how she'd spent it, but he figured it would be rude to ask. He crossed the room until he stood on the opposite side of the horse from her. "Is it hard being in here?"

"A little," she answered, her voice breaking to betray her.

"Come here," he said softly, ducking under the horse's neck and coming around to her side. He held his arms open.

Laney stood, uncertain at first, but stepped into the circle of his arms, sliding hers around his waist and laying her head down on his chest.

As he wrapped his arms around her, he couldn't help but notice how right it seemed, how well she fit next to him. She smelled fantastic, a fragrance that made him think of a fresh, summer peach imbued with sweet sunshine. He closed his eyes and breathed her in.

Her muffled voice came from his chest, "I'm okay."

But I'm not. Give me a second. Reluctantly he let her go.

"I'm sorry," Laney mumbled.

"Don't say that, Laney," he responded, with a sharpness he didn't intend. She looked up at him. He switched gears to cover his own puzzlement. "Now...I need to see anything which may give me a clue as to why someone would want to kill your sister. Personal papers, a tablet, laptop..."

"Her office is this way."

Cooper sighed. He was going to have to do a better job of controlling the emotions she seemed to bring out in him. He followed, trying not to watch the rhythmic sway of her hips, but thinking he had never seen anyone move in such a tantalizing way before. It was natural and graceful and he had to shake his head to rid himself of the fantasies it brought on. When she glanced back to see if he was following, he wished like hell he could get inside her pretty little head. What was it, besides the obvious, which drew him to her like a beacon light? He knew part of it was the vulnerability he sensed in her. It appealed to whatever it was inside him that called him to be a cop, a deep-seeded need to protect the good and innocent. But there was more to it than that. He felt a companionable ease around her. He simply enjoyed being with her.

She stopped at a set of French doors opening into a cozy office, although he thought it could be called a library. Books lined both side walls from floor to ceiling, with twin ladders on tracks, which could move the length of the shelving. The far wall had a recessed, arched window, surrounded by the familiar whitewashed adobe walls. On either side of the window, behind a large mission-style desk, hung enormous posters of two of Sydney Essex's book covers. Facing the desk were two, large red chairs. He spotted a laptop open on the desk.

"This is my favorite room." Laney sank into one of the red chairs, curling her legs up under her.

"Somehow that doesn't surprise me," he said with a grin, moving the mouse to wake the laptop. He sat behind the desk and began to read.

After a while, she got up and roamed around the room, pulling books off the shelves and paging through them restlessly, or picking up knickknacks to study, then replacing them.

He found himself getting caught up in the story in front of him, so much so he wasn't aware of Laney's closeness until her voice was in his ear.

"Did you find something?"

Again, her sweet fragrance enveloped him and he had to steady himself before answering. "I can see why your sister sold a lot of books. It's very interesting. It seems like it's a story about a businessman who has two families in separate cities, neither of which knows about the other."

"Hmm." She bent next to him, scanning the page. She was so close, her creamy skin was inches from his. He felt gripped with momentary paralysis.

"Does it mean anything or is it...?" She turned and swallowed the rest of her sentence. She froze, their gazes locked briefly, then hers strayed to his lips momentarily before moving all over his face. Her breath came more quickly through her parted lips.

He wanted her, no need to deny it. He wanted to possess her unlike any woman he had ever met. He reminded himself he had known her for less than twenty-four hours, but it didn't matter, the pull between them was indisputable. He saw it in her eyes right before she withdrew.

"M-maybe I should look somewhere else."

Cooper remained still as she flew from the room, but groaned as the doors closed behind her, pushing the laptop away and laying his head down on the cool wood of the desk. He was startled when the phone rang in his pocket. In slow motion he pulled it out.

"Cooper Sullivan," he answered with a sigh.

"Coop, it's Aidan."

"Oh, geez, Aidan. I forgot to call you. I'm at Sydney Essex's house, check-ing out the—" As he spoke, he reflexively paged through a leather bound planner on the desk. It opened with a paper clip to the night of the murder. Written in big, bold letters he read, "TELL LANEY!" As Aidan interrupt-ed him, he picked up a pen and started underlining Laney's name without thought.

"And how'd you get into there?"

"Laney had a key."

"Laney? Oh, I see, the cute sister, right?"

He set down the pen. "Yeah, so?"

"So—" He could hear Aidan smiling into the phone. "—stay out of the bedroom, would ya? She lost her sister. She's vulnerable."

"What kind of loser do you think I am? I'm not trying to seduce her in her murdered sister's house."

"But you are trying to seduce her."

"Shut up, Aidan. You don't know what you're talking about."

"All right. All right. Calm down. I didn't mean to insult your sensibilities, for God's sake. Have you found anything?"

"No. Not yet."

"Well, keep me informed."

"Hey, Aidan," Cooper interjected before his partner could hang up. He hesitated, wondering if he should bring up her name again, but decided to take the chance. "When you ran financials, what did Laney Essex's show?"

"Nothing, man. She inherited two-point-five million five years ago when her father died, but she has given most of it away. She tends to donate to children's funds, you know, literacy programs, community centers, gave a big chunk to her alma mater..."

"Okay. Thanks."

"Sure. See ya tonight."

Cooper hung up, staring off into space for a minute. Laney Essex was an interesting person, all right, and he thought it would be fun to discover more about her, on a very personal level.

Pulling himself back into the moment, he began searching through desk drawers. At first, he found nothing more than copies of electric bills and receipts for furniture. All of the drawers had locks on them, but were unlocked, until he tried the bottom one.

Wondering if Laney would know where a key would be, he got up to search for her.

CHAPTER SEVEN

He found her by the pool. She had dark sunglasses on, but somehow he sensed she had been crying. "Hey. You okay?" He sat in the chair next to hers.

As confirmation of his suspicions, she brushed at something on her cheek. "It's weird being here. Going through her things. Sydney was always very possessive of her belongings." After a beat, the corners of her lips tugged upwards. "One time...she had this teal sweater...it looked better on me than it did on her—" Cooper had no doubt. "— but she wouldn't let me wear it. So, I borrowed it one night, without permission. But, it was like she had radar or something. Whenever I wore something of hers, she seemed to know. When I got home, I tried to sneak in through the back, but she was waiting for me out by the pool. Scared the living daylights out of me." She chuckled, remembering. "She was mad. Boy, was she mad. We got into a tussle, and she literally ripped the sweater off me. I'm standing there in my bra and jeans—" Cooper did his best not to visualize that. "—feeling humiliated, and I went nuts. Started flailing at her and tried to drag her into the pool, and—" Laney broke off, laughter rolling up, making it too hard to finish her sentence.

"You both fell in," Cooper guessed.

"Yeah. And then my dad comes out, and when he sees me in my bra, he starts screaming that he told us there would be no skinny-dipping in the pool." She chuckled. "If he only knew."

"What? You did skinny-dip?"

"Once or twice," she said slyly. She paused, lost in thought, but then sighed. "That's why it feels weird. Sydney wouldn't like me pawing through her stuff."

"So you guys didn't get along?"

"Actually, she was my best friend. As adults. But growing up...growing up it was a different story. When I was little, my dad was my champion, defending me against Mom's verbal attacks, which were frequent. But after he died, Sydney took on that role for me. It's time I did it for myself. I'm twenty-three, about time I grow up."

"I don't know. You did a pretty good job of standing up to your mom today."

"Yeah." She thought about it. "Maybe I did." They sat in silence for several moments, the sun shining down on them with benevolence. "So, did you find anything?"

"I found a locked drawer. Do you have any idea where your sister would have kept a key?"

"No. Not really."

"People tend to keep them near the locked object—but I've searched the office pretty thoroughly so I don't think it's there—or somewhere with other valuables, somewhere personal to them, somewhere they consider safe." He gave her a keen look.

"Her bedroom?"

"That's what I was thinking."

She stood, seeming rejuvenated. "Let's go then."

SYDNEY'S BEDROOM WAS, well, Sydney. It was expansive, with a raised, windowed area at the back of the house that provided room for a couch and chairs and a small table. Near it, French doors led to a wide terrace. In the middle of the enormous bedroom was a huge canopied bed, its four posts carved like tree trunks. The comforter looked like true leopard skin, and Cooper wondered for a minute whether the pelts had been snuck into the country illegally. The wall behind the bed was a beautiful painted rain forest, with trees, vines and paths that snaked their way through the foliage. To the right was a short hallway to a master bathroom with walk-in closets on either side, hidden behind mirrored doors. The bathtub was a work of art, the sides covered in bamboo, surrounded by tropical plants, some flowering and dropping their petals into the water, and the piece de resistance, a waterfall that came, miraculously, out of the wall, cascading into the tub.

Cooper was impressed by the engineering, but Laney seemed to find it a bit disconcerting to hear the noise of the waterfall in the empty house. She sat on the edge of the tub, and stuck her hand in the water as it flowed out of the wall. She spread her fingers wide, or brought them together under the stream, watching how the path of the water changed.

"What are you thinking about?" he asked quietly, but even so, she jumped. He was sitting close to her on the edge of the tub.

"Oh...I don't know." He watched as her face shifted and changed with her thoughts as she continued to play with the water. "That's not true. I was thinking about the day Sydney had this installed. She was so thrilled..." Her voice trailed off.

Cooper came and squatted in front of her. "Hey," he said, trying to get her to raise her eyes. "Laney." He reached up and touched the side of her face again, her skin so incredibly soft under his hand. "If this is too hard..."

She shook her head, and a teardrop flew from her eye. Then she closed her eyes and leaned into his hand for a minute, a gesture that stopped his heart. When she opened them again, he saw the pain there, and the resolve. "No. I want to help." She stood with such suddenness he almost lost his balance. "I'll start on the dresser."

He rose and watched her walk away, wishing, illogically, that he could take this all away from her, and remembering with chagrin Aidan's warning not to take her into the bedroom.

As she started opening drawers, he entered the hallway and chose the closet to the left. He pulled down an obscene amount of plastic boxes with shoes in them, but didn't discover anything more. Then, when he was reaching back into the farthest corner of the shelves that hung above the clothes bar, his fingers found a stack of books. Pulling one down, he saw it was actually a photo album. Page after page showed pictures of two little girls, here dressed in matching Easter dresses, here, older, with braces and Band-Aids on their knees. Often the girls' heads were bent together, with bright smiles for the camera. He would have thought they were twins had he not recognized one was Sydney and the other one, Laney. So absorbed was he in the photographs, he didn't hear her enter behind him.

"Find something?"

He jumped, wishing he could shield her from this. She came forward when she saw what was in his hands and took it carefully from him. She sat crisscross and began paging through it without speaking. He watched her for a moment, concerned, but then turned back to the shelves. He was surprised to see a small key hanging down from a pink ribbon. He reached up and pulled it down, and a second book came crashing down with it. Laney jumped up from her place on the floor.

"Syd's diary," she blurted out, running her hand over the worn cover reverently. It had a picture of pink ballet slippers on the cover and it locked with a tiny, golden latch. "You don't know how many times I tried to break into this when I was a girl." She looked at him with comic seriousness. "This holds all of the secrets of a twelve-year-old girl, it's priceless." She laughed, still rubbing her hand over the cover. "Wait...this isn't the right key. This is too big."

Cooper examined it. "You're right. It looks like it's about the right size for a desk drawer, though. Come on."

They raced downstairs to the office. Laney sat behind the desk as he bent and slid the key right into the lock. They shared a look of delight, excitement, and apprehension. Slowly he opened the drawer. It was empty except for a pile of envelopes tied up with a red ribbon. He reached in and pulled them out, setting them on the desk in front of her. The envelopes had yellowed some but were addressed to her father, David Essex, and were from a woman named Lea Essex who lived in Phoenix. "Who's Lea Essex?" he asked.

"I haven't the faintest idea." She picked them up and began to page through them. "There must be ten letters here, all from Lea Essex." She carefully slid a letter out of its envelope. Her face paled as she read. "They're love letters," she murmured, incredulous. She let the sheet drop on her lap. Cooper got a sinking feeling. Could David Essex be the basis for Sydney's novel about a man with two families?

"Simple love letters, with everyday commentary, like you'd share with someone you were close to." She picked her letter up again and read out loud. "'Missed you at bridge club. Don and Susie said to tell you hello. Jay was not the partner that you are. We lost all four rubbers.'" She paused, her breath catching a few seconds later. "Further down she goes into some more intimate details about how much she missed him and how she was going to welcome him home. Home? I don't understand. Who is this woman? Was she deranged? And if so, why did my father keep her letters?"

Cooper perused one that he had opened. "Laney, I think you better read this."

"'I was so happy you could come to the sonogram with me this morning, honey. It's nice to put a face with the name we came up with, isn't it? And to think, in a few months our Scottie will be here.' Oh, my gosh!" She jumped up and began pacing behind the desk.

"Laney, what is it?"

"Scott was going to be my name if I was a boy." She looked at him, her eyes wide. "My father had another family in Phoenix. He had a son. He had a son..." she repeated faintly, settling back down into the chair with a shocked expression on her face. After a few minutes, she turned to Cooper and asked. "How can we be sure?"

"If I could borrow the laptop..."

She hopped out of the seat and let him take over. "Do you think your sister had wireless internet access?" He looked up to catch her are-you-kidding-expression. "Right." He started to type in Lea Essex, but as soon as he typed the first three letters, a dropdown appeared with her name in it. The pair exchanged a look. "Are you sure you want to know all this?"

"I'm in this far. I need to know the answers."

"Okay." He clicked on the name and maneuvered deftly around the web. He pulled up Lea Essex's obituary, and there it was in black and white. She had died in an automobile accident, killed by a drunk driver, and was survived by her husband, David, (42) and son, Scott (10).

"Oh, my God," Laney started pacing again. "That was my tenth birthday."

"What?"

"The day she died. I remember. My parents had a huge fight. I heard them, even over the chatter of all the girls at my birthday party. I snuck outside his study and listened, peeking through the door crack. He told my mom that he had to go, that something had come up at the office in Phoenix. She said, 'You're not leaving Laney's party to go to her. I won't let you.' and then my dad broke down and cried. I'd never, in my whole life, seen him cry. He put his head in his hands and cried out, 'She's dead, okay? Is that what you wanted to hear? Dammit, Camille. She's dead,' and that's all I heard because my mom turned around to march out and I had to run away before she caught me. I always thought that they were talking about my Great-Aunt Martha, who lived in Phoenix. She and my mom never got along, so I thought..." She stood still, lost in thought. "My mom knew and she never said a word. Never. Not even after he died. I have a brother, or half-brother, I guess. This is crazy." He watched as the realization dawned on her. "This must have been what Syd was going to tell me. She was doing research and somehow stumbled upon these letters."

The real question was who wanted to keep Laney from finding out? Who needed to keep Sydney quiet? He glanced at her. She looked utterly befuddled and shell-shocked.

He closed the laptop. "I think you've had enough for today. I'm taking you home."

She glanced up as if remembering he was in the room with her. "Okay."

CHAPTER EIGHT

Laney didn't say a word on the way home, just stared forward, in a daze. She got out slowly when the car came to a stop in her parking lot. Cooper hurried around to her side of the car where she had closed the door and was now leaning against it.

Laney had so many thoughts and emotions churning through her she felt like a witch's cauldron with things popping up at random to the surface, not the least of which was her confused feelings for Cooper. She felt pulled to him like no man she had ever met before, but she also knew the kindness he offered was little more than an obligation to his job, and her frustration over that, along with her grief and shock, were kindling for the fire under her boiling pot.

"Man. I can't even begin to imagine what you must think of me."

"What do you mean?"

"I mean, first you see my mom hit me—no, no, revise that, first you almost get into a fight because of me, then you witness a family throw down, and then you find out my dad was a lying, cheating bastard." She moved past him, muttering, "Yeah. I got the whole package, all right. A mom that freaks out from time-to-time and strikes people in public, a dad living a dual life...oh yeah, it's a barrel of laughs with the Essexes." She set off at a pretty fast clip across the parking lot.

"Laney, wait."

She spun to face him, her face hot with anger and pain.

"This isn't any reflection on you."

"Oh, you are the eternal optimist, Cooper." She whirled continued toward her townhouse.

"Laney? Laney?" He scrambled after her and grabbed her arm. "Wait a minute."

She shook him off. "Your duties here are finished, Officer," she said cool-ly. "You've done a great job of offering comfort to the deceased's sister. I'll commend you to your superiors."

He stood there for a moment, mouth hanging open. "What? Now you're mad at me?"

"No, Officer Sullivan, not at all. Your goddamn professional courtesy is appreciated, now leave me alone." The tears which threatened earlier ran down her cheeks now. She didn't even know what she was shouting at him, let alone why.

"Laney, let's talk. You're upset."

She struggled with the key in the lock. "I'm okay. I'll handle it the way all we Essexes do." She jerked the door open. "I'll drink 'til I'm blind, deaf, and dumb and then maybe I'll do a header off the balcony." She tried to close the door on him, but he wedged his foot in it. She stared at him through the crack, her eyes burning from tears and lack of sleep. "I'm kidding, Officer. Don't worry. You won't have to scrape me off the pavement. Now, if you could please, leave me alone."

"Lane," he said, his voice soft and desperate, "is that really what you want?"

She struggled to find words, looking down, the anger dissipating, leaving her tired.

"Yes." Her voice was a mere whisper. "Yes," she said more firmly, looking him in the eye with a hint of residual anger stirring.

He took his hands from the door frame, where he had been trying to force his way in, and pulled his foot out. She slammed the door in his face and turned the deadbolt. She laid her forehead on the door, her hand still on the bolt. It was dead silent. She'd never felt so alone.

She turned and plodded up the stairs to her bedroom and curled up on her side in her bed. The words from the letters kept floating through her mind. "Come home soon, honey. We love you-Lea and Scottie."

Her father had been her staunch supporter, her advocate, and all the while he had been lying to her. Her mother knew the whole time but had never bothered to say anything to her. And Sydney had gone and left her with this mess. She couldn't cope. She cried until she fell asleep.

In her dreams, someone was standing over her, speaking her name tenderly, but when she woke in the dark room later, she was alone.

She got up and dragged herself to the kitchen to warm up a bowl of soup. She caught her reflection in the microwave. Her eyes were so puffy they looked like swollen pickles, her nose was sore, and the exhaustion of sleepless nights showed on her face. Why would Cooper want me? Why would anyone want me?

She turned away from her reflection and took her soup to the kitchen table. As she sat stirring her soup, with no real interest in eating it, there was a soft rap on the French doors that led to her back patio. She saw her neighbor, Steve, outside. She got up and went to unlock the door.

"Hi, Steve," she mumbled dully. She abandoned the soup she'd just made and shuffled to the living room. Steve was 6'3 and gangly, with curly brown hair and a killer smile. He had moved in several years ago and they had become friends.

"I brought you some cookies."

She looked up and noticed, for the first time, the plate of chocolate chip cookies he held in his hand. He knew they were her favorite. The sweet gesture penetrated the haze of pain. Unable to speak, she patted the chair next to her.

"I don't think I'll be very good conversationalist tonight," she got out after a bit.

"Oh, Laney." He came to sit by her. "I didn't expect you to be. You don't have to say anything at all. I thought you might like some company."

His unexpected kindness broke the dams. Her shoulders started shaking. "Oh, Laney. Poor baby."

She wept until she fell asleep again, in his arms.

COOPER LEFT LANEY'S and drove straight to the precinct house. He typed up all he had learned that day and, with several interruptions—not the least of which was the informal inquisition Aidan had given him about he and Laney—wasn't finished until well after seven. He hadn't eaten, but he didn't feel hungry either. He went home and turned the basketball game on, but had trouble following it.

The words Laney shouted at him in the parking lot kept repeating in his head. Every time she had called him 'officer' had been like a bullet to the heart, emphasizing how wrong it was to have these feelings for her. But what bothered him the most were the images of her face he couldn't shake, the stark pain and confusion. More than once he picked up the phone to call her then hung up without doing so. She made it clear she wanted to be by herself. He needed to respect that.

When he went out for a drive, he had no idea he would end up over at her place. He sat in the parking lot for a while. *This is silly. I'm here, I might as well check on her. She was upset. It's what any caring individual would do,* he further rationalized. He simply wanted to see her again, to make sure she was all right. But, if he were completely honest with himself, he wanted more than that, but he knew it wasn't right.

He got out of his car and ambled up to her townhouse. He raised his hand to rap on the door, glancing in one of the long side windows. He saw her curled up, her head on another man's lap; the man was stroking her hair. He turned and hurried away.

Of course she had a boyfriend. Why had the thought never occurred to him before? Maybe because *if I were her boyfriend, I would keep better tabs on her, at a time like this. I wouldn't allow her to walk into some bar and dance with some strange man...and look so good...and...* He shook his head. But then again, Laney wouldn't have listened to anybody. And that was one of the things he liked about her, he realized. When she made a decision, she was strong-willed and fearless.

And she belonged to another man.

WHEN LANEY WOKE UP in Steve's arms, she felt embarrassed. They were good friends, but not fall-asleep-in-your-arms kind of friends. She felt utterly awkward until he left.

Meandering around her condo, she reviewed the day's events over and over, feeling like a caged animal. She couldn't believe how much her life had changed over the past couple of days and she wished, desperately, to have her old life back—the life of papers and red pens, teenaged angst and poor grammar. Not the life she had inherited—a life of murder, betrayal, and deceit. She felt incapable of handling the situation she had stumbled into.

And again and again, she kept coming back to the end of the day, to the hateful way she acted with Cooper, the nonsense that had come out of her mouth. One thing was for certain, she owed that man an apology.

So, apologizing was what she had in mind when she showed up at the precinct house the next morning. She wandered the halls, amazed by how big the building was. *I wonder if the people who work here ever feel like a mouse in a maze.* She turned a corner and almost ran into someone. In fact, he had to take her arms to prevent them from ramming into each other. He was mopping sweat from his face with the ends of the towel slung over his shoulders. He wore a sleeveless shirt and sweats.

"Oh. I'm so sorry. I wasn't watching where I was going."

"No problem," he said with a grin. He was tall, with dark hair and a tanned complexion. "Can I help you find someone?"

"You wouldn't, by any chance, know where Cooper Sullivan is, would you?"

"I would," he answered brightly. "I just left him. He was giving me one hell of a workout, and he's still at it. Down the hall to your right."

"Oh, thanks." But before she could turn to go, he stopped her.

"I knew something was gnawing at him and now I see why. You're Laney Essex, aren't you?"

"Why, yes. I...how did you know—"

He stuck out his hand. "I'm Aidan. Aidan McConnahy, Cooper's partner."

"Oh. Well. Very nice to meet you. I didn't even realize he had a partner."

He eyed her. "Yeah. Well. He's been kind of lone wolfing it lately. May I say...you don't look anything like I expected."

"Oh, I don't?" She glanced down at her faded blue jeans and t-shirt. "What did you expect?"

"Somebody more...I don't know...uptight."

"That would be my mother."

His grin widened. "So I heard." A uniformed police officer rounded the corner with some papers in his hand and stopped short. Aidan didn't look up or acknowledge him.

"And I'm plenty uptight."

"You don't look it. You look more like the kind of girl that every designer in Europe would be dying to get to walk down the runways in their latest fashions."

Laney felt a wave of heat rush to her face. "Oh. Well...thank you. You may have suffered some oxygen deprivation in that workout." *This is shaping up to be one of the strangest conversations I've had in a while.*

He laughed. "Sense of humor, too. Yep. Coop's in trouble."

"Uhh...McConnahy? I'm kind of in a crunch here."

"Keep your shorts on, Bohouser. I'll be right with ya." He took her hand and bent to kiss it. "Nice meeting you, Laney Essex." He gestured again. "Down the hall and to your right. Take it easy on him."

"Oookay," she replied.

He swung around and slapped the uniformed officer on the back with a, "Now what can I do for you, Jack?"

Laney stood for a second and then laughed and shook her head. Aidan McConnahy was one of a kind.

She continued down the hall and paused outside the door to the weight room. A window took up half the door, so she was able to look in and see Cooper right away. He was preoccupied with adjusting his machine, so he didn't see her. Her heart stopped for a minute as she watched him. He had his shirt off and sweats on. His shoulders were huge, and the muscles in his back and arms, well defined. When he turned and sat on the end of the bench, she could see the rest of him, and she had to remind herself to breathe. He looked like he should be on the cover of a romance novel with some exotic woman running her hands down his chest. She wished she could be that woman. When he started to lift his eyes, she dropped into a crouch below the window and waited anxious, holding her breath, to see if he had observed her outside the door. She duck-walked out of view of the window and then straightened. Spotting a women's restroom down the hall, she tore off in its direction. Behind the closed door, she leaned against the wall, breathing heavily and feeling foolish. What had she done? Had she really ducked like some junior high-schooler caught staring at her crush? What an idiot. She laughed at herself. *Geez, Laney, maybe he'll ask you to the senior prom*, she chided herself. *For goodness sakes, pull yourself together.*

She opened the door a crack and saw him coming out of the gym and into the hall. *Okay, time to act like an adult.* She exhaled and stepped out.

Cooper had put on a t-shirt, but she still imagined his bare back as he walked in front of her. She was about to call out to him but his name died on her lips. Coming toward him, a pretty blonde launched herself into his arms. "Cooper!" she squealed.

He laughed, picking her up off her feet. "Kenz!" he shouted happily.

Whatever he said next was drowned out by the sound of the blood rushing through her head with a loud swish that turned into a hum. Of course. He had a girlfriend. Of course. She knew it all along. So, why did seeing him with her feel like a punch to the stomach? She spun on her heel and hurried blindly down the hall toward a stairwell. When she was safe behind the door to the stairs, she kept moving. She wanted to get away from the police station, and Cooper Sullivan, as soon as humanly possible.

CHAPTER NINE

"K enz! What are you doing here?"
"Came to see if my big brother might be available for lunch later."

"What time?"

"Noon?"

He thought about it. "Sure. I can rearrange a few things." He placed his hand over her shoulder easily. "So, where do you want to go eat?"

"You choose," she said, skipping off. "I have a meeting next door. I'll be back to pick you up."

"Okay," he said, laughing at his exuberant sister. A lunch with McKenzie was what he needed to get his mind off Laney Essex, he decided, opening the door to the locker room.

A HALF-HOUR LATER HE was back at his desk making phone calls. Aidan glanced over at him when he jotted something down on a notepad. He hung up the phone.

"What is it?"

"Get this...Scott Essex is out of town on business."

"So?"

"You wanna guess where his business took him?" Cooper leaned back in his chair and folded his hands behind his head with a smug smile.

"Los Angeles?"

"You got it."

"And get this, Coop, Scott Essex inherited a bloody fortune from his father. Twice what Sydney and Laney did. Had Camille Essex discovered that, she may have tried to sue him to recover funds that she thought should go to her girls. I'd say 6.5 million is a good enough motive for murder."

"He's staying at The Standard Hotel, downtown," Cooper said decisively. "Wanna get out and take advantage of this gorgeous Southern California sunshine?" Aidan stood and pushed the chair into his desk. "Lead the way."

"MR. ESSEX." THE GIRL behind the counter waved at a tall, slender man who was walking by.

Aidan flashed her a smile. "Thanks."

"Scott Essex?"

"Yes. What can I do for you gentlemen?" the man said with a smile. He had the unmistakable mark of an Essex about him, blond hair and blue eyes the same rich color of Laney's.

Aidan and Cooper showed him their badges. "We had a few questions concerning the murder of Sydney Essex."

"Sydney Essex, the author? I'm afraid I can't help you. That's a different Essex family altogether. Sorry about that." The businessman tried to get around them but Cooper laid a restraining hand on his shoulder.

"Funny," he said, pulling a picture of Sydney out of his pocket, "cause you two look an awful lot alike." He smiled, but gave him a hard stare.

Scott Essex turned to Aidan hopefully, but the detective nodded his head. "The spittin' image," he agreed.

"Okay," the man said with a sigh. "But can we talk somewhere private?"

Cooper bowed and gestured for him to lead the way. Scott ducked into the breakfast nook where a large, African American lady was cleaning up after the morning crowd.

"Do you mind leaving so we can have some privacy?" Scott snapped.

The woman paused in mid-swipe as she brushed crumbs into her hand, giving him a bland look. "Um-hum, I'll do that," she said, in a tone that made it clear that she had no intention of leaving. She continued wiping the table without giving him a second look.

Scott made a frustrated noise and crossed the hall, opening the door to the pool area. The place was deserted except for a pair of noisy kids doing cannonballs, and a mother who was absorbed by the latest tabloid, but they were at the other side of the big room, and for that matter, she could have been standing right next to them and not heard the conversation over the din the kids were making.

"All right. What questions do you have for me, Officers?" Scott Essex looked nervous, the bead of sweat on his forehead coming from more than the heated pool area.

Cooper went for the jugular. "For one, can you can tell us where you were Saturday night during the time of Sydney Essex's murder?"

Scott dropped his head with a sigh, then, seeming to make a decision, he raised it to look him straight in the eye. "I was at Phat Jack's." Cooper and Aidan exchanged surprised looks.

"I know I probably should have come forward, but I didn't see what the point was. I didn't see who killed Sydney, and to tell you the truth, I didn't want to deal with the hassle."

"You didn't want to deal with the hassle? This was your sister lying strangled in the parking lot."

Scott Essex blanched. "My half-sister," he corrected. "Listen, up until a week ago I didn't even know I had a half-sister, and then she appears from out of nowhere, tells me about our connection, and goes and gets killed. Just when I was starting to really like her."

"Well, I'm pretty certain that's not what Sydney had in mind either," Cooper said wryly.

"I know, I know. I'm coming off as a big jerk here, and maybe I deserve to be." The businessman yanked on his tie, succumbing to the heat, and pulled out a chair at a nearby table, gesturing for them to take a seat. Cooper pulled out his notebook.

"Sydney Essex showed up on my doorstep a week ago with a pile of letters written by my mom to...our...dad. I was flabbergasted. I had no idea Dad had any life other than the one he had with Mom and I. He was gone on business a lot but, another family? No way. Anyway, there was no denying the resemblance, like you suggested earlier, and the letters were pretty much stone cold proof."

"And how did you happen upon the scene of the murder?"

"Sydney had asked me to meet her there. She seemed, well, fairly theatri-cal, and she wanted to sort of spring me on Laney, my other half-sister. I got there early and had a drink. And then I had another, Sydney was late. The longer I sat there, the more nervous I became." He folded his hands on the table, leaning forward. "I started to think that maybe this wasn't the best way to break the news to Laney, so I paid my tab and left. It wasn't until I hit the parking lot that I knew something was wrong. A woman was screaming and a man yelled for someone to get the police. A man rushed past me, warning me to stay inside, someone had been murdered, but I didn't listen. Something was drawing me outside, curiosity I guess, and maybe a little bit of a sixth sense or something. I started thinking, was Sydney late, or had she been way-laid in the parking lot? Still, nothing could have prepared me for seeing her there on the ground—" He broke off, staring into space and shaking his head. Cooper raised his eyes to Aidan's to see if he thought the story was credi-ble or not. Aidan gave him a shrug. Before Cooper could prompt him, Scott started talking again. "I guess I was in shock because people started gather-ing outside and I stood there, not moving, staring at Sydney's body. I don't know how long it was before the police arrived and started shoving people back and setting out that yellow tape, and then she came...Laney. I knew her right away. I saw her searching the crowd for Sydney. And then I saw her turn and see the body. She rushed forward but the cops scooped her up.

I've never heard anyone cry like that. It was like an animal or an insane person. I had to get out. I saw the pain on that beautiful face, a face that looked so much like my daughter, Paige's, and I had to get out of there. I've regretted it ever since. She had no one, and I left her. But, you see," he said, looking up at them now with pleading eyes, "she didn't know me. I couldn't comfort her."

Aidan nodded to reassure him.

"That was one of the worst nights of my life. My sister, who I had just met and started to like, was dead in front of me. And my other sister in anguish, who I hadn't even been introduced to yet, but I still felt a sort of...bond with. It was bad," he said lamely, wiping the sweat from his upper lip. "It was real bad."

Cooper looked at Aidan again. Someone was going to have to play the hard ass here. "Mr. Essex, you mean to tell me that you just happened to be in L.A. the night of the murder."

"I didn't happen to be. I came because Sydney asked me to."

"And you weren't a little bit afraid that your two new half-sisters might try to take back some of the six-point-five million dollars you inherited?"

His face became red. "You're not insinuating I had something to do with Sydney's murder, because I most certainly did not. And as for the six-point-five million, well, I never wanted that money. As far as I was concerned, that money was blood money. Money I was given because my dad, the man that I looked up to the most in this cruddy world, had died. I didn't want that money. So, I spent it. Not in the way you're thinking," he barked, seeing the two detectives exchange a glance. "I gave it away to special charities...Amnesty International, One, which is a group trying to annihilate extreme poverty in Africa...I gave to churches, community centers, hell, I even built an iceskating rink for underprivileged children...that money never changed my lifestyle one iota. I got nothing from it other than the satisfaction of helping others."

Cooper frowned. *He's a lot more like Laney than he knows.*

"And I could have never killed Sydney. I hadn't known her for long, but I liked her. And what was done to her was horrible. Just horrible. And, she was my sister," when Cooper looked ready to correct him Scott amended, "half-sister, but a sister all the same."

Aidan looked to Cooper. He had already closed his notebook. "So how long is your business going to keep you in town, Mr. Essex?"

"Until the end of the week."

They all rose from their seats. "Make sure you don't travel too far."

"Phoenix and here, that's all," he reassured them. "Umm, do you know...does Laney know about me yet?"

"Yes. She and I discovered the letters you talked about. That brought us to you."

"If you could—" He reached into his pocket and pulled out a business card. "—please give her this and tell her she can call me—anytime of the day or night—if she wants to talk."

Cooper hesitated. "All right. But I don't know if she's ready for that yet."

"I understand. But maybe later."

"Yeah. Maybe."

CHAPTER TEN

As the two detectives approached Cooper's Corvette in the parking lot, Aidan asked, "Wanna grab some lunch?"

"Actually I have a lunch date with—"

"Laney Essex. I saw her at the precinct house."

"Huh? No." Cooper shook his head. "I was going to say, with McKenzie. You saw Laney at the precinct house?"

"Yeah." Aidan had walked around to the other side of the car and they now stood talking to each other over the roof. "And I've got to say, you didn't do justice to her hotness quotient. She's smokin'. Definitely 'special' material."

He tried to ignore the irritation that sprang up when he heard Aidan talk about Laney that way. "What was she doing there?"

"I don't know," he replied, shrugging. "She was looking for you, and I told her you were in the weight room. Didn't you see her?"

"No." He frowned, opening his door to get into the vehicle.

"Maybe she changed her mind."

"Yeah. Anyway, you can join Kenz and me if you want."

"No. No. I wouldn't want to interfere with brother/sister bonding time. Besides, I'm gonna call Jenna and make some—" He cleared his throat suggestively. "—lunch plans for myself."

Cooper chuckled as he pulled out of the parking spot. "I just bet you will."

"COOPER? EARTH TO COOPER," McKenzie nagged. "You haven't said two words. I should have just had lunch with the guy at the desk who spoke Japanese."

"I'm sorry, Kenzie. How's work?"

"Boring. We'd have to hit the snooze button for that conversation," McKenzie said with a grin. She sold advertising airtime at one of the local radio stations. The only part of her job she liked was sometimes scoring concert tickets to sold-out events. "What's been going on with you, bro? I heard you landed the big Sydney Essex case."

"Yeah, I did."

"So, how's it going? What sort of bad guy are we looking at here?" McKenzie whispered conspiratorially. "Was it a drug deal gone bad? A jealous lover? A family squabble of some sort? What?" She waited, breathless, her eyebrows arched for dramatic effect.

He smiled, finishing his bite before answering. "You know I can't tell you anything."

"Oh, you're such a poop," she said, miffed, punching him in the arm.

"Ouch."

"Sorry about that," she said mockingly.

"Just like I'm sorry about..." He reached under the table to grip her kneecap in an old familiar torture move, one that would be sure to give her terrible Charlie horses.

"No, Coop. Not that. Please!" She laughed with a hint of hysteria.

"All right, all right." He released her knee with a conciliatory pat.

"Softee," she commented, moving her chair away and kicking him in the shin.

"Ouch!" He reached down to rub his leg. "Man, you don't fight fair."

"Has it really been that long, Cooper?" She grinned as she ate her meal daintily, not looking the menace he knew she was. "How's your love life?" she said, with more interest than the question usually got.

"Nonexistent."

"That's not what I heard," she cooed, twirling her chopsticks at him.

"What have you heard?"

"Aidan said you've got the hots for the dead girl's sister," she responded with glee.

"I've got the hots for...? 'The dead girl', as you so tactlessly put it, was named Sydney Essex. And as for her sister, whose name is Laney—" he emphasized, "—any guy with a pulse would have the hots for her, so it's not like it's a news flash."

"It is when it comes to you. You haven't exactly been doing the horizontal bop with anyone in a long time."

Cooper laughed. "You kiss Mom with that mouth?"

"Oh, come on, Coop. Give me the scoop. What's she like?"

"Is your love life really that boring that you have to delve into mine?"

"Low blow. Okay, if you won't dish, I'm going to tell Mom you said her gravy was lumpy."

"I like lumpy."

"But I might not mention that."

"Go ahead," he challenged, trying to look nonchalant.

"Okay." She opened up her cell phone, hit speed dial and stared across the table at her brother, her eyes sparkling. "Hi, Mom...just a minute." Cooper was waving his hands frantically. She covered the receiver with a triumphant grin.

"I'll tell you whatever you want," he whispered in desperation, afraid of the wrath and/or hurt feelings of his mother.

"Thanks, Bree." McKenzie snapped the phone shut.

"Why, you little dog."

"Uh-uh-uh." She opened the phone again and paused with a finger poised over the buttons. "I'll do it for real, and you know I will."

He studied her features. "You would, you brat. What do you want to know?" he sighed, resigned to his fate.

"What's she like? What do you like about her?"

"Well...she's funny, and sweet, and sexy all rolled into one."

"Sounds like a keeper."

"Yeah—" Cooper replied, taking the opportunity to signal for the check. "—only you've got to have something first, before you can keep it."

"What? Just work your old school charm on her." She punched him lightly in the arm this time.

"Nah. I don't think that would work."

"Why not?"

"I don't know. She's from money."

"Oh, she's highfaluting." Her face displayed her disdain. "You're right, you don't need that."

"No. She's not like that at all," he blurted out. "She's a teacher. At Walter Davis."

"A teacher—at Walter Davis, no less—but she comes from money? She must be crazy." McKenzie rose.

He laughed. "I think the word is dedicated, which you wouldn't know anything about Miss I've-Had-Five-Jobs-in-Four-Years."

"I just haven't found my calling yet," she replied petulantly, grabbing the fortune cookies from the table.

"Yeah, right."

"But, back to you." Cooper smiled at his sister's persistence. That was one thing about Kenzie, he thought, if she got something in her mind, it was impossible to shake her. "Have you let this girl know about your feelings for her?"

"No. I'm not even sure what my feelings for her are. This is in the very early stages, Kenzie. And besides, I met her on the job and you know how Dad would feel about that."

"Oh, for heaven's sake. When are you going to stop trying to live up to that man's expectations?"

"I hope never." Thaddeus Sullivan was a tough man, especially with his boys, but he had a good heart and a lot of wisdom under his belt, and Cooper had looked up to him from the day he was born.

"You know Daddy's proud of you. So I say, screw it. If this girl's what you want, then go for it."

"McKenzie Marie Sullivan. I'm not sure I like you hanging out with all those foulmouthed rock stars."

"Oh, now you're sounding like Momma. Eat your fortune cookie," she ordered, tossing it at him.

He caught it and opened it. "'A lifetime of surprises is about to begin,'" he read, then crunched into his cookie as they headed toward the cashier.

"In bed." McKenzie giggled.

"Huh?"

"Don't you know how to read a fortune cookie? You read whatever it says, then add 'in bed.'" She cracked her cookie and tried to slide her fortune out. "'A lifetime of surprises is about to begin in bed.' Sounds pretty good, Coop."

He grinned. "What does yours say?"

"'Life is bound to have its share of disappointments' ...in bed. That sucks." McKenzie stood on her tippy toes to give her big brother a fond peck on the cheek and then slid her hand through his arm. Cooper was quiet while he was walking her to her car, mulling over what she said about giving things a go with Laney.

When they got to her car, she turned to him. "You know, Cooper, you may have made the Dean's List every semester of your life, but I am the one in the family with the common sense, even if I can't hold down a job."

He grimaced. "I'll think about it."

She poked him in the chest. "Do."

CHAPTER ELEVEN

Cooper made it back to his desk, but found himself distracted from the work in front of him. Deciding he would go back to Phat Jack's later, he knocked off early to swing by Laney's place, and find out why she had stopped by without talking to him.

But when he got there, no one responded to his knocks. As he was turning away, a man on the adjacent stoop asked suspiciously, "Can I help you?"

Cooper glanced over to see the curly-haired man he had spotted through Laney's window the night before, holding grocery bags. He had an instant dislike for the man. "I'm here to see Laney."

"She's gone."

"I can see that." He sized him up. "Are you her boyfriend?"

"Maybe," he answered, evasive. "What's it to you?"

He bristled, but replied pleasantly enough, pulling out his badge. "I'm the officer assigned to the murder of Ms. Essex's sister, so...I was wondering if you knew where she was."

"Oh." The neighbor's guard dropped a fraction. "I'm not sure." He balanced one of the bags on his knee so he could get his key in the door.

"Well, my name's Cooper Sullivan, you are...?"

"Steve Bertrand."

"Steve, nice to meet you. What do you do for a living?"

"I own my own security business and teach karate on the side. In fact, I installed the system at Walter Davis, the school where Laney teaches," he added with an air of pride.

"Ah. Well, we may need to install a system here for Laney if we don't catch the killer soon."

"Why?" he asked, concerned. "What does that have to do with Laney?"

"We don't know if this has to do with just Sydney, or if they may be targeting other Essex family members."

"No one would want to hurt Laney," Steve said defensively. "She's not like Sydney. Sydney thought she was hot stuff. But Laney, Laney is sweet...she's different. No one would want to hurt her, believe me."

"Yes, I agree. Well, if you should see Laney, would you tell her I stopped by?"

"Sure, sure," he said, still wary. Cooper doubted the message would ever get through.

"Okay, thanks."

Cooper crossed to his car, but when he threw a glance back over his shoulder, the neighbor still stood on his stoop, watching him.

Laney paced the office. The door opened behind her.

"Kent," she breathed, relieved to see him. Kent Heaton strolled into the room.

"Laney," he walked up and gave her a quick hug. "I wasn't expecting to see you so soon. How are you?" he said, taking her hand.

"I've been better," she admitted. "But you can help me out." She smiled at him, hopeful.

Kent crossed to sit behind his desk. "Anything, Laney. You know that."

"Good. I was hoping you would say that."

"What is it that you need?"

"I want to come back to work. The day after tomorrow, if possible."

"The day after tomorrow? You haven't even had the funeral yet."

"I'm well aware of that, Kent," she snapped. But then, seeing his look of surprise, she added, "I'm sorry. It's just...I need something to do. I can't sit around my condo anymore. Time to think is too painful."

"Yeah, but Laney..."

"Really, Kent, I can hold it together, I swear."

"Laney. You need time to heal."

She bolted out of her chair and circled to stand behind it. "If I have any more time, I'm going to lose my mind. I have to have something to do to take my mind off things."

He studied her. "You look tired, and this edginess is uncharacteristic of you."

"Come on. You know what it was like after..." She was taking a risk here. "After your break up with Jan." His jaw tightened and he crossed his arms but she went on. "You threw yourself into your work to numb the pain. And, because of that, you rose up the ranks."

"Yes. But we both know I made some big mistakes, too." Laney knew what he was referring to. When she first came to Walter Davis after student teaching there, Kent was her mentor teacher. He had been younger then, and much more foolish, and erred by making a pass at his even younger first year teacher. Even though troubled by the breakup with his long-term girlfriend, he must have known it was wrong to initiate anything with Laney. She had let him down with as much grace as she could, and because of that, they had always remained friends. He stood and walked around the desk, leaning on its edge. "It's because I know you better than most of my teachers that I know this is tearing you up inside."

She lowered her head, unsure of what to say next.

"I'm not sure this is such a good idea, but... I'll let you come back next Monday, if you are up to it. No sooner."

She flew around the chair to plant an unexpected kiss on him. "Thanks, Kent. I knew you would understand."

He smiled. "I can't say no to you. But Laney, if you change your mind, I want you to let me know. I'll keep Liz on standby for another week just in case."

"Thanks. That will be perfect. I'll get out of your hair."

She left his office feeling better. She would be returning to school. She may not be the same person she was before Sydney's death, but she'd be back in the classroom.

"YOU'RE NOT GONNA START another fight tonight, are ya?" the bartender said with a grin.

"Hey," Cooper retorted, "I didn't start it. But—" He held out his hands. "—I took off the gloves. I'll behave, I promise."

"Just kiddin', man. That guy was an ass. And three-times your size, dude. I wouldn't have had the balls."

He shrugged. "He pissed me off."

The bartender gave a robust laugh. "Well, good thing you're light on your feet, Mac, or we'd still be picking up your pieces."

He laughed with him, pulling his money out to order a beer.

"Put your money away. This one's on me. What'll you have?"

"Thanks. I guess I'll take a scotch, straight up, then." He let his eyes wander while the bartender poured. "It's quiet tonight," he commented.

"Yeah. I guess all the curious folks came out the last few nights. Now everyone is spooked off."

He feigned ignorance. "And why's that?" he asked, raising his drink at the bartender in a salute and taking a sip of the smooth, top-grade scotch he was served.

"Because of the murder."

He swallowed, his eyes wide, giving his voice the proper note of alarm. "Someone was murdered here?"

The bartender leaned on the bar. "Don't you read the paper, buddy?"

"Just the sports page. Name's Cooper by the way," he added, offering his hand.

"I'm Joe. You never catch the news?"

He shrugged again. "Sometimes at the gym. Man, I thought this was a nice place. Somebody shot someone in here?" He searched around as if looking for the blood splatter.

"No, man. Out in the parking lot. A woman was strangled. Sydney Essex."

He stared at Joe blankly. "Who's she?"

"You never heard of Sydney Essex? She writes all those sappy romance novels my wife reads. But it gets her in the mood sometimes, so I don't knock it, ya know what I mean?"

Cooper chuckled and nodded, playing along. A customer down the line waved a hand. "I'll be right back." Joe took off to fill the customer's order, giving him a chance to eyeball the place for a while.

After several hours, he had zeroed in on a large man with a dark beard and bushy eyebrows. He wore an expensive suit, like the others, and lots of jewelry. People kept stopping by his table near the end of the bar and shaking hands, but not staying around for long. He tried to inconspicuously watch the handshakes, to see if anything was being exchanged, but in the dim lighting, he wasn't having much success. "Hey, Cooper," Joe said, his voice low. "Look who walked in. Blondie."

His jaw hardened.

"Is she a friend of yours?"

"No. I just met her the other night," he said truthfully, his voice with an edge.

"Maybe she came back looking for you. You know, her knight in shining armor and all."

"You read too many of your wife's romance books," he commented, not taking his eyes off Laney's reflection in the mirror.

"I don't know, man. I'd give it a try if I was you. She is one appealing lady."

"I'd have to agree with you there." Cooper watched as the bartender waltzed down to pour some kind of shot for her. Her hair was loose and curly, as it dropped beyond her bare shoulders. She had on a turquoise number that was even sexier than the one she wore before, if that was even possible, but as he strode toward her, he felt his anger beginning to rise again. What the hell was she doing? *I thought I'd made it perfectly clear that she was not to come back here.*

Laney downed her drink and raised her hand to order another. Cooper brought his hands down on either side of her on the bar. She raised her eyes and caught his in the mirror. He wanted to get her alone and chew her out. "Let's dance."

She turned on her stool to face him. Her eyes were fearful, but she raised her chin in defiance as she stared at him. That little cocky lift of her chin almost undid him. He knew how torn up inside she was and how she was fighting the pain that threatened to engulf her. He recognized her need to rebel against him, to defy somebody, anybody, to do something to turn back the tide of grief. But at the same time, the mild irritation, which had turned into anger, continued to seethe inside of him. Why would she return to the place where she had run into trouble before? And then, there was the second question that continued to bother him, why had she been in the arms of another man last night? He knew it was crazy to be upset by what he saw, after all, he had no claim on this woman, but all rationality concerning her had left a long time ago.

CHAPTER TWELVE

Before Laney could react, Cooper took a hand and pulled her toward the dance floor. Just as they hit the parquet, the same sultry song that had been playing the last time he saw her dancing began. He rolled his eyes. Perfect.

He turned to face her. Gazing into her eyes, he was struck by a charge of electricity. Her face was exquisite, hair glowing in the dance floor strobes like it was part of the light show; she absolutely took his breath away. He raised her arm and let his other hand circle her waist and rest against the skin of the small of her back. She shivered and he sensed it was with something stronger than fear. They began to sway to the music, their eyes locked, first with the heat of his anger, but changing to something even more charged. He wasn't certain whether she had moved her hand, or if he had released it; it happened almost at the same time. She linked hands behind his neck, and he brought both of his to her back. By secret agreement, their hips began to move in rhythm with each other.

His hands dropped to her hips as they moved, but he was unsure of who was leading who. He just knew he was completely and utterly turned on and his heart ached for her in a way that caused him physical pain. His stomach felt hollowed out and filled with only the strong urge to be with her, touching her like this, forever. He'd never felt such all-consuming desire for anyone before and it rocked him to the core, both thrilling and confusing.

He knew the moment the shot hit her as she became more fluid underneath his hands, a slow, sexy smile spreading across her face. He could not smile in return; he could only want and be guided by his private temptress. He was lost in her eyes' ocean of blue, but he felt himself wading in further. Without thinking, he began to lower his head to hers. As he tilted his head, her eyes traveled to his lips and he was so close now he could feel the sweet warmth of her breath. But the music had changed and while the others around them were dancing, they were standing still.

She put one fingertip to his lips for a second, then took one of his hands from her waist and moved out across the dance floor to the end of his arm, her smile bright. She twirled into his arms and they rocked together, her back against him, engulfed in his arms.

Cooper breathed in the scent of her hair and thought he would go crazy. He tried to nuzzle her ear, but just like that, she moved away again. She laughed, holding on to him by only the tips of her fingers and he laughed too, releasing all the pent up tension, catching her contagious, playful attitude. She crooked a finger at him and he pulled her into his arms, hands on her hips again as they shimmied. He smiled as he bent close to her again. She turned her head and pressed a cheek to his, extending their arms in a tango. Laughing still, he played along, even grabbing a flower to put into her mouth as they glided by one of the tables surrounding the dance floor. It was a carnation, not a rose, but it would suffice.

A few seconds later, she stuck it in his coat pocket and began to flamenco dance around him. She hiked up one side of her dress and held it there as she shook her hips, trailing a hand across his chest and around his back. He knew it was the alcohol making her feel so free, guessing that normally this was something she would never do, but he couldn't say he minded one bit.

COOPER'S HANDS FELT strong on her hips as Laney moved within the circle of his arms. She prayed what she saw in his eyes was what she wished it to be, a longing similar to hers. She knew she was in more danger in his arms than in the man's who had her on the dance floor the last time, because Cooper now held her heart in his hands. Without even realizing she was giving it away to him, it had gone from her. She had never felt for anyone the things she was feeling for him, or even known she was capable of such strong emotion. He awoke a part of her she never even knew existed. She wouldn't think about the woman she saw him with in the hall. She wouldn't torture herself with the thought she was misreading him. She would only bask in this moment, in the feel of his hands on her hips, their thighs touching and moving together to the rhythm of the music. There was something undeniably sexy about being within arms that could crush her, but instead touched her with great care. She gazed up into his face and, although hair was falling into his eyes, he was looking at her with a smoky intensity. She stopped breathing for an instant, mesmerized by the longing she saw there.

As the music neared an end, he dipped her. She laughed, throwing her head back so that her hair almost touched the floor, but as he brought her back upright, they both became serious. He moved to kiss her again, but her borrowed valor disappeared and she felt a surge of panic. She turned from him and strode across the dance floor back to her bar stool. When she reached it, she grabbed for her shot, but before she could throw it back, he took it from her and slammed it back on the bar. He was angry again.

"Uh-uh. You've had enough."

Her own ire rising, Laney picked up the glass and downed the drink sloppily, wiping her mouth with the back of her hand. "Now I've had enough," she hissed, but she could feel tears mounting behind her eyes. She pulled a bill from her purse without looking at it and laid it on the bar before turning to leave.

"Aren't you going to wait for your change?" he called after her, but she continued to march away from him. She bumped into an attractive, dark-haired man as he chatted with friends. He caught her by the arms as she was knocked off balance by the impact.

"Hey, what's the hurry?" he said, his voice kind, perhaps seeing she was upset.

Laney looked up at him, feeling confused. Cooper laid his hands on her shoulders. "She was leaving," he told the dark-haired man, his eyes hard.

Not even knowing why she was doing it, she stepped closer to the man she had jostled.

"Actually, I decided to stay."

"Laney," his voice was a warning. "We need to talk."

The man looked from his angry face to hers. "Is that what you want?" he asked, extending himself to his full height. "You want to leave with this man?"

She never took her eyes from Cooper's. A tense pause hung between them as she exhaled and lowered her face. "Yes. I'm sorry." She turned to hurry out ahead of Cooper.

She was halfway across the parking lot when she felt his hand on her arm as he jerked her around.

"What the hell are you doing?"

Tears stung her eyes, but she shook herself free, saying honestly, "I don't know."

She pulled out car keys, her hands shaking as she tried to press the unlock button. He snatched the keys out of her hands.

"You are not driving home."

"Fine!" she spat, and started tramping across the parking lot again.

"Now, what are you doing?"

"Walking," she answered without turning around.

"You can't walk home from here," he yelled after her.

She stopped. "Fine. I'll get a cab." She took one step into the street and started waving her hand to flag down a taxi. Cooper reached her and pulled her back onto the sidewalk just as a driver bore down on them, blaring his horn.

"Are you crazy?"

She started storming away from him again. "Apparently."

"Laney, wait. Wait! Dammit, Laney, stop, would ya?" He caught up to her again, grabbing her. "What's going on here?"

"You're hurting me."

He loosened his grip a fraction while still keeping her in place. "Come on. Don't say I'm hurting you. I would never hurt you."

So why is this tearing me up inside? "You're stronger than you think, Coop," she threw back. "I mean, the way you toss around those dumbbells—" She shut her lips, realizing her mistake.

"So you were at the precinct earlier. Why did you leave without talking to me?"

"Well, I didn't want to interrupt you and your gorgeous, blond-haired girlfriend," she yelled, furious. *Oh, geez. Why did I say that? I should have never had that second shot. I sound like an idiot.*

"Girlfriend?" he asked with a puzzled expression. Then he started laughing, "Oh, you mean Kenzie." He let go of her, sticking hands in his pockets, and wearing a smirk.

She tried to act like she didn't care. "Oh. Is that her name?"

He chuckled. "My, my, Laney. If I didn't know better, I'd say you were jealous."

"Jealous?" she squealed, trying to sound incredulous but coming off as shrill. "Not everybody falls for that incredible body of yours and that playboy hair—"

His eyes twinkled. "Careful. You're letting your lust show."

"Ugh!" she screamed in rage, turning to stomp away again.

She had gotten several feet before he shouted after her, "That was my sister."

She stopped dead in her tracks. Without turning she repeated, "Your sister?"

"Uh-huh."

She hung her head a minute, defeated, feeling foolish.

He trotted up to her, reaching out to stoke her arms. She leaned back into him for a second, tired. He spun her around, softly putting his hands on either side of her face. He seemed to be searching for words and ended up settling on, "Let me take you home."

CHAPTER THIRTEEN

They didn't speak on the way home, but at one point Cooper reached over to take her hand, and she smiled weakly, still hanging her head some. When they got back to her place, he opened the car door for her, and then took the keys he still had in his hands and opened the door to her condo. She trudged in, dropping her purse on the floor.

He closed the door behind them and turned to her, having thought out what he was going to say on the ride home.

He turned her to face him, rubbing her arms up and down as he spoke. "Laney, I'm sorry if I've been sending you mixed messages." She lowered her chin, but he reached down to lift it up so he could look her in the eyes. "I'm very attracted to you, and not just in the physical sense...but, as a cop, there are some lines I can't cross. So, no matter how much I want to act on these feelings I have for you, I can't. Do you understand?" She nodded, her eyes downcast.

He lifted her face again, reflexively running his thumbs across her lips. "So we're okay?" Her lips were moist and they parted under his touch. She squeezed her eyes shut and managed to nod.

"I should go then."

He stepped back but she grabbed his arms, her eyes wild and desperate. "No. Don't go!" She stepped toward him and her words came tumbling out. "Please, Cooper. Stay. I can't bear the thought of having to attend the funeral tomorrow. Please, stay with me." She paused, but when he didn't answer right away she blurted out, "We can have meaningless sex."

He laughed. "Laney. I could never have meaningless sex with you."

Her voice didn't even sound like her own. It was faster, more urgent. Desperation flashed in her eyes. "Please." She reached up to stroke his face, then pulled him down and pressed her trembling lips to his.

A wave of warmth and passion spread through him and he was paralyzed. "Please," she said again, her voice husky, "Make love to me, Cooper."

Her lips were on his again and he felt himself giving in. His hands caressed the bare skin of her back and shoulders. She unbuttoned his shirt, running her hands across the smooth skin of his chest, moaning with pleasure. The sound shook him; it took all he had in him to push away from her. He turned away, unable to witness the hurt in her eyes. He ran his hand through his hair. Why wasn't he able to control himself around her?

"Laney..." he said in a warning tone.

"Come on, Coop," she coaxed. She came around to face him, searching his face in the streetlight that filtered in through the windows. "What if I told you I'm a virgin? You could teach me the ropes. That's supposed to be a turn on, right?"

He didn't even know what to say to that. She threw her hands over her face.

"Or not." Her hands moved to her temples. "I can't believe I said that. I'm losing my mind." She turned away.

He tried to soften his reaction to her statement. "Laney, I can't. I just can't." Before he could say anything more, the phone rang. They both jumped at the sound. It was far too late for anyone to be calling. She turned and stared at him for a second, her eyes dead, then moved like a mummy to pick up the receiver.

"Hello?"

Cooper watched Laney's mouth fall open and her eyes get wide as saucers.

"Laney, what's wrong?" Cooper asked. Her mouth moved, but no sound came out.

He could now make out a male voice that seemed to be yelling. He stepped over and grabbed the receiver out of her hand but there was a click and the line went dead. She closed her eyes and swayed on her feet.

"Lane!" he cried in alarm, taking her arms to steady her. She reached back to feel the couch and sat down carefully.

"Who was that? What did they say?"

"Go, Cooper. Just go," she murmured.

He sat next to her. "I'm not going anywhere until you tell me who was on that phone." She sprang off the couch and turned, glaring at him and screaming, "It was him. Okay? It was the guy who k-killed Sydney." She covered her face with her hands again and wept.

Cooper shot off the couch and took her into his arms. "What did he say?"

She shook her head, "I...I don't know."

"Laney, calm down," he said, trying to keep his own voice level. "Take a deep breath." He could feel her starting to hyperventilate, her shoulders shaking.

"Just go, p-please!" she wailed.

"I'm not going anywhere," he repeated, this time more gently. She buried her head in his chest, hands still covering her face. "Did he threaten you?"

She nodded her head. He pulled her closer, glancing around the room to make certain there was no immediate threat. He moved her to the couch. "What did he say, Laney? Please try to remember."

"I don't know..." she said on the verge of hysteria. "He didn't make any sense...he said 'what are you doing, Laney? Why are you betraying me?' He kept saying that I was betraying him...betraying?" she questioned, bewildered.

"An old lover?"

"Apparently you weren't paying attention. I'm a virgin, remember?" she spat at him.

"Okay, okay," he patted her arm, thinking. "What about the guy next door?"

"Steve? You met Steve?"

He frowned. "Yeah."

"No. Steve would have no reason to believe I betrayed him. We're just friends."

"Well, it didn't look like that the other night," Cooper muttered.

"The other—you saw us?"

"I came back to check on you," he answered, defensive. "And he was...you were..."

Her face turned bright red. "I was upset. I fell asleep in his arms, that's all, I swear. It was a mistake, and I felt uncomfortable when I woke up." They were silent for several minutes, while Cooper digested that information with satisfaction. "Besides, Steve's a nice guy."

"He looked like he wanted to be more than friends, Laney."

Her face registered surprise. "You think?"

"Yeah," he said sarcastically, some of his old anger resurfacing. "I think."

"Oh." She seemed to think about this. "I would have recognized his voice. It wasn't him."

"What else did he say?"

"He said...he'd kill me like he 'fucking killed my sister'...and that I'd 'pay dearly.'"

"Okay," he said as if making a decision. "I'm staying here tonight. That's not a question, it's a statement." She nodded her head without saying anything. "I'll sleep on the couch. Stay here while I check the locks."

Cooper found French doors off the kitchen opening onto a stone paved patio, unlocked. He shook his head and locked them, peering out into the darkness. He checked all the windows and doors on the first level, and then returned to her side. She hadn't moved an inch. "Let's get you to bed." He climbed the stairs, holding her hand behind him and she followed.

The top floor was one large bedroom and bathroom with a small balcony off the front and a larger one off the back. He checked both sets of French doors to the balconies. He wasn't happy with the flimsy locks, but he saw it was a long way down with no access from below, so he was satisfied. He'd talk to that Steve guy in the morning about installing a security system. A top-notch one. Laney could afford it.

In the bathroom, she mechanically brushed her teeth. He took the opportunity to phone Aidan.

"I'm at Laney's."

"Well, I'll be damned. Fast worker."

"Shut up, it's not like that. We ran into each other at Phat Jack's—"

"What the hell was she doing back there? She shouldn't be in there."

"I know. I know. I told her that. But she can be kind of stubborn." It was one of the things that made her so sexy. "I'm staying here."

"Ahh. Good for you."

"Shut up, would you? I told you. It's not like that."

"Why are you staying then?" Aidan teased.

"Because she got a phone call from Sydney's murderer."

"No shit?"

"Yeah. And he threatened her."

Suddenly Aidan was all cop. "Did you secure the premises?"

"Yeah. We're locked in good and tight. No one's getting in here."

"Call me if you hear anything."

"All right, see you in the morning."

She shuffled out of the bathroom and pulled pajamas out of a dresser drawer. Seeming unaware of his presence, she unzipped her dress and let it fall to the ground. Surprised, he forced himself to turn his eyes away. He ordered himself to think about the room, not the fact the figure he saw silhouetted in the outside lights was impossibly perfect. Luckily, the room gave him something to think about. He noted a simple antique wooden dresser, a brass bed, unadorned except for a bright quilt and a few pillows, everything a glaring contrast to the décor downstairs. This room was without a doubt Laney, warm, unassuming. He stole a look over his shoulder and saw her just as she unsnapped her bra; he groaned inwardly, spinning his head around. He could tell when she was finished by the lack of noise. When he turned, she lay curled up in bed with her back to him, facing the rear doors. He felt the chill coming from her, but was drawn to the bed anyway. "Lane?" he whispered, stroking her hair. She flinched, hands tightening their grip on the covers. He withdrew his hand. He could see that her eyes were open wide, staring, unseeing, into space. He supposed the shock of the past several days and the threat on her life had hit her hard. "Good night, then." His voice was hoarse, sorry for the part he had played in it all.

He descended the stairs, still thinking about her and whether or not he had made the right decision to pull away, and whether that would be something he could continue to do. He sat on the couch and only then remembered his shirt was unbuttoned. He rubbed his hand over his chest, recalling the way her hands had explored his skin there, her touch electric. With a sigh, he removed his holster from the back of his pants, where it was hidden by his jacket, and placed it on the coffee table in front of him. Having second thoughts, he snapped the holster open and removed his pistol, setting it out where it would be handy. He unfolded the quilt he had picked up from a trunk at the end of Laney's bed, and stretched out on the couch. He lay with his hand flopped across his forehead, knowing sleep was a long way off.

He reflected over the day, especially the parts containing her. Even with his eyes closed, he still saw her face. He saw the fear and defiance in her eyes when she turned on the barstool, caged by his arms, staring into his face. He took a deep breath, remembering the way her hair had smelled, and felt so soft when he leaned in and whispered in her ear before she turned. He thought of her now, lying upstairs under a quilt, imagining how warm and supple she would be, and drove himself insane.

A virgin? Was it really a virgin's hips that had moved under his hands on the dance floor? How could it be possible, that someone as striking, as fun, as she was—dancing the tango with that silly carnation in her mouth—how had she never been with anyone? And how did he feel about that? It made her more fragile, more vulnerable, than before. He felt the need to protect her even more strongly. But a turn on? He had to admit, it held a certain mystique.

With a frustrated sigh, he threw off the blanket and sat. He might as well get up and check on things. He stuck his gun into his waistband and went to the back doors and searched outside, returning to the front to inspect the shadows of the parking lot. The killer had said, "What are you doing?" Had he been watching them? Could he feel betrayed because he saw them kissing through the windows? Cooper saw nothing outside, but as he turned to go back to the couch, he heard a noise upstairs.

He was instantly alert. Keeping in mind the possibility Laney had gotten up to go to the bathroom or something, he ascended the stairs, trying not to make a sound. As he neared the top, he could hear her rhythmic breathing. He drew his gun. Breaching the top of the stairs, he realized the back balcony doors were wide open, a breeze rustling the sheer curtains surrounding them. Did she open them to get some fresh air and then fall back asleep? Staying close to the bed in case he had to dive in front of Laney to protect her, he made his way over to the doorway. He edged out on the balcony but found it deserted. He looked over the edge. No rope, no ladder, no anything. He inspected the door handles and found scratches, and deep gouges that indicated someone had forced their way in. In alarm, his eyes searched the dark recesses of the room. The intruder could still be in the room, or in the bathroom. He knelt on the bed and crept next to Laney. For a minute, he was frozen by the sight of her peaceful face in the moonlight. He covered her mouth with his hand and bent to whisper in her ear.

"Laney."

She started and looked up at him with round, confused eyes.

He removed his hand. "Did you open your balcony doors?"

"Sometimes they open on their own," she explained.

"When? Have you ever seen it happen?"

"No. It happens mostly at night, or when I've been away."

He didn't want to alarm her, but..."I think someone has jimmied your lock. And from the looks of it, more than once." Her eyes opened wider in realization. She shook her head as if to deny it.

"It's okay," he reassured her, but she could now see the gun in his hand. "I want you to get behind the bed, behind me."

She listened and moved as he asked, squatting behind the protection of the mattress. "Stay here," he instructed, starting to move around the end of the bed.

"Cooper!" she said, grabbing his arm in a panic. "What are you doing? You could get hurt."

"This is my job." He shook her off. "Now stay down," he ended, fiercer than he had intended, the concern for her safety coloring his words.

She shut her mouth, surprised by his tone. Anger flashed in her eyes, but she complied. He inched forward until his back was pressed against the edge of the door to the bathroom. She watched tensely from her side of the bed. He listened but could hear no breathing or any other indication someone was present. He reached in to switch on the light, ready for someone to spring out, but there wasn't even the slightest movement. With the fresh light, he again searched all the dark recesses of the room, his eyes scanning. Seeing nothing, he took a deep breath and burst through the door of the bathroom, yanking the shower curtain back. To his relief, the tub was empty.

"Laney, honey, it's okay."

She rushed from her side of the bed and into his arms. He could feel her shaking. He tucked his gun into the back of his waistband so that he could put both of his arms around her.

"You're okay?" Her voice sounded strained against his chest.

"Yes, I'm fine." He breathed a sigh of relief, and ran his hand over her hair as he pulled her closer. After a minute, he held her at arm's length. "Are you okay?" She nodded. "Are you sure?"

Instead of answering, she wrapped her arms around him again. "I have never been so afraid in my life. You shouldn't have done that." She began pounding on his chest. "Dammit, Cooper, you shouldn't have done that. You could have been killed."

He smiled at her fit of temper. "Laney, this is my job. This is what I do for a living—"

"I don't care. If something had happened to you..." She shivered.

He pulled away to look at her face. "Nothing happened. I'm fine. Now," he changed the subject, "I want you to pack your toothbrush and anything else you might need. I'm taking you back to my place, for tonight. We'll fig-ure out what else we need to do in the morning. Okay?" She nodded. He placed his hands on either side of her face, concerned about how pale she looked. "Are you sure you're all right?"

"I'll be fine when we get out of here," she answered, starting to sound like herself again. He moved over to the bed with her, his arm over a shoulder, rubbing her smooth, still-warm skin. He reached down to turn on the lamp on the bedside table and she gasped. He looked down at the single red rose lying on her pillow, inches from where her head had been. Her trembling hand reached down to remove it.

"Leave it!" he barked, unintentionally harsh.

She pulled her hand back in surprise.

"I'll have it dusted for prints," he said, with more control, but his jaw was tight.

The killer had crept in somehow while he was lying downstairs and been close enough to Laney to feel her breath. He felt an unfamiliar rage inside him. The rose was the killer's way of mocking him, asserting he could get to Laney any time, even when Cooper was feet away. He smiled grimly. He wasn't about to let that happen again.

While Laney gathered her things, he went back out onto the balcony to check again for clues, looking back every few seconds to make sure she was all right. Looking down, he discovered nothing new. He looked up. The bal-cony extended beyond the roof line by several feet, so it would be easy for someone who had accessed the roof to jump down on her balcony. But how would they access the roof?

She came out to join him, looking up along with him. "You think that's how he got in?"

"Possibly. Do you know of any way to get on the roof?"

"Well, there's no staircase that I know of, if that's what you mean."

He nodded thoughtfully then looked at her. She had pulled on an oversized Missouri Tigers sweatshirt, making her look even smaller and more vulnerable.

Seeing the way he was studying her, Laney glanced at the sweatshirt. "Sydney got it for me. She wrote one of her books about a pair of college sweethearts and went to Columbia for 'research.' She got this at the bookstore." She shrugged. "It's comfortable."

He put both hands on her shoulders. "I think you look cute in it. Are you ready to go?"

She nodded and they left the balcony. He closed the doors securely, although he knew it meant very little.

CHAPTER FOURTEEN

B y the time they got to Cooper and Aidan's apartment, it was well after one. Laney had fallen asleep on the ride over and was apologetic.

"That's okay. You're wiped out. I'm glad you got more sleep." Cooper opened the door and let her in. "I'll show you to my room and I'll sleep on the couch." He was grateful Aidan had cleaned up in anticipation of his date with Jenna ending up at their place.

While he was getting her settled in, a tousle-haired Aidan appeared in the doorway. He grinned when he saw them together in the bedroom, sliding his hands up the door frame and looking self-satisfied.

"You dog," he started to say before Cooper shot him a warning look. He cleared his throat. "Nice to see you again."

Laney's face was red and she was avoiding direct eye contact with Aidan. Seeing he was only wearing his boxers, and she was in his roommate's bedroom in the middle of the night, Cooper could see why she was uncomfortable.

Aidan looked at him with one eyebrow raised, his way of asking Cooper why the change of plans. He gave him a little head jerk to indicate he would fill him in.

He seemed to have gotten the message. "I'll let you get settled in." Aidan smiled. "Sleep well." With a wink to Cooper, he left the pair alone.

Laney looked at him, sheepish. "I'm sorry about all of this."

"Don't be silly. Is there anything you need?"

"No. I think I'm set. Thank you so much, Cooper."

"Sure." He felt unexpectedly awkward. He made a move to leave, but turned back, framed in the doorway. "If you need anything, I'll be in the living room, just down the hall."

She sat cross-legged, on the bed, the light from his ancient lamp giving her hair a magical glow. *She looks good in my bed.* She smiled, appearing tired, but no longer afraid. "Good night," she murmured.

"Good night, Laney," he replied, his voice sounding husky to his ears. He closed the door and stood outside, gathering himself before going to the living room to talk to Aidan.

"What's up?" he asked as soon as Cooper entered the room.

"The killer was there."

"There? As in where, exactly?"

"In Laney's room. I had turned in, but couldn't get to sleep."

"A little keyed up, were ya, Coop?"

"Shut up." He smiled, but continued talking. "I heard a noise, and when I went up to check on Laney, her balcony doors were open. He was in there, man, when I was lying right at the bottom of the stairs."

"He didn't hurt her, did he?"

"No, she slept through the whole thing." His lips twitched, but then he frowned. "But he left a rose on her pillow. He could have hurt her. I should have known he was there." His heart clutched, remembering.

"You don't generally expect someone to break in on the upper floor."

"Yeah. But I should have—"

"Coop," Aidan interrupted, "you took care of her. You brought her here, and she's safe. Don't beat yourself up."

"Yeah, I guess."

He smirked. "She's pretty, even rumpled up."

Cooper glared at him before nailing him with the pillow he was carrying. Then, he ambled over and retrieved the pillow. He sat on the couch, running his hands through his hair. Aidan sat next to him, waiting. "Geez, man. You should see her dance."

"There was dancing?"

"Y-yess. Is your love life so pathetic you have to live vicariously through me?"

"You wish." Aidan turned to leave. "And, hey, Coop, try to keep it down in the morning, would ya? I'd hate for you to wake Jenna."

Cooper smiled and shook his head. "And I'm the dog?"

"Good night, Coop. Enjoy the couch." He ducked, chuckling when the pillow hit the wall.

Unbelievably, he fell asleep right away. Somewhere in the middle of the inky night, though, he woke up. He heard footsteps. He swung off the couch and snatched his gun from the coffee table in one smooth move. Knowing his way in the dark, he made his way to the opening of the hall. In the murky light, he could see the door to his bedroom open. Keeping his back on the opposite wall, he slid along, his gun at the ready. He felt a vibration at his back as a door opened. He swung across the hall, his back slamming into the wall on the other side, his gun up.

Laney swallowed her shriek, hands coming to her chest. He lowered his gun. She leaned against the bathroom doorjamb, both breathing heavily. He rubbed his hands over his face. As one, they stepped to the middle of the hall and into each other's arms. "God, Laney, I'm sorry. I heard a noise..." His voice was muffled by her hair.

"No, Cooper, I'm sorry. I was trying to be quiet. I couldn't sleep."

"Come here." He looped his hand over her shoulder and led her to the living room. He sat on the couch and pulled her between his legs. His hands began to work her shoulders.

"Mmm..." she murmured, her voice low and sexy. "You're good."

He smiled as she leaned back into his arms. "Better?" he growled in her ear.

"Much."

He rested his hands on her thighs and she leaned into him. She turned her head toward him. "I don't want to leave here," she said wistfully.

He gazed down into her face, moving a strand of hair from her eyes without speaking, his throat tight. He shifted until he was lying behind her on his side, his back to the couch, his arms wrapped around her. She copied his position, leaning her back into him, and was asleep in minutes. Her breathing and the warmth of her closeness soothed him, and he drifted off soon after.

WHEN COOPER OPENED his eyes, he saw Aidan leaning against the wall, his arms crossed, a snide smile on his face. "Well, I'll be damned."

"Shh. You'll wake her," he hissed, sitting up quickly, but trying not to jostle Laney. "I just freaked her out a little, so she slept out here with me. I heard a noise in the hall and ended up pulling my gun on her by accident."

"Geez, Coop. I didn't think you'd have to pull a gun on a woman to get her to sleep with you."

"Shut up."

Laney took a sudden deep breath and stirred. When she opened her eyes and saw Aidan watching her, she scrambled into a seated position, almost knocking Cooper in the chin. "Oh, Aidan. G-good morning," she sputtered.

"Good morning, Laney." He seemed tickled by her reaction. "Did you sleep well?" He could hardly keep from laughing.

"I...well...I..."

Aidan couldn't keep it in any longer, he put a hand up to try to hide his snickering. Cooper hit him with a well-aimed pillow. "Get out of here." He laughed, turning to Laney. "I'm sorry."

"No, no. I guess I deserve it." She moved away from him sooner than he would have liked. "I'll get my stuff together and get out of here."

"I'm afraid I'm not going to let you out of my sight for a while. Not until we catch this guy."

"But I have the funeral today."

"We'll go with you."

"Okay."

He wished he could read her expression, but before he had much of a chance, she left the room.

Aidan joined Cooper and Laney when they returned to her condo to get her suit for the funeral. Cooper preceded her up the stairs to make certain it was safe, and was the first to see her bed.

"Uhh, wait, let's—" He tried to shield her from the sight, but it was too late. A strangled noise left her mouth as she moved around his side.

She held the shredded quilt up to her cheek. "My grandma's quilt."

"I'm sorry. I had a car sent out here to watch your place, but it must have been too late."

Hearing the disruption, Aidan followed them upstairs. He surveyed the damage. The quilt looked like it had been hacked to bits, the top of the trunk was torn off its hinges and thrown across the room, and deep gouges were scraped into the top of the antique dresser. Clothes were spewing from dresser drawers, some of them ripped, and one of the drawers was removed and cracked down the middle, dumped upside-down on the floor.

He whistled. "Somebody has some serious anger issues."

Cooper glared at him and Aidan mouthed, "What?" Both men watched as Laney walked over to the closet and opened the door fearfully, but it appeared the killer hadn't had enough time, or, perhaps, enough energy, to make it that far. She pulled out a dark grey suit and white blouse, which were untouched.

"At least I have something to wear today."

"I'll call it in," Aidan offered, taking his phone out and backing down the stairs.

Cooper moved over to peer into the bathroom and make sure it was safe for her. Everything inside was still intact. She approached him, her suit in hand.

"Just try to touch as little as possible. You okay?"

"Yeah. I'm tired of this man trying to intimidate me, trying to make me a victim. I'm not comfortable with that role. It's not me. Besides, he already took from me the most valuable thing I had. Beside her, none of this—" She gestured to include all of the destruction in the room. "—means anything." She edged past him into the bathroom. "I'll be down in fifteen minutes."

That a girl, Laney. There was the defiance he liked in her.

CHAPTER FIFTEEN

When Cooper hit the bottom of the stairs, he kept walking. Aidan had finished dialing in his report on the vandalism, and was asking for crime scene technicians to come and have a look. He jumped up and followed.

"Where you goin'?" He tried to keep up with Cooper's angry strides.

"To talk to the neighbor." He pounded on the door. It opened almost immediately.

"What do you want?" Steve droned.

"Steve, this is my partner, Aidan. Aidan, this is Laney's neighbor, Steve. I was wondering, Steve," Cooper pronounced his name like he was referring to some sort of repulsive bug, "if you heard any kind of disturbance last night as somebody trashed Laney's room."

"That's a shame," Steve replied, his face impassive. "But I'm afraid I didn't hear anything." He smiled, while Cooper stood, his hands clenching and unclenching. "Too bad you didn't have me install that security system for her."

"Yeah, too bad." The two men stood staring at each other while Aidan looked from one to the other.

"Well," Aidan said, breaking the awkward silence. "If you should remember anything, please give us a call." He handed him his card.

"Yeah," Steve said, taking it, but still staring at Cooper, "I'll do that." He stepped back and closed the door in their faces.

COOPER WATCHED LANEY as she stood at her mother's side. She had made him promise not to say anything to her mother about the killer threatening her, not wanting her to worry, though he didn't see Camille as the worrying sort. Neither Essex woman shed a tear during the entire service; he figured such a thing must be "unseemly" in her mother's eyes, but it looked like it was killing Laney. When Aidan and Cooper approached her afterward, she appeared half-dead with the effort.

"Ahh, Detective Sullivan. So good to see you again." Camille bubbled upon his approach, although her eyes were cold as she surveyed him.

"Mrs. Essex. Again, I'm sorry for your loss. I'd like to introduce my partner, Aidan McConnahy."

Aidan offered his hand. "How do you do?"

"Officer McConnahy." Camille nodded stiffly, but then she turned on Cooper. "And why haven't you been keeping me informed of the progress on my daughter's murder investigation?"

"Mother," Laney interrupted, "Cooper has been keeping me informed. I haven't had the opportunity to talk to you about it."

"Did you expect me to hear it from the tabloids, Laney? Like everything else about Sydney? I guess it should be no different from hearing about which Hollywood hunk she was screwing."

"Mother!"

Camille seemed to realize her blunder and glanced around to see if anyone had overheard them. Laney whispered fiercely, "I was trying to save you a little pain. My mistake. Did you want me to show you the autopsy photos, Mother? Did you want to see her the way I saw her that night, lying on the pavement beside her car, knowing she had been alone at the end, with no one to help her?" She made a slight gurgling noise, somewhere between a sob and a gasp.

Camille took Laney by the hand and marched her out of the room, leaving Cooper and Aidan behind openmouthed. They hurried to follow. Stopping at the opening to the short, empty hallway Camille had dragged her into, they watched the pair's interaction. Laney's mother grasped her by the shoulders and shook her, like she was a child afraid of the dark. "Don't you fall apart on me, Laney Cassandra Essex. Don't you dare fall apart on me. I won't have you embarrassing me like some silly school girl." Cooper imagined the woman's long, manicured fingernails biting into Laney's skin.

She pulled away from her mother's claw-like grasp, gazing at her with fire in her eyes. "The only one who is embarrassing herself here is you, Mother."

She turned and marched off, almost bowling him over as she entered the lobby. He put his hands on her shoulders. "Hey, you okay?"

"Nothing a strong drink wouldn't cure."

He smiled. "I'll remember that."

She smiled and exhaled, laughing. "That woman gets under my skin."

"That woman would get under Gandhi's skin, no offense," Aidan interjected with a shake of his head. She laughed and Cooper pulled her to his side for a quick squeeze.

The rest of the funeral went off without Laney or her Mother speaking to each other; the ice wall had been erected. Cooper watched the interactions between mourners. He watched one man approach and take Laney by both shoulders and kiss her on the cheek, ignoring the way it made his hair stand on end. "Isn't he going to let her go?" he mumbled under his breath.

"Huh? What, Coop?"

"Nothing," he muttered. Then he saw Steve. Cooper strolled casually over behind Laney so he could catch some of their conversation.

"I heard someone broke into your condo. That's awful. You should let me install a security system for you. I won't take no for an answer."

"Thanks, Steve. Maybe in a couple of weeks. I'm not comfortable there at all right now."

"Where are you going to stay? With your mom?"

"No."

Hell no! Cooper thought.

"I'll find a hotel somewhere. Thank you for coming, and for taking care of me." She hugged him.

"Of course. Let me know if you need anything."

Steve moved on and shook Camille's hand coolly, offering his condolences, and then proceeded past the coffin. Cooper was about to turn away, when he saw something. Was he imagining it, or did Bertrand have a smug look on his face as he looked down on the corpse? Now that the karate teacher thought no one was looking at him, his face, which had been bright and friendly seconds before, changed, the lines becoming hard and sharp.

"Aidan, look at Steve Bertrand," he said out of the corner of his mouth, but just as he said it, his face turned back into the benign visage, which was in place when he talked to Laney. It reminded him, somehow, of a puppy.

"What about him?" Aidan whispered, eying Steve.

They looked on for several seconds, but Steve seemed to have his mask firmly back in place. "Never mind. It was nothing, I guess." Cooper took out his phone. "I'm going to make arrangements for a uniform to stay with Laney at her hotel tonight."

For the second time in as many days, Kent Heaton had visitors waiting in his office.

The two men rose from their chairs as he entered. "Good morning, gentlemen," he said, extending his hand. "I'm Kent Heaton."

Cooper recognized him as one of the mourners from the funeral. The one who had seemed a bit too friendly with Laney. "Cooper Sullivan."

"Aidan McConnahy."

"Nice to meet you." Kent crossed behind his desk and all three took their seats. "What can I do for you, officers?"

"As we mentioned on the phone," Aidan began, "we were looking for some information about Laney Essex."

"Yes, you said that. But I'm curious..." He looked from one to the other. "I understood you were investigating her sister's murder. What kind of information would you need about Laney to help you with that?"

Aidan threw a glance in Cooper's direction, but his partner was concentrating on studying the principal, so he took lead. "Well, sir, it would appear whoever murdered Sydney Essex may also be after Laney Essex."

"After Laney?" he repeated, alarmed. "Are you sure?"

"We're fairly certain, yes."

"Well, I'll be happy to give you whatever information I have then."

"Good. First off, we were wondering how well you know Ms. Essex. You must have a very large staff here—"

"Yes. But Laney and I are very close. When she first came to the school, we worked together in the classroom. In fact, I feel I know her better than anyone else on the entire staff."

"Good. That'll help. Could you tell me, would Ms. Essex have anyone here at the school you would consider an enemy?"

"Laney? Of course not. Laney's about the sweetest person I've ever met."

"What about an ex-boyfriend? Or anyone who may have, I don't know, maybe made a pass at her and been turned down?"

He straightened some papers on his desk. "W-well, I'm not sure...if Laney would...share something like that with me."

Cooper sensed he was hiding something and sat straighter, watching his face with interest.

"After all, I am the principal..." He trailed off, looking from one face to another. "She told you about us, didn't she?" he blurted out.

Cooper was so taken aback by the "us" he didn't jump on it fast enough. Aidan cleared his throat. "Not directly," he baited, "but we came to that conclusion."

"Listen, I was young and foolish back then. I knew it was wrong to make any sort of move on her, but I was going through a rough patch with my girlfriend, and Laney was so understanding, and..." He leaned forward, both palms flat on his desk. "Come on, you've seen her. Tell me you wouldn't have done the same thing in my position."

Cooper was silent, but his jaw tensed.

"We're not here to judge, Mr. Heaton. We only want to be certain that was as far as it went."

"Of course it was." He got up to stand behind his chair and gripped the top of it in a wringing motion as he talked. "Laney shot me down right off the bat. At least she knew it was wrong. She rejected me with more poise than a girl fresh out of college should have. I apologized, and, luckily, we were able to get around it and become friends."

"You're certain there is no unresolved anger over it?"

"None whatsoever. I was never let down with such grace before. If anything, it made me love her more, but I've never made a move on her since."

"Okay. Do you know of anyone else who would harbor ill will toward her?"

"No." Kent was eying Cooper now. "Like I said, Laney is well-liked by her peers. Everyone has missed her since she's been gone."

Aidan rose, and the sound of his chair moving back woke Cooper from his stupor of sorts. "Thank you for your time. If you should think of anything, here's my card. Don't hesitate to call us."

"Certainly." Kent shook hands with him and returned Cooper's level stare as he shook his hand as well.

CHAPTER SIXTEEN

Laney crashed for a solid two hours. She had nothing to do when she woke up in her hotel room, so she invited her guard, Officer Dave Preston, in for a hand of cards. As she dealt the cards, she listened to the officer's account of his newest daughter's birth.

"So, you say she was your third?" He nodded. "All girls?"

"Yep. But I don't mind. I've got the whole girl thing down now. Besides, girls worship their fathers. It's their mothers they can do without."

"Tell me about it," she mumbled.

A half hour later, she began to notice Dave yawning frequently. "Is Gabrielle still keeping you and your wife up a lot?"

"Uhh..." He yawned again, then, laughed. "Yeah. I guess you could say that."

"Why don't you go get a soda while I shuffle? I saw a machine at the opposite end of the hall when we came in."

"Okay. But you lock this door behind me and don't let anyone in until you're sure it's me."

"Yes, sir." She gave him a grin and a salute, the cards still in her hand. She followed him to the door and locked it behind him.

Five minutes later, she heard a rap on the door. Hopping off the bed, she went to the door and listened.

"It's me, Laney," Dave's voice came.

"Okay, Dave." She had turned the lock when she heard a loud bang on the door. She listened, but heard nothing more. "Dave?" There was no answer. A tingle rolled up her spine. She turned the lock back. "Dave? Are you there?"

"Yes."

But the voice wasn't right. With a chill, she recognized the smooth voice of her personal nightmare. Her whispered "no," was almost inaudible, but he seemed to sense she identified him.

"Laney, open this door."

She stumbled backward and ran for the phone between the beds.

"Open this door, now!"

Her clumsy hands dropped the receiver, but she picked it up again and dialed the front desk.

She barely registered the sweet voice at the other end. "Front desk, can I help you?"

"Yes! Yes. This is L-laney Essex in room..." *What the hell is the room number?* Her eyes scanned the phone's face. "424. 424!" She screamed at the sound of a body crashing against the door.

"Laney!" he snarled.

"There's someone trying to break into my room."

The teenager at the front desk was slow to catch on. "Do you want me to call the police or something?"

"Yes. Yes! Call the police!" She screamed again with the *crack* of the door frame splintering. She dropped the receiver, leaving it dangling from the bedside table, and hunted around for a weapon.

In between the thuds of her would-be-assailant's body hitting the door, she heard the neighboring door open. A man cried, "Oh, my God!" and slammed and bolted his door.

Then, a bang much louder than the others shook the room, followed by the sound of wood rending. She ran into the bathroom and slammed and locked the door just as the front door gave in. She searched for something, anything to protect herself with. The towel bar was made out of little more than aluminum foil, so she ruled it out, and the shower curtain rod was not a spring rod; it was built into the wall.

"Laney." He laughed. "You might as well save me the expenditure of my energy and come on out now. Because, one way or another, I'm coming in there."

Why isn't someone coming to help me?

COOPER WAS DRIVING with Aidan back to the station house when his phone rang.

"Cooper Sullivan."

"Cooper!"

"Laney? What's wrong?"

"He's here, Cooper. He's here!"

"Who's there?"

"The killer. He's right outside." She gave a short scream. "He's getting in. The door's breaking!"

He switched his Corvette's grill lights on and yanked on the steering wheel. "Where are you?" Aidan braced himself, one hand on the dashboard, one on his door as the sharp turn slammed him against the side. The 'Vette took a wide swerve into oncoming traffic and then jerked and fishtailed as it reached the end of its 180 degree arc.

"I-I'm in the tub. But he's getting in, Cooper. He already got in the front door. My God. No one is coming to help me."

"Where is Dave?"

"I don't know," she cried. "I don't know! He went for a soda..." Cooper could hear the dull *thuds* of a body crashing against the bathroom door, and someone cursing, though he couldn't make out the words.

"Okay, Laney. I'm a couple of minutes away. Hang in there."

He heard her terrified scream like something out of a horror show, only this wasn't a movie. After a loud series of clanks like she had dropped the phone into the tub, the line went dead.

"Dammit!" He handed the phone to Aidan. "He's there. He's in her fucking room!"

"Holy shit!"

Cooper passed a driver who was too slow getting over by detouring into the momentarily vacant lane for oncoming traffic. He saw the approach of headlights and heard horns honking. He screeched back over in front of the slow driver just in the nick of time. Now they could see the rolling lights of squad cars coming from the opposite direction. With unerring accuracy, Cooper hit the driveway of the hotel in front of a police car, launching his vehicle before slamming to a stop. Aidan took a breath but Cooper leaped out of the car on the run. Aidan followed without stopping to fill in the uniformed officers who were yelling at them. Cooper was taking the stairs two at a time.

I can't be too late. If anything happens to Laney, I will never forgive myself.

The first thing he saw when he reached the broken door was blood, everywhere. When he crossed the threshold, he saw Dave Preston lying unconscious in a pool of blood. He heard Aidan not far behind, so he moved on into the room, pointing his gun into all corners as he progressed forward. When he reached the bathroom, he could see a large, bloody knife stuck in the door.

"Laney?" he shouted.

"Cooper!" Her voice was flooded with relief.

"I'm here. But I want you to stay in there for a minute." He turned to an EMT who had just squatted next to Dave. "Do you have an extra glove?"

"Sure." The EMT handed him one from his bag.

Cooper removed the knife from the door and gingerly slid it inside the glove, handing it to one of the uniforms to place into evidence. He didn't need Laney to be stuck with that image in her head. "Okay, Laney. It's safe to come out."

She scrambled with the door's lock and then she was out and rushing into his arms. He held her close, laying his chin on the top of her head. She didn't say anything, but squeezed his waist for several minutes. She looked around and noticed the EMTs. She couldn't see Dave on the other side of the bed but must have guessed.

"Oh, my God. Dave!" She started to rush forward but he held her back.

"You don't want to see that."

"Dave's hurt, isn't he? He hurt Dave. Oh, my God! This is all my fault."

"Laney, no."

"Yes. It's all my fault. Dave wouldn't have been here if it weren't for me. Oh, Cooper," she cried, "he has a baby..." Her voice came out weakly and she leaned on him until he was almost supporting her weight. Tears ran down her face as they watched the EMTs work from a distance. At one point, Aidan reentered the room. He shook his head at Cooper, letting him know the attacker hadn't been apprehended.

After several minutes, the medical technicians had Dave stabilized, and as they prepared to take his girder out, one of the paramedics in charge came over to Laney and Cooper.

"The good news is, it doesn't seem as if anything major was hit by the knife, as far as I can tell. His vitals are all pretty good, considering. The bad news is, he's lost a lot of blood. But he's young, and seems to be in good health, and that'll work in his favor."

Laney nodded dully. When he left, she turned to Cooper. "I want to go to the hospital."

CHAPTER SEVENTEEN

Cooper waited with Laney for hours while Dave Preston was in surgery, playing with her hair, fingers restless. She lay with her head on his chest, waiting. She never talked about what had happened in the hotel room, and he didn't press her. They had been unable to contact Dave's wife; it appeared she had taken the kids to her sister's, but no one was home there. Police were waiting at her sister's house in San Diego to bring her to the hospital as soon as they returned.

When the surgery was over, the doctors came out and told them it had been a success. Dave was expected to make a complete recovery. Laney was visibly relieved, but insisted on waiting around until he woke up.

"Okay, but let me get you something to drink," Cooper suggested. He came back with coffee for himself and a Diet Pepsi for her, but stopped inside the door to have a whispered conversation with Aidan before returning to her. "Laney, I need to go back to the police station to write up a report, but Aidan's going to stay with you."

"I won't leave your side," he reassured her.

"I think I'll be okay." She was almost giddy now Dave was in the clear. She looked pointedly around the room where a half dozen cops waited along with them for Dave to regain consciousness, most of them wanting the opportunity to rib him for letting someone get the jump on him, their convoluted way of showing they cared.

"I'll be back soon," Cooper added, giving her a kiss on the forehead.

COOPER RAPPED ON THE chief's door and waited for his curt "Enter," before turning the handle.

"Hey, Coop. Good to see you." The chief leaned back in his chair, lacing his fingers behind his head. "Have a seat. Have a seat."

"Thank you, sir," Cooper said with a smile. These meetings with the chief were always awkward for him. He'd never quite gotten over the fact that he'd once called his boss "Uncle Eddy." Eddy Royanovich had been his father's partner up until "Sully" had been shot in the leg and had to leave the force five years ago. He had been at Cooper's birthday parties since he was in grade school, and now Cooper sometimes didn't know how to act when they spoke about official business.

"Well, I don't see you much in my office, so this must be important."

"Yes, sir."

"Well, what can I help you with, Coop?"

"Well, sir..." He cleared his throat. "I'd like to ask to be taken off the Sydney Essex case."

Eddy Royanovich couldn't have looked any more surprised. Cooper knew he had given the case to Cooper as a sort of gift. A high profile case like this one could get a guy a lot of mileage in the department.

"Well, well." Royanovich studied him, still shocked. "When you called earlier and told me you wanted to talk about the case, I went ahead and looked up what you had in the computer. It's a very impressive start, Cooper. Why would you want to throw all of it away? Is it because of what happened to Preston? Do you feel that is somehow your responsibility? Because it's not. Preston knew what he was getting into."

"No, it's not that, sir."

"Well, what is it then, son?"

Cooper had thought out what he wanted to say while sitting in the hospital. But thinking about it, and actually saying it were two different matters. "It is a question of professionalism, sir. I have...developed feelings for Laney Essex...and I don't think it's appropriate for me to continue on the case in this situation." He said the last part in a rush, feeling somewhat foolish and staring at a spot somewhere over the chief's head.

He leaned back in his chair. "You're just like your dad."

Cooper didn't see the connection. "I'll take that as a compliment, sir."

"Well, you both have an overdeveloped sense of professionalism, if you ask me."

He didn't know what to say to that.

"Have you talked to your dad about this?"

"No, sir, I haven't. But I know what he would say."

"Yeah." He chuckled now. "I bet you do." He shifted in his seat. "All right, Cooper. You are officially off the Sydney Essex case." He turned back to the paperwork he had left undone on his desk.

"Thank you, sir." Cooper was surprised by how easy it had been. He hesitated then got up to leave, but was stopped at the door by the chief.

"Oh, and Cooper," Eddy said, looking up at him, the light from the table lamp giving his face a friendly glow, "I don't have anyone to take over the case right now, so you can still work it, although you are officially off of it. Do you understand?"

The chief was giving him a way out. "Yes, sir." He gave his Uncle Eddy a grin and left his office.

MINUTES AFTER THE CHIEF'S door closed behind him, Cooper's phone went off.

"Coop, I think you need to get back here. Laney's acting...different."

"What do you mean 'different'?"

"She was fine, energized even, when you were here, and Dave had just come out of surgery. I have to whisper so she doesn't hear. I haven't taken my eyes off her, I swear."

"Good."

"But since you've left, she's been...well...like a zombie or something."

"Maybe she's feeling a little shy with all you guys around," he suggested.

"No, Coop. It's not that. It's kind of eerie. It's like she's checked out. I'm telling you...her face doesn't even look the same."

"All right, Aidan," he replied, concerned now. "I'll be there in a few minutes. Thanks for watching her for me, pal."

"Hey, Coop, you know that's not a problem. I like her. I do. I'm just concerned."

"All right, man. I'll be there as soon as I can."

When he arrived, she was staring out a window with her arms crossed. He had to admit, she looked a little...stunned. He came up behind her and laid a hand on her shoulder. She jumped. "Are you okay?"

She smiled at him weakly. "Yes, thank you." Her eyes had a vacant look.

After a few minutes, Jenna, who it appeared had joined Aidan when he left, called to him. "Hey, Cooper, can I talk to you for a minute?" She and Aidan were on one side of the room with their heads together. He sidled over to them, still keeping his eyes on Laney.

"I see what you mean," he said to Aidan.

"Oh, no, Coop. Compared to when you weren't here, she's lively right now." He stood with his arms crossed, his anxiety for Laney written on his face. Cooper flinched, thinking she had been worse than her current semi-comatose state.

"Can I give you my professional opinion?" Jenna asked in a hushed tone.

"Please."

"Okay. Here's how I see it." She seemed excited about using her new skills as a grief counselor/victim's advocate. "Before Dave came out of surgery, her mind had something to do, worry about him. Now that he's okay, though, her mind has gone back to the hotel room and to her utter terror. Frankly, I don't know how she's doing it. If some guy had come after me with a knife and I had been trapped in a hotel bathroom waiting for him to hack his way in, or whatever, I'd be a babbling idiot by now."

"Yeah," Cooper said, distracted by his worry. "So how can I help her?"

"Well...I suggest getting her to do something normal. You see, her mind is having trouble right now wrapping around the fact that someone was trying to kill her. It's outside of her norm, she can't comprehend it, can't compute." She tapped the side of her head. "It's like when a record player gets caught on a scratch. It's stuck there and it can't get past it. Her mind's playing over and over, 'he was going to kill me,' and she can't get around it. But if she could do something normal, or fun, she would be able to see things are okay now. In other words, her reality was altered and we need to get things back on track again. Does that make sense?"

"Complete sense."

They all thought for a few minutes, but it was Jenna who came up with an idea first.

"How about we propose a trip to the beach? Get her out of here?"

"I'm not sure she'll leave."

"Try to convince her."

Aidan slapped him on the shoulder. "Yeah. Go on, Coop."

He moved over to where she was, staring blankly at the window. He stood behind her and put his hands on her arms. She lifted her head a little in acknowledgement of his presence. "Hey, Lane. How about we all go to the beach? Get out of here for a while? It's nice out."

She turned to look at him with alarm. "I c-can't go. I've got to be here when Dave wakes up. He doesn't have anyone here."

"Actually," he said, trying to reassure her, "I heard they got a hold of his wife, and she's in there with him right now."

She bit her lip, thinking about this new information. "Can we come back later and check on him?"

"Sure. If you want to."

"Okay." She smiled, but it seemed forced.

He was relieved. Without letting Laney see him, he gave Aidan and Jenna the high sign. The four of them strolled down the hall together, Cooper with his arm draped around Laney's shoulder, as Aidan had his around Jenna's. They made a point of creating mindless chatter to make things seem as "normal" as possible.

She interrupted. "But I don't have a swimming suit." It was totally out of context, as if that's what they'd been talking about the whole time. She sounded panicked.

Jenna answered her slowly. "That's okay, Laney. You can borrow one of mine."

That seemed to alleviate Laney's concerns. Cooper reasoned that maybe she was frightened about the prospect of returning to her place to get a suit.

They drove to Jenna's and got changed, then stopped by Cooper and Aidan's. They decided to take Jenna's car, as it was roomier. Cooper was surprised when Laney fell asleep on the way over. He ran his hand over her hair as she leaned into his chest.

"All the work her brain is doing is extremely draining," Jenna said, catching his eyes in the rearview mirror. He nodded without replying. "I'll head farther south. Give her an opportunity to rest."

When they got to the beach, they found a spot in some light shade and spread out. As late as it was in the afternoon, the beach was fairly deserted. Aidan and Jenna took off to play in the waves, leaving Cooper and Laney alone. She sat with her hands around her knees in a relaxed position, staring out at the waves without speaking. At first, he talked about this and that, ignoring that it was virtually a one-way conversation. After a while, he fell silent, trying to come up with something else to say. He stared out over the waves like she did.

"Laney. When I went to talk to the chief, I asked him to take me off your case."

Her head spun in surprise, but then she seemed to swallow the information with resignation. "I understand. It's a good decision. It's not safe to be around me."

"No. Oh, no, Laney, you don't understand." He turned her so he could look into her eyes and make sure he had her full attention. "I asked him to take me off the case because...I tried to explain before, but I guess I didn't do a very good job..." He sighed, and then started over. "I didn't ask to be taken off the case because I'm worried about the danger, I asked to be removed from the case because... Laney, when I'm with you, my thoughts aren't...very professional." He saw a glimmer of understanding in her eyes. "In fact," he lifted a couple of locks of her hair, sliding his fingers down the strands all the way out to the ends, and then released them to touch her face, his gaze flicking back and forth between her eyes, "my thoughts when you're close to me, like this, are about as far from professional as you can get." His heart was in his throat. He leaned in and softly kissed her lips, meaning to stop there, but, he felt himself falling deeper and deeper into the kiss.

There was a point at which Cooper knew the kiss would explode into something else—something so intense it wouldn't have mattered if every man, woman, and child on the beach had been watching them, he would have had no choice but to lay her back onto the sand so he could begin to tear off her borrowed swimming suit—and that point was approaching like an express train. The gentleman in him overcame the pure animal lust and he pulled back. As he did, he opened his eyes to take in her reaction and saw, to his great pleasure, she was having trouble resurfacing.

"Wow," she breathed. Then, she giggled, warming his heart.

He laughed. "I don't think any woman's ever reacted to one of my kisses like that."

She ducked her head. "I find that hard to believe."

"No, it's true. But I don't think I've ever kissed anyone that way before, nor have I ever wanted to as much." This was why they called it being a fool for love, he realized; people were filled with an overwhelming desire to share all of themselves with someone else, blurting out anything which came to mind, no matter how private or asinine. But her smile was so lovely, he didn't care. "Do you want to take a walk?"

"I'd love to."

They strolled along the beach, hand-in-hand or with Cooper's arm around Laney's shoulder. Whatever happened to her after Dave's surgery, the fog that had made him so uneasy had lifted. She smiled and laughed and chatted as if she had no concerns in the world.

"I like that suit, by the way," Cooper commented suggestively. It was a simple black bikini with a silver rectangular-shaped metal loop in the middle of her chest connecting the two sides, and identical loops on the bottom half on each hip, connecting the back to the front. She filled it in well.

"Oh." She blushed. "Well, I asked Jenna for a cover up, and she gave me this." She gestured to the sheer blouse she wore over it. "It's not covering up much," she added, laughing.

"And why should it?" he queried, stopping in front of her and reaching under the sheer cloth to run a finger up and down the straps which tied behind her neck.

She ran her hands up his broad, bare chest. He had abandoned his t-shirt when they first got to the beach, and wore long, solid navy trunks. "You keep doing that, Officer," she said coyly, "and you'll have to arrest me for lewd and indecent behavior on a public beach."

He grinned, pulling her close. "I'm willing to take my chances."

This time, she initiated the kiss, running her long fingernails through the back of his hair and sending his system into overdrive. "You keep doing that, ma'am," he teased, "and they're going to have to arrest us both." He kissed her again, feeling happy to be himself with her, no longer having to consider whether the emotions she stirred up in him were out of bounds for a cop.

When he pulled back, she commented, "The sun's going down. You up for a swim?"

"Sure, if you are."

"In that case," she said, already cheating toward the water, "last one in's a—whoo!" She was unable to complete her sentence as he surprised her, scooping her up from behind and carrying her toward the water. As he waded in, she seemed to realize his intent. There would be no gradual getting used to the chilly water for her; he was planning on giving her an instant full immersion.

"Ohh no. If you take me down, you're going down with me." She clung to his neck.

"Okay. Okay," he acquiesced. He shifted to place her on her feet, and she loosened her grip. Then, he changed tactics and launched her out into the Pacific before she could readjust. She came up sputtering and laughing harder than he had ever seen her laugh.

"You! You're going to get yours. You just wait." When he got closer, she splashed him until he fought through the froth she was creating and grabbed her wrists.

"Promises, promises." He pulled her in by her hips to nip at her bottom lip playfully. The water sparkled on her skin in the sunlight. She pushed her wet hair back, still laughing for a minute, but then she sighed.

"Cooper..." She squinted up at him, the setting sun getting into her eyes, "Thank you for this. For today. For coming when I called."

It was the first time she had mentioned anything related to what had happened earlier. He became serious, too. He wrapped his arms around her waist and she twined her legs around his, her hands crossed loosely behind his neck, buoyed by the water. He spoke with sincerity. "I'll always be there when you call, Laney." He watched as her eyes filled with tears. She turned and laid her head on the front of his shoulder, closing her eyes and seeming to bask in the feeling of being safe with him. The simple gesture melted his heart and he held her close, neither of them moving or speaking for several minutes. After a bit, she pulled away. A breeze made her shiver. "It's getting late."

"Yeah."

They turned and trudged in together, holding hands. She looked up the beach where Jenna and Aidan were sitting, lip-locked, on the blanket they had spread out.

"I'm starved. Let's get those two knuckleheads and go get something to eat."

When they got near the blanket, Cooper made a show of clearing his throat loudly. Aidan ignored him and continued to kiss Jenna, until Cooper kicked some sand onto their blanket.

"That's it!" Aidan yelled, jumping up and running at him. He chased Cooper back into the waves and tackled him, both of them going down together.

"AND THERE GO A PAIR of world-class doofuses. Or would that be doofesi?" Jenna smiled. "But they sure are cute, aren't they?"

Laney sighed. "Yeah."

Jenna put her hand around her shoulder. "You feelin' better?"

She nodded, wary, afraid Jenna would ask her to discuss things.

"Good. Help me shake this blanket out and then we'll get those bozos to take us out to dinner somewhere."

She smiled. "Sounds good." By the time they were finished, Aidan and Cooper had returned, wearing hang-dog expressions.

"Sorry," they said in unison, both looking contrite. Then they shook the water out of their hair simultaneously, carrying out their evil plan to spray the unsuspecting girls with water.

"Hey, cut it out." Jenna laughed, giving Aidan a little shove in the chest. After he wrestled his arms around her, they looked up. Cooper and Laney were watching them, his arms around her, linked with hers in front. She was leaning against his chest, smiling. Jenna and Aidan smiled back. "You boys hungry?" Jenna hinted.

"I'm not," Aidan replied. "Are you, Coop?"

"Nah."

"Oh, shut up. You're always hungry. I need to wash this salt out of my hair first though," she said, grabbing her beach bag and heading in the direction of a public shower/restroom. "Are you coming, Laney?" She turned back to catch Laney and Cooper kissing. "Ahem."

Laney laughed, running to catch up with her. They walked arm-in-arm, as if they'd been best friends forever. The shower room was bright, but deserted. Laney trotted over to the bench nearest the shower stalls and started pulling clothes and a towel out of the bag she had borrowed from Jenna. "Oh, shit." Jenna searched her own bag. "My shampoo must have fallen out in the car. You get the water all warmed up for me and I'll be back in a minute."

"Okay." Laney slipped out of her wet suit, letting it plop to the floor, then, padded into a stall and turned the water on, giving a little shriek when she discovered how cold it was. She bravely ventured into the next stall, turning that one on as well. After a couple of minutes, the water began to get warm. She stepped into the spray, letting it soothe her as it washed over her sand-chafed skin. She threw her head back and let the water flow over her hair with a sigh.

All of a sudden the lights went out. Laney's hand went out to the side of the shower stall in the dark.

"Cooper?" she called out, guessing he inadvertently turned the lights off, thinking she'd left.

"Your boyfriend's not here, Laney." A voice came out of the shadows, much closer than she would have thought possible, but she realized the sound of the running water had covered his footsteps. It was a voice she had come to recognize. Fear swamped her. She had to get out. Trying to keep her head, she grabbed a towel from the old wooden bench in front of the showers. She wrapped it around her, praying she would be able to make her way in the blackness surrounding her. As she reached the end of the row of showers, some unseen force grabbed her. She was slammed up against the wall, her arm torqued from behind and pressed into her back. Fingers locked into her hair and her face was pushed, a cheek smashed onto the cold cinderblocks of the wall. "What are you doing, Laney? Huh? Huh?" With each question, he jerked on her head and hair. She could feel his hot breath on her face and knew he was inches away.

Her lips were able to form the words her head had been screaming ever since he had taken hold of her. "P-please don't kill me."

"Please don't kill me." He pitched his voice high, mocking her. It seemed familiar now… "I'm not going to kill you, Laney," he said, laughing. "I'm just going to mess you up real bad." With that, he threw her across the room. She landed, sprawled on the floor, the towel coming open, but, thankfully, staying over her. The concrete scraped her chest and hands, arms and legs as she slid and crashed into the wooden bench. A blinding light shot through her head. She reached up and felt a warm oozing she didn't believe was the water, which still ran in the shower stall. She could hear him coming, so her hands searched for a weapon. She found the lower support arm of the bench, which had cracked in two on impact, and she wrenched it free from the base, rolling over and swinging blindly. She was rewarded with a loud thud, but she could tell she hadn't made solid contact. His reflexes were quick, and he jerked it out of her hands. She could hear it clatter in the dark somewhere far away. "Not a good idea." He was on top of her, gripping her hair again and pressing her face into the water, which was pooling into a drainage hole nearby. She spit and tried to move her head out of the water, but he forced it back in. He was going to drown her.

"Laney?" It was Jenna.

With the kind of strength purchased with adrenaline, she lifted her head and screamed.

"Run, Jenna, run. Get out of here!" Belatedly she added, "Get Cooper! Get Aidan."

She paid for issuing her warning. Her assailant struck her hard, once, across the face.

She felt intense pain, and then the sensation that everything was slipping away.

CHAPTER EIGHTEEN

Cooper and Aidan were leaning against the hood of the car, their feet stretched out in front of them, joking around. When Cooper caught Jenna's frantic movements as she exited the shower building, which was down a hill and across an expanse of sand, he knew something was wrong. He took off running. It was several seconds before Aidan realized what was happening and followed.

"Laney's in trouble!" Jenna was screaming.

Cooper rushed through the door. He ran his hand along the wall impatiently, searching for a light switch. He called out her name, but heard nothing but the sound of showers running. He inched his way forward.

"Coop?"

"Over here."

Aidan was by his side in an instant, even in the dark.

"I couldn't find a—OOF!" Cooper crumbled to the floor. "He went to the left," he rasped. He tried to draw in breath to his aching lungs. He had been rammed hard in the stomach and had the wind knocked out of him.

Aidan's voice came from close by. "Are you okay?"

"Yeah. Get going." Cooper dragged himself to his feet, keeping a hand wrapped around his middle, and caught up with Aidan.

They felt their way, using a set of lockers as a guide, listening for breathing and footsteps. In seconds the blackness was cut by a ray of light, and for another second or two, they got a glimpse of where they were. Lockers stood to the left and right. Aidan had been about to trip over a bench. The outdoor light came over the top of the lockers to their left and Cooper could see the arc of brightness on the ceiling getting slimmer and slimmer as a door closed and they were immersed in the blackness again.

"He's outside now. I'm going for Jenna. You find Laney."

"Okay. Good luck."

Cooper felt again along the wall, heading toward the sound of the water endlessly pelting the walls and floor. The room flooded with light. Aidan must have flipped the power back on. It registered in his mind now that there had been a large power box on the outside of the building. It took a second for his eyes to adjust, but he could make out the wide entry to the shower room. He flipped more switches until the whole place lit up, still calling out Laney's name. When he came around the corner to the shower stalls, he drew in a sharp breath.

What he saw had his heart racing. Laney lay, face-up, with a towel crumbled at an angle over her lower body. It looked as if the whole room was splattered with blood, as it commingled with the running water, swirling red around the drain. "Oh, my God," he whispered. He stood frozen for a second.

Not now, God, not after I've fallen in love with her.

Jenna and Aidan came running up, and she pushed past him to Laney's side, kneeling down in the water. Cooper started moving forward, too.

"Cooper, get out of here," Jenna ordered.

"What?" he asked confused. "I want to help."

"Dammit, Cooper, get out of here. She's naked. She wouldn't want you to see her like this."

"What the hell? I don't care—"

"Out!" she screamed. "Aidan, get my bag out of the trunk."

Cooper fumed and listened while Jenna tried to revive Laney, speaking to her with a calmness he did not possess. Aidan returned with her EMT bag. "Thanks," she said shortly. "You get out, too." She gestured with her head to the door and he left without a word.

Cooper was out in the locker area pacing around, his face white and tense. "Shit, man. Did you see her? Did you see what he did to her?"

"Yeah, man. I saw it. She's gonna be okay, Coop."

There were a few seconds of quiet. He wished to hell he could turn off those damn showers. What kinds of wounds did she have? Were they knife wounds? Could he have had a gun with a silencer?

He ran his hands through his hair. "Did you see anything?"

Aidan shook his head. "No sign of him. Not a car, nothing. Too many footprints to tell what direction he might have gone."

They waited while Jenna worked.

"I shouldn't have left her. What was I thinking? She had just been attacked a few hours ago, for God sake." He slammed his hand into a locker and then laid his forehead on it, whispering, "What was I thinking?"

Aidan came over and put a hand on his friend's shoulder. "None of us was thinking about there being any danger here. We're at the damn beach. We were having a good time. None of us were expecting this. It's not your fault, Coop. No way."

With a squeak the showers stopped running, and a few second later, Jenna stepped out, and both men looked up. "She wants her clothes," she said, looking a little sheepish.

Cooper stepped forward. "She's conscious?"

"Yeah. But she's pretty beat up, Cooper. When I get her dressed, you can come back there. I don't want her to sit yet. I'm afraid she'll pass out. I'll call you." And then she was gone.

Aidan clapped him on the back. "See, Coop. She's gonna be fine."

"Yeah." He breathed a huge sigh of relief, but he still felt horribly guilty.

After a few minutes, Jenna called out to them. Cooper rushed back. He knelt on the other side of Laney in the water.

"Hey. How are you doing?" He smoothed the hair away from the side of her face left unbandaged. Her forehead was creased, face tight with pain.

"I'm okay," she replied weakly, seeming embarrassed by all the attention.

"I'll feel better when I get you to the hospital and have a doctor check you out."

"Oh, no, Cooper. I don't need to go to the hospital."

"It's out of the question."

She looked up at Jenna desperately. "Jenna, tell him. Tell him I'm okay."

Jenna pulled the bandage away from Laney's head wound for a moment. Cooper fought back a wave of nausea when he saw the opening.

"I'm afraid I'm going to have to agree with Cooper on this one, Laney. This hasn't stopped bleeding yet and, since you lost consciousness, I think you need to be worked up."

Her eyes traveled to Aidan, hoping to find an ally, but the stubborn set of his chin showed no quarter would be given there.

"Fine," she said, resigned.

They all heard the ambulance and police cars Jenna had called earlier arriving at the same time outside. Cooper used his connection with law enforcement in order to ride along in the ambulance. She looked up at him at first, almost as pale as the sheets beneath her, but after a few minutes she closed her eyes. He bent over her, holding her hand, his face grim.

At the hospital, he waited impatiently in the hall, his hands clasped behind his head, his feet sticking out in front of him, oblivious to those who were having to skirt them on their way by. Aidan and Jenna sat across from him, subdued.

Jenna cleared her throat and leaned forward. "Cooper, I want to apologize for yelling at you. I—"

"No, Jenna. You were looking out for your patient. That's what a good EMT does."

"I was a little freaked out, to tell you the truth."

Cooper turned to look at her. "You? Freaked out?"

"Yeah. I thought I was going to puke."

He raised his eyebrows.

"Don't get me wrong. I've worked some pretty gruesome cases before. But it's different when it's someone you know. And you're not at work. I didn't expect to have to deal with something like that today."

He put a hand on her knee. "I'm sorry, Jenna."

"Oh no, Cooper. I was where I wanted to be. I'm glad I could be there to help. It was just...scary."

"Yeah." He rubbed his hand over his face. "Yeah."

More time passed. Cooper got up and paced. He wanted to punch something. He sat. Minutes later, he straightened so fast he startled Jenna.

"What I don't get—" he began, as if they had been having a discussion all along, "—is how does he keep finding us? I was sure no one followed us to the hotel, and today, the only people who knew where we were going were the four of us. How does he always know where she is?" His frustration was like bile, eating away at him.

Aidan was thoughtful. After a few minutes, he began to speak slowly. "The other day I was talking to Greg Montgomery—" Greg was a fellow police officer. "—and he was mentioning his son had gotten into trouble. He's a teenager, and he told Greg he was going to his best friend's house, but Greg felt like his kid was lying to him." Now Aidan straightened, too, excited. "So he tracked his son through the kid's cell phone's GPS. Kid was at his girlfriend's."

"So you think he's tracking Laney, somehow, through her cell phone?"

"I don't know, man. Let's give it to Guido and let him figure it out."

Denny "Guido" Sardoni was one of the tech-heads in the department. Anyone who needed a photograph enhanced, an audiotape deciphered, or a wiretap set up, went to Guido. To retrieve data from a computer, they went to Guido. If they wanted to figure out their kid's iPad, they went to Guido.

"Brilliant." Cooper smiled broadly, extending his hand to knuckle Aidan.

The doctor walked out and Cooper bolted out of his seat. "Can I go in now?"

The doctor eyed him. "You do this to her?"

"Did I do this to her? No! Some maniac did."

Aidan stepped between them. "We're police officers."

"Ahh," the doctor responded, tapping his pen on the chart he held. "Well, take it easy on the questions. She's been through a lot."

Before Cooper could respond, Aidan grabbed his elbow. "Thank you." He guided him through the door.

"How ya doin'?" Aidan was the first to ask.

"Better," she responded, ducking her head self-consciously.

Aidan rubbed her knee as she sat on the side of the bed. "I'm glad. I'll be outside," he added to Cooper.

When they were alone, he spoke up. "What did the doctor say?"

"He said I was fine and could leave."

"Really? I thought sure they would keep you." She glanced away.

"Laney?"

"Well, he wanted to keep me at first but I convinced him I was okay."

"Laney—"

"Listen. I passed all his tests. I'm fine." That tilt of the chin. It got him every time.

He stood in front of her, his hands on the side of her thighs. "Laney, I want you to stay with me tonight." As if anticipating an argument, he held up his hand. "I won't put any moves on you or anything, I promise. I need to be right by your side tonight. For you and for me."

She looked down for a second, but then gazed again into his eyes. "Cooper. This is getting dangerous for you. I don't know if I can put you in that position."

"It's either here at the hospital, or home with me, Laney," he said firmly. "Those are your two choices."

She smiled. "You don't play fair, you know?"

"Of course I do," he deflected. "I'm a cop." He bent to kiss her, being gentle with her swollen face.

The doctor bustled in with her discharge papers, and before they knew it, they were on the couch at Cooper and Aidan's. They were wrapped up in their own thoughts while Aidan and Jenna were throwing together a salad for the four of them.

After a while, Laney broke the prolonged silence. "Aren't you going to ask me about what happened?" She looked at her hands on her lap.

"Eventually I was going to have to, but I was waiting until you were ready." He could hardly bear to look at her bruised and swollen face or at the scrapes that covered most of her body.

"I want to get it over with."

"Okay. Do you mind if I record it so I won't have to ask you to repeat things later?"

"No, I don't mind." Jenna and Aidan walked in with the salads. "Can Jenna be in here?"

"Of course."

"What's going on?" Jenna asked, wary.

Cooper stood to get his phone. "Laney wants to tell us about what happened today."

Jenna looked at her, her eyes wide. "Are you sure, honey?"

She nodded and patted the seat next to her Cooper had vacated. Aidan set the salads down and prepared to leave. "No, Aidan. You should be here, too. I guess we're all in this crazy thing together."

When Cooper had the phone in place and recording, he began. "Now, any time you want to stop, tell us and we'll be through, okay?" He sat on the coffee table in front of her.

She nodded. "I don't know if anything I have to say will help at all, it was too dark for me to see."

"That's okay. Just tell me what you can."

"I was in the shower...and the lights went off. Jenna had gone to get shampoo, so I thought maybe you had accidentally turned the lights out, thinking I was with her." She paused. Jenna held her hand, and Laney looked at her with gratitude.

"I called out your name." The words seemed to choke her. "But he was already there." A single tear fell out. "I guess I didn't hear him because of the sound of the water running. I tried to stay calm. I didn't scream, thinking it would help him to find me, at first...and later, I...couldn't."

Cooper squeezed his pen, looking at Aidan, both men fighting to control their anger.

"I snatched my towel and put it around myself, but when I was leaving the shower area, he grabbed me and shoved me up against the wall." Her hand went to her cheek, as if she was remembering the feel of the cold cinderblocks. She swallowed and closed her eyes, but kept going. "I was scared. I begged him not to kill me." A small sob escaped. "I'm sorry," she cried, putting a hand over her mouth.

"Do you want to stop, Lane?" Cooper put his hand on her knee.

She shook her head, sending a few isolated tears flying, and tried to collect her emotions. Her voice became hollow. "He mocked me. Told me he wasn't going to kill me, just mess me up really bad."

Cooper's stomach rolled. He was only a few feet away. He should have been able to stop this from happening to her.

"That's when he threw me across the room and I hit my head on the bench. But when he came toward me, I thought, I'm not gonna let him do this to me. I grabbed the rung from the bench and swung. I hit him, but...I couldn't see anything, and I don't think I made solid contact."

"That's good, Laney. It could help. If you made him bleed, maybe the crime scene people will find some physical evidence which could help us tie this to someone."

She nodded.

"What happened next, Laney?" Aidan prodded.

"Well...he wrenched the bar out of my grip and told me I'd made a big mistake."

She began to shake, and Cooper got up to sit on the other side of her. "Maybe you've had enough."

"No!" she shouted at him. She put her face in her hands. They exchanged glances. It was gut-wrenching to hear. She took a deep breath. "I'm sorry, Cooper, I didn't mean to yell at you. It's just...I don't want this to have a hold of me. I want to get it out there. Demystify it."

He nodded.

She thought again. "He shoved my face into the water from the shower. I couldn't breathe, but over the sound of the pounding water, I heard Jenna call out. I fought my head out of the water so I could warn her. I was dizzy. He hit me, I think...and I don't remember anything else except waking up with Jenna there." She blew out her breath, squeezing Jenna's hand. "You saved my life."

"No. I just patched you up until the ambulance got there."

"You saved my life," Laney insisted. "He would have drowned me. Thank you." Jenna looked up at Aidan, tears in her eyes. He smiled at her.

"What I don't understand is," Laney continued slowly, "why? Why is he doing this to me? What could I have done to make him so angry at me?" She looked up, her eyes wild with anxiety.

"Laney, this isn't your fault," Aidan answered.

"No, honey. You can't think that." Cooper put both hands on her shoulders and turned her to face him, ducking his head to catch her lowered eyes. "You did nothing wrong here." She let herself fall forward and laid the top of her head on his shoulder, weary. He pulled her all the way into his arms and she leaned on him. "I know that wasn't easy for you to do," he breathed. "But you did a great job."

"It was very brave," Jenna added, patting her back.

Laney lifted her head to give Jenna a wan smile. "I couldn't have done it without your help...all of you." She looked at Aidan to include him, too. "I'd be an even bigger basket case if I didn't have you guys to lean on."

Aidan stood up and rubbed her hair in a brotherly fashion. "Well, you lean whenever you want to, babe. We'll be here for you." He put his arm around Jenna, who had gotten to her feet.

"And as far as I'm concerned," Jenna put in her two cents, "you're no basket case. You're amazing."

Cooper stood. "You want to eat something?"

"Umm...yeah, sure."

They all sat down to eat, trying to act as normal as possible. Laney picked at her food for the others' benefit, but seemed glad when the meal was over and everyone decided to go to bed.

"You guys turn in. We'll get these," Jenna said, taking Laney's bowl.

"Oh, no. You made dinner. We can—"

"You look exhausted. Go. I don't want all my fantastic healing work to go to waste." She gave Laney a wink and headed into the kitchen with Aidan.

Cooper and Laney moved to the bedroom. Later, when Aidan walked past, the door was still open and a lamp was on next to the bed. Cooper was sitting with his back against the headboard, fully-clothed, with Laney asleep in his arms. She had changed into pajamas, which Jenna lent her, and he was stroking her hair above the bandage covering her stitches. As Aidan peeked in, Cooper put his lips to her hair and kissed her. Aidan caught his eye.

"How is she?" he whispered, leaning against the door frame.

"She's beat, but she's okay."

"She's quite a girl," he commented.

"Yeah." Cooper looked into her face, peaceful in sleep despite the bruises.

"We'll get him, Coop.'"

He didn't comment.

"Good night."

"'Nite, Aidan. And thanks."

"Sure thing."

A few hours later, Aidan was awakened by the sound of Laney screaming. He snatched his pistol from the bedside table and rushed into the hall, leaving Jenna still sleeping. In the hall, he could hear Laney whimper and the murmur of Cooper's voice as he reassured her.

"It's just a dream, babe. No one's here, I swear."

When Cooper got up a few minutes later, he met Aidan in the bathroom.

"She okay?"

He noticed the gun in the waistband and put two and two together. "You heard that." Aidan nodded.

"Sorry, man."

"No, don't worry about it. She freaked out?"

"A little. Her head's pounding now. Although she's trying not to let it show," he commented with a small smile. "She's afraid I'll make her go back to the hospital. I got up to get her some pain killers." He reached into the medicine cabinet.

"I'll get her some water." Aidan filled up a Dixie cup.

"Thanks." He took the cup, but made no move to leave, leaning against the sink and jiggling the pills around in his hand.

Aidan waited for him to say something, but when he didn't, Aidan prompted. "Something on your mind?"

He spoke, still looking at the small red pills in his hand. "He could have stabbed her, or...done whatever he wanted with her, and I was out there goofing around with you."

Aidan didn't respond. A few seconds ticked by. "We're going to protect her now, Cooper."

He lifted his head and they exchanged a long look, an unspoken pact signed between them. They would keep this from happening again, no matter what. Cooper nodded, and the two returned to bed without another word.

CHAPTER NINETEEN

Cooper's eyes opened slowly. He saw the empty bed beyond his finger-tips—the sheets still warm and wrinkled—and raised his eyes to see Laney sitting on the edge of the mattress. In the morning light, he could see the mass of bruises on her right shoulder blade, traveling all the way to her side. The delicate, pastel green spaghetti strap of her top stood in juxtaposition to the black and blue marks of a prize fighter. As he watched, she stretched, but then sucked in a breath, grasping her arm with a quiet sound which was somewhere between a yelp and a groan.

"You okay?"

Her head spun around in surprise. "Hey. Good morning." She smiled, but her mouth was still tight around the edges from the pain. "Did you sleep okay with me hogging the bed?"

He smiled back. She was so beautiful in the morning, with her hair falling loose around her. He loved the smattering of faint freckles on her cheeks and upper chest, not to mention the way her soft curves were just visible where her camisole squared off. He reached a finger up and trailed it down her arm. "I liked having you here." He gazed into her eyes. "I think I could get used to it."

He loved that deer-in-headlights look she got whenever a spark of electricity passed between them. It made him feel powerful, and in control, until she did something to make him feel as wonderfully off-balanced. "Are you hungry?"

"Starved."

He bounded out of bed. "Let's get you some breakfast then."

AFTER BREAKFAST IT was decided Laney would go with Aidan and Cooper to headquarters. Jenna had to go to work, and was reluctant to say goodbye to the trio before they set off, the gruesome events of the day before having formed a bond between them, making it hard for her to leave.

At the precinct house, they met up with Guido Sardoni. He was a heavy-set, sloppy looking man in his early thirties with wild, black hair and a bushy moustache under his long nose. Black, thick-rimmed glasses made him appear slightly bug-eyed. With the patience and delicacy of an archeologist uncovering an ancient artifact, Guido removed a razor-thin chip smaller than a dime from the inside of Laney's cellphone.

"See this—" he announced, holding it up with a miniature tool that was a cross between a tweezers and a set of pliers, "—is not supposed to be here."

"What is it?" Laney asked, fascinated.

"It's a tracking device," Guido told his pupil, smiling at her.

"That's how he knew where you were," Cooper added. "He's been tracking you through your cellphone. Who has access to your phone?"

"No one. I always keep it in my purse."

Aidan and Cooper exchanged a look. "Ever left it at home?" Aidan queried.

"Yes, from time to time. You mean, you think he did it when he snuck into my condo?"

"It's a possibility."

Guido made a move to throw it into the trash can.

"Wait. I've got an idea." Everyone focused on Cooper. "We know how he's been tracking Laney, but he doesn't know we know. Why don't we set a trap for him, lure him into a spot where we could nab him."

Aidan thought about it. "I don't think it would work unless Laney was there. If he doesn't see her, he won't make a move."

"Trash it then."

Guido leaned toward the trash can again.

"No, wait. Cooper—" Laney began.

"No, Laney. It's out of the question. It's too dangerous."

"The way I see it, it's my only way out of danger. He won't just go away. I know that now. He'll continue until he gets whatever it is he wants, which seems to be punishing me, for some reason. At least this way we even the field of play. We know he's coming, and we're ready."

Aidan smiled, putting a hand over her shoulder. "She makes sense."

Cooper glared at him. "I don't like it."

"We'll make it someplace public, with scads of people around. But, like on the beach, or at the hotel, he won't be able to resist. We'll have a bunch of undercovers with us and we'll stay close. Laney will never be out of our sight. And we'll have her wired so she can speak to us if she wants to."

"Aidan, even if I agreed, the chief will never go for it."

He paused, then, his eyes lit up. "But you're no longer on the case."

"So?"

He spread his arms wide. "You're simply out for a walk in the park. Off-duty."

Cooper rubbed his chin. "But you can't do it. You'd get suspended for using a civilian on an operation like this. I'm not gonna let that happen."

"I just decided to take the day off tomorrow, too." He smiled and folded his arms across his chest, rocking back on his heels.

"No. No. It's not enough. I'm not taking a chance with her life," he gestured in Laney's direction, "with only the two of us to—"

"How many?"

"What?"

"How many officers would it take, in your estimation?"

Cooper thought. "Four or five. At least four off-duty officers."

"I'll take care of it."

"You'll take care of it?"

"I'll take care of it. Consider it covered." They all thought it out in silence.

Aidan's face fell. "We couldn't use equipment. There'd be a record."

Guido spoke up. "But you still have your wires from the Patroli bust."

Aidan didn't catch on. "Guido, I turned those in last week."

Guido turned around and reached into a box on the table behind him. He pushed a mic set across the table. "No you didn't, Aidan. You forgot."

Now it was Aidan's turn to smile. "Oh. I forgot. Damn the luck." He picked the equipment up and slipped it inside his jacket. "I must be slipping."

Guido nudged Laney. "I'm sure a lot of cops forgot, huh?"

"Oh. Undoubtedly. Very busy, these police officers."

They all looked expectantly at Cooper. "I still don't like it."

"But what choice do we have?" Laney asked. He stared into her determined face for several seconds and the others waited without speaking. He looked at Guido for help.

"I'll get you the best equipment ever," he responded.

Cooper sighed, gazing back at Laney and brushing the hair from her face. "I don't like it," he repeated. "But I guess I'm outnumbered."

THEY RETURNED TO THE apartment to change clothes. They chose an amusement park as the location for the trap, so casual clothing was required. While Laney was changing, Cooper and Aidan argued in the living room.

"She's not a goddamn piece of meat to be dangled in front of a wild dog, Aidan."

"Don't you think I know that, Cooper," he hissed back. "But she's right. We can sit around and wait until he tries something again—in a place of his choosing, at his time— or we can take action and force his hand in a place of our choosing, where she's surrounded by cops. And—"

Cooper heard footsteps approaching and raised a hand, stopping Aidan in midsentence.

"I'm ready."

They exchanged a wordless glance, and then both rose.

"Okay," Cooper said with a sigh. "Let's go."

He was quiet on the ride over. He tried to keep his mind away from worst case scenarios. Tried, and failed. They pulled into a back section of a superstore parking lot a mile from the park. They got out and car doors began to open, people rising from vehicles and strolling toward them. He was surprised by how many.

"You got all of these people to help out?" he asked Aidan out of the corner of his mouth.

"I had to turn some people away. Once word got out, everybody wanted in."

"Wow." Cooper was touched but as they formed a loose circle facing him, his inner cop surfaced and he took command of the group of ten officers, including Aidan. After getting their orders, the group split off in singles and pairs to return to their cars, all of them wearing hidden radios.

They filed into the amusement park lot and left their vehicles in different sections. When Cooper got out he placed his hand over Laney's shoulder casually, but every nerve in his body was on alert. They entered the park under the big archway of lights and strolled through the grounds to the big carousel in the middle, where they would wait for the killer to show up. Laney swung up onto the back of one of the painted horses while he stood at her side.

After fifteen minutes or so, she leaned down and whispered. "Aren't you going to go now?" The plan had been to leave her seemingly alone, Cooper taking off to get some popcorn. But, in reality, he would be watching her, and other officers were posted within feet of the carousel.

His eyes scanned the crowd, mentally checking people off. Couple with a child, they're okay. Teenagers making out, harmless. Older couple...

He saw one man by himself wearing a ball cap. Could he be their man? He wanted a better look, to see if he could identify the man, but she was leaning toward him again.

"I trust you, you know."

He was sure her words were meant to reassure him, but, instead, they made him feel ten times worse. She trusted him with her life. Why, he didn't know. So far, she had been watched over in her sleep by the killer while he was feet away. She had the maniac try to attack her in a hotel room, and had the crap beaten out of her on a public beach, all while under his care. Yeah, he was one trustworthy S.O.B., that was for sure.

"If you see anything, recognize anyone, speak and we'll hear you through the microphone." She nodded, looking more put-together than she had a right to be, still harboring bruises from the man they were waiting for. He gave her hand a squeeze, then left, hopping off the carousel and striding purposefully toward a vendor. He tried to see where the stranger with the Dodgers hat had gone. He was straining his neck, peering around, taking mental photographs of every face he saw as he waited in line while a man ordered a lemon shake-up in front of him.

Her voice broke through his thoughts. "He's here!" She sounded terrified.

His eyes flew to the carousel, but her horse was out of sight. "You see him, Lane?"

"No. But I can feel him."

Cooper shut his eyes. He should have known better. She was too raw for this. Of course, she would jump at every shadow.

Laney seemed to sense his feelings in the long pause before he answered her. "I know it sounds crazy, Cooper, but I swear, he's here."

Another second passed. He made a decision, pushing his mike button. "Heads up, everyone. Our guy is here."

Aidan jumped on board the carousel from his nearby spot and started walking casually forward. Cooper's heart was racing as he watched and moved in his direction. He could see Laney was alone. Aidan had almost reached her when he stopped and bent over, reaching into a stationary sled that was part of the ride. It offered a couple a spot to sit together, should people desire to.

His voice sounded in Cooper's ear. "He's here." He straightened, a single red rose in his hand.

Cooper searched the people that mobbed the area, zeroing in on a figure hustling off, wearing a baseball cap. "He's headed toward the main entrance, wearing a Dodgers hat." He ran around to the left. As he cleared the carousel, he saw the suspect rushing down a path toward the main gate. Cooper broke into a run, his blood pounding, screaming, *Get the bastard!* He hurdled the low chains that bordered the pathways wagon-spoking the carousel. He angled his path to intercept and timed himself, launching into the air. His arms wrapped around the suspect and brought him to the ground.

The stranger grappled with him. "What the hell...?"

Belatedly, Cooper warned him, "Police."

He secured the man's arms behind his back as Aidan walked up, holding the rose. "He left this."

Cooper wrestled the man to his feet.

"What the hell is this all about?" The man sounded both angry and frightened. He looked at Aidan. "I didn't leave that."

Laney hastened forward, bookended by two officers.

"Laney," Cooper demanded. "Do you recognize this guy?"

She peered at him, her face white. "No." The word came out choked. "I've never seen him before."

Cooper got a sinking feeling. His gaze skimmed the surrounding area, seeking an answer. Many of the park visitors had stopped what they were doing to stare at the group openmouthed, but he passed right over them looking for someone else.

"What's this all about?" the tackled man asked.

Aidan strode forward, getting in the man's face, the veins in his neck bulging. "What? Do you get some kind of sick kick out of beating up on innocent women you don't even know, you little prick?"

"What are you talking about? I never..." The man looked from him to Laney, and seemed to notice the deep bruises on her cheek and the bandage above her eye. He began to stammer. "I-I s-swear...I..."

"If you're so innocent," Aidan continued, his anger boiling over, "then why were you hurrying out of here like the place was on fire?"

"B-because my wife's having a baby."

The answer was so unexpected, everyone stared at him.

"She just called. She went into labor."

"Oh, no," Laney moaned.

"Oh, come on." Aidan sounded less confident now. "Why would you be at an amusement park by yourself without—?"

"I came to meet my folks. They've got our son, Timmy, for the afternoon, so I thought I'd take half a day and meet them."

Aidan was stymied. Ted Waters, one of the officers with Laney, interjected. "What hospital, sir?"

"St. Vincent."

"Your wife's name?"

"Virginia. Virginia Coltrain. I'm Peter Coltrain." Waters stepped away and made a call.

"But I was so sure," Laney mumbled, dazed. "I felt him here. Or I thought I did, but I was wrong, wasn't I?" She peered up into the stranger's face, searching for answers.

He stared at her, perhaps seeing the pain in her eyes, which went deeper than the bruises. He nodded.

"You weren't wrong, Laney." Aidan showed her the rose.

Her eyes flew to his. "He left it?"

Aidan nodded.

Her hands went to her arms, and she began to rub them. "He was here."

"What's with the rose?" Peter Coltrain asked.

A female officer standing closest to him responded. "It's sort of the killer's calling card. He killed her sister," she added, jerking a head in Laney's direction, "and now he's after her."

Coltrain absorbed the information without speaking, looking at Laney now with both curiosity and pity.

"Sir," Ted Waters said to Cooper, "his story checks out. There is a Virginia Coltrain at St. Vincent's."

Cooper closed his eyes for a second, letting the defeat wash over him. He turned to the man he tackled minutes earlier. "I don't know how to tell you how sorry I am, sir. I thought—"

"That's okay," Coltrain said. "I understand. We all make mistakes." He glanced at Laney. "I'd want to get the bastard, too."

Cooper sighed, grateful the man was forgiving. "I can arrange for a police escort to St. Vincent's for you."

The man smiled broadly. "That would be great."

Cooper nodded to two officers who moved to follow Coltrain from the park, but he hesitated, mumbling to those closest. "God, I hope I don't read about her murder in the paper this week." Then he hurried off with the policemen.

Aidan stepped forward. "I'm sorry. I overreacted."

"No, I'm the one who rode the man to the ground." Cooper turned his hand over as he spoke to examine the scrapes on his palm that he'd received from sliding across the pavement.

"Oh. You're hurt." Laney came out of her silent revelry, taking his hand.

He snatched it back. "It's nothing." *What that bastard did to her is so much worse. And he's still out there, thanks to me.* "Let's get out of here."

When they reached the 'Vette, he turned to see Aidan walking with his arm over Laney's shoulder. He helped her into the car while Cooper thanked and dismissed the other officers.

A minute later, he stood leaning against the car with Aidan. "That was great," he ranted. "We'll be lucky if that guy doesn't sue the damn department."

"I think he's okay with it. He—"

"Dammit!" Cooper turned and pounded his fist on the car's roof. Inside, Laney jumped.

"Sorry," he yelled through the glass. She nodded, but then turned to stare forward again with a blank expression on her face. He faced Aidan. "We almost had him."

Aidan's jaw was tight. He nodded his head in Laney's direction. "You need to take it easy on her, Coop. She's near the edge."

"I know. I—"

Aidan held up a hand to silence him. "When she was looking at your hand back there and you jerked it away, I don't think you saw it, but she flinched." He paused. "You kind of acted like an ass."

He exhaled, shaking his head and looking skyward. "I know. It's so frustrating. This guy always manages to stay one step ahead of us somehow."

"I know," Aidan responded with a measure of sympathy. He stepped forward and tapped lightly on the window, bending to peer into the glass. "See ya."

Laney waved and smiled halfheartedly.

Cooper walked with Aiden to his car, two empty parking spots away.

"You know. We've had problems like this before on other cases, and you were able to keep your cool," Aidan prodded. "What makes this one different?"

Cooper turned back to look at Laney in the car. He shrugged, but then leaned against Aidan's car with a sigh. "Everything."

"Or just one thing," Aidan said pointedly, looking at her, too.

Cooper glanced at him. "Well, how would you feel if it was Jenna?"

Aidan smiled. "Ahh. The Mighty Cooper Sullivan has fallen."

Cooper punched him in the shoulder. "Shut up."

"She's 'special' isn't she?" he egged. "Isn't she?"

He walked away. "Shut up, you moron."

"She is special." Aidan roared with laughter, taking great delight in his partner's uneasiness.

"I'm out of here." But he turned around halfway to his car. "Promise me, when we get this guy, you'll let me have a few minutes with him alone."

"No way, Cooper. I'll give you a few shots, but you'd kill him if I left the two of you alone."

"Yeah. Your point is...?"

He grinned. "I'd be stuck cleaning up the mess." He pulled out his keys. "See ya back at home."

Cooper nodded and got behind the wheel of the 'Vette. He put the car in gear and pulled out. Laney sat silent beside him, still looking numb. Unsure of how to approach her, he filled the car with senseless rambling. She did her best to add to the conversation, but he could tell her mind was elsewhere. After a while, he reached over and laid a hand on her leg. "I'm sorry for jumping on you back there."

"No, I understand," she said. "I was wrong. I was too nervous. I blew it."

"No. I—"

"Yes. The bait isn't supposed to panic."

Cooper winced. "I should have never put you in that position."

"Still, I understand why you would be mad at me."

"Mad at you?" He took his eyes off the road for a moment to gaze at her in surprise. "Laney, I'm not mad at you. You didn't do anything wrong. He was there. We just got the wrong man. I acted too quickly. I didn't think. I was letting my emotions get in the way of my judgment. I want to get this man so much."

She studied his profile. "Because he keeps eluding you? It's a matter of ego?"

He laughed at her bluntness. "Yeah, I guess. That, and..." He reached over and touched the side of her face. "Because it's tearing me up inside to see what he's doing to you." He put his hand back on the wheel, staring ahead. "And thinking about what he wants to do to you..." He gestured vaguely. *That scares the shit out of me.*

He glanced over. Her head was lowered and she was rubbing her hand along her shorts. He couldn't see her expression through her hair where it fell forward to cover her face.

Her voice was small, hesitant, as it seeped through the blond wall. "Why does it matter to you so much? I mean, you see cases like mine all the time, don't you?"

Her words echoed Aidan's. He nodded, although she hadn't turned to look at him. He waited for her to complete her thought, but she seemed to change horses in midstream.

"So," she said with what sounded like false cheerfulness. "You'll catch him and then this will all be over." Her voice caught and she stopped talking.

But what she said struck a chord. What would happen after this was done? When she was free to go back to work. When the danger that had forced them together was gone. Would she walk away without looking back? A sweet goodbye, perhaps, and then...nothing. The thought left a hollow feeling in the pit of his stomach.

LANEY ENTERTAINED SIMILAR thoughts. She would be another case solved, stamped "CLOSED" in red, put away in a manila folder and locked inside a metal drawer. She wouldn't have him to lean on anymore, and there would be no Sydney to comfort her.

She had no close friends, only acquaintances. She had never felt confident enough to open up to anyone other than Sydney, always fearful of the rejection her mother inundated her with. It was safer not to risk, she knew, not to try at all. Then she couldn't be rejected. But, somehow—whether it was because she was mourning the loss of Sydney and was weak, or if it was the unsteadiness of her current reality, hunted by some maniac who wanted to hurt her—somehow, she had let him in. She dreaded the thought of being alone again, of being without him. She wrapped her arms around her middle, feeling nauseous.

As they drove, the tires beat a slow, mournful tune to accompany their bleak thoughts and neither one spoke until they pulled into the parking lot at Cooper and Aidan's.

He switched off the ignition and turned to her, again putting his hand on her leg. "You okay?"

She nodded, and tried to force a smile. Aidan was walking toward their car, so they got out.

"Hey," Aidan said, his easiness a stark contrast to their somberness. "I was thinking on the way over here, this place isn't safe anymore. If he was tracking Laney through her phone, then he knows about this place."

"I thought the same thing," Cooper said with a frown.

"My mom has a place I bet we can use," Laney interjected. "I've never been there, so he won't know about it. I'm sure there's room for all of us."

"Are you sure she'd let us borrow it? I don't think she's very fond of me. After you left the table that day I first met your mom, I kind of suggested that she owed you an apology."

Laney stared at him. "And how did she take that?"

He shrugged. "I didn't stick around to find out."

Laney smiled. "No one talks to my mom like that, except for maybe Syd."

"I guess I don't have any manners." He laughed.

She took his hand and gave it a squeeze. "I'm glad."

His heart did a little cartwheel as he gazed into her sunny face. *Man, when she smiles, she's the most gorgeous thing I've ever laid eyes on.*

Aidan cleared his throat. "Not that it's not a great offer, Lane, but I was thinking of staying at Jenna's place. Unless you think you may need backup."

"No. If he doesn't know about the place, we'll be fine."

Aidan held out his hand to shake Cooper's. "But you'll call if you need anything?"

"Yeah," he said and clasped Aidan's hand, putting his other hand on his friend's shoulder. "I'll call."

"Good. Let's get our stuff then."

While they packed duffle bags, Laney called her mother and arranged to meet with her, ironically, in the same ritzy restaurant where they had all met before. Her things were still packed in a bag a female officer had retrieved from her condo the day before, so they were off in no time.

CHAPTER TWENTY

Camille Essex sat in the same booth she had been in on their previous visit. She eyed the pair appraisingly as they approached the table. They exchanged greetings and sat. Camille's gaze zeroed in on the bruises and bandage on Laney's forehead.

"Tsk, tsk. You are such a klutz, Laney-dear. Did you trip down the stairs at your condo?"

Out of the corner of her eye, Laney saw Cooper's mouth twitch. His jaw was tight and she hurried to answer before he had an opportunity to, squeezing his hand underneath the table. "Yes, Mother. I tripped down the stairs." She sent Cooper a warning glance and he had to bite his tongue to keep his promise to her.

"Why, Officer," Camille said, letting a bit of her southern drawl seep through, "every time I see you lately, you are in the company of my daughter." She sipped her highball, measuring him over the rim of the cut crystal.

"Mother, please don't start."

"Nonsense, Laney, I want to know what this young man's intentions are. Who are your people, son?"

"Mother."

He laughed. "I belong to the Sullivans of Orange County."

"Mother, I won't have you insult Cooper. He—"

Camille shot her daughter a sharp look. "I see your manners haven't improved since the last time we met here," she declared, her voice steel. The implication was clear. Laney would remember exactly what had happened the last time she spoke back to her mother. "Maybe you've been hanging out with this one too much," she added, indicating Cooper with a jerk of her head.

"His manners are impeccable. He would never make anyone squirm by being self-righteous and...and..." Her mind seemed to search for the words to express her indignation but she gave up with a loud sigh, trying to rein it in.

Camille took a long sip of her drink. "Oh, Laney, you are so naïve. All he wants to do is get into your pants."

She gasped.

Now it was Cooper's turn to be irate. "For your information—"

"I'm not interested in anything you have to say." She gave him a cool gaze.

"Mother. We are not here to discuss Cooper or his intentions, good or otherwise. I simply wanted to ask you if I could use your house in Malibu."

"What?" She looked from one to the other. "Are you two looking for a place to shack up?"

"You know—" Cooper began, his eyes blazing, but Laney interrupted. "Cooper."

When he turned to Laney, he expected to see a warning look on her face, beseeching him not to tell her mother about the killer stalking her, but instead she said calmly, "Let me tell her." She turned back to her mother, laying her folded arms on the table. "Mother, I need the house because the man who killed Sydney broke into my house, followed me to a hotel room where he stabbed a police officer and tried to get at me while I cowered in the bathroom, and then attacked me at the beach and did this to me." Her voice shook with a cold fury. "I need a place where I can hide myself away until Cooper can figure out who's doing this, so...can I stay there or should I look for something else?"

"He-he struck you?" Camille stuttered in shock, her hand over her heart.

"He knocked her out cold," Cooper said, happy to see she was taken aback.

"And you...where were you?" she turned on him, her voice shrill.

Laney stood, jarring the table and splashing water from the goblets onto the tablecloth.

"This isn't worth it." She reached for his hand as he slid out of the booth. Camille stared at them, open-mouthed. They turned and walked away.

"That felt good," Laney whispered to him.

"Laney. Wait," her mother called.

They halted but didn't turn at first, looking at each other. Then Laney sighed and spun. Camille was scrambling to pull something out of a beaded bag on the table. Laney slowly walked back to her side.

"Here," she said, sliding a piece of paper she had scribbled on into her hand. "This is the name and address of the property management company that maintains the house for me. I'll call ahead to let them know you are coming." As she reached for the paper, Camille grasped her hand. "Be careful, Laney," she said, her voice hoarse. "You're all I have left."

Her voice sounded tight when she responded. "I will, Mother." She kissed her on the cheek and left. She returned to Cooper shaking her head. "Unbelievable. She had to point out how horrible it would be for her should I be killed." She sighed. "But at least she said it would matter to her. I wasn't at all sure whether it would."

COOPER FOLLOWED THE sky-blue sedan up the steep, twisty drive to the house. Before he and Laney headed for the management company, he pulled over on the side of the road so she could toss her cell-phone over the cliff and into the waves below. It was important for her to do it herself, her way of thumbing her nose at the killer and taking back control. He had been right; she relaxed for the rest of the ride.

Now, as they pulled up to a small, unassuming cottage, she peered out the window uncertainly. "This is it? This is my mother's place?" They got out and walked with the young man from the property management service to the front door as he pulled out the keys. "I'm surprised by how...modest this place is. Knowing my mother, I expected something more, well, splashy."

The young man laughed. "This is just the tip of the iceberg, so to speak. Most of the house is built into the side of the cliff." He opened the door and stepped back so they could enter.

As Cooper and Laney crossed the threshold, they found themselves standing on a sort of balcony/entryway about twenty feet above a living room the size of a casino lobby. A wide, curved staircase cascaded to the floor below which was illuminated by a wall of pure glass on the far side of the room. Camille knew a home built into the side of a cliff would have a limited area in which to install windows, so she had twenty-foot high windows that spanned the entire length of the room. Laney leaned against the railing overlooking the room below. "She is a piece of work," she muttered under her breath, a smile twitching at the corners of her lips. She descended the staircase, trailing a hand over the satiny-smooth wooden banister as she went.

Cooper turned to the man from the property company, pulling out his badge. "Listen, Jarred...it's Jarred, right?"

The young man, who was now nervous, nodded his head vigorously.

"It is important no one know Ms. Essex is here. No one. Not your mom and dad, not the guy you work out with at the gym, not even the mailman, okay? Ms. Essex's safety depends on it. Do you think you can do that for us?"

Jarred's eyes strayed to watch Laney as she ambled down the long staircase and he nodded.

"Good, good. I think we can find our way around, and if we have any questions, we'll call you."

"Yes, Officer." Jarred passed the keys off and was out the door without further comment, closing it behind him.

Cooper pocketed his badge and the keys, turning to locate her. When he saw her, his breath caught in his chest. There were times, like this, he was taken off guard by the way his feelings for her swamped him. She stood at the bank of windows, her back to him, her arms crossed. He stepped down the stairs slowly, watching her the whole way. She didn't move an inch. He was captivated by her, not observing the resplendent surroundings as he passed, taking in only the glassy shimmer of her hair in the sunlight, the tantalizing curves of her bare back, where it was revealed by her halter top dipping low and the sweet allure of her hips, sensual even in the khaki shorts she wore.

He was thankful for the long walk as he anticipated touching her, letting his hands claim what he wanted, breathing in her subtle, tempting fragrance, a scent that had its own power to arouse him, as it required his closeness to smell it and he had come to associate it with their most intimate moments. As he approached her, he almost felt like some sort of wild animal stalking its prey, and, indeed, she jumped when his hands touched her, sliding around her waist and pulling her close to him. He buried his face in her hair and she leaned back into his arms with such delicious trust and familiarity, it made him smile. He could see she had closed her eyes, a faint smile playing over her lips, her hands folded up to touch his arms. She stoked, following the curves of his muscles as they basked in the warmth of the sunlight, coupled by the heat of their closeness.

There it was. That smell. The clean, floral scent that rose from her skin, making him want to sink his teeth into her flesh. His lips ran the length of her neck, although they were not parted, and he was consumed by the velvety softness of her skin, along with the silky feel of her hair against his cheek.

Oh, God, how I want to do so much more to you that would feel nice. He tried to temper his need. "Your mom has...flair."

She laughed at his understatement, the noise bubbling up from deep inside her, spilling out like tinkling bells. "Do you think?" she countered, turning in his arms. "I hope we don't get lost in here. I forgot to ask Jarred for a map."

Now his deep, low laugh mixed with hers, dancing together in the sunlight that blazed through the window. "What do you want to do now?" he asked suggestively, his voice a low purr. He was certain he saw her guard come up for a minute, a wariness floating behind those beautiful blue eyes of hers.

"Well-ll...I need to go to the grocery store to get stuff for dinner." She looked at him with curiosity.

"I'll go with you."

"You don't need to. I'll be safe here."

"Well, I'm not taking any chances. And besides, I love grocery shopping."

"Wow. You use that line a lot, Sullivan?" Her lips turned up in a sexy grin, a twinkle in her eye.

With his hands on her hips, he shimmied her closer, bending his face to hers. "Only on girls I'm trying to score with."

"Oh? And how does it generally work for you?" She smiled, running her fingertips up his chest.

He shrugged, feeling his own smile a mile wide. "I do okay."

"Not this time." She laughed, pushing off his chest and dodging when he moved to pull her back. She grabbed her purse from a chair and hurried up the long steps, her laugh floating back to him. She left him feeling like he'd been doused with a bucket of cold water.

Ooh. He groaned. *I like her.* He chased after her, out the door.

CHAPTER TWENTY-ONE

Who knew the grocery store could be so much fun? Laney loved having someone to talk to, someone to push the cart and trail along with her, or run and get something on the list. Cooper turned out to be pretty handy to have along, as he seemed to know his way around a grocery store better than she expected.

"Do you cook?" she asked, after he had successfully retrieved some fresh rosemary for her.

"Aidan and I used to take turns," he explained. "But I ended up teaching myself how to cook in self-defense. Aidan is terrible."

"Ahh."

"Besides," Cooper added, grabbing her up by surprise, "the grocery store is a great place to pick up girls." Before she could make any evasive moves he kissed her, stealing her breath away and leaving her off balance enough she had to reach for the cart handle to steady herself.

"Cooper!" She giggled. "There's a boy watching us." She tried to squirm away from his arms.

He looked up, following her gaze to where the cute little red curly-haired boy was observing them from the end of the aisle. "So?" he responded, brushing his lips temptingly over hers again. "Let him find his own girl."

"Ahem."

He glanced again. Now a heavyset, redheaded woman frowned at them as she ushered the boy away.

"Killjoy," Cooper muttered, but he released Laney and behaved himself for the rest of the trip.

When they left the grocery store, the sky had turned dark and the Santa Ana winds had picked up in intensity. A storm was brewing.

"Boy." She helped to load the groceries into the car. "I hope you can get the barbecuing in." The wind was whipping her hair into her face. She tried to push it out of her face with one hand, while reaching back into the cart for another bag.

Cooper placed his hand over hers. "Go ahead and get in. I've got the rest of these."

When he got in, she had stolen his yellow and brown San Diego Padres hat from the dashboard and placed it on her head as an attempt to control her hair.

"Do you mind if I use this?"

Cooper stared and then grinned. "Of course not."

"What?" She pulled the visor down to check the mirror. "Does it look weird?"

He smiled. "No. You look cute. You know," he added, taking her hand, "I don't want you to worry about anything tonight. Forget about all the craziness for a while. I want to have a normal, quiet evening with you."

"I want that, too." She brought his hand to her lips.

When they got to the house, she set about seasoning the chicken while he hunted down the grill. He entered the kitchen through some French doors a few minutes later. "I've got it going," he informed her. "And boy, is she a beaut. Much nicer than my little charcoal grill. It even had a button to ignite it."

"Yes," she said slowly. "They have those now, caveman." He picked up a radish and threw it at her, but she caught it, surprising herself with her dexterity.

He came up behind her, placing his hands on either side of her on the counter.

"Whatcha doin'?"

She squirmed. "Making the salad. Do you want to open the wine?"

"Thought you'd never ask." In minutes, he had it open and was handing her a glass of Chardonnay. He leaned back against the counter, watching her face as she worked, peeling pieces of carrot into the bowl. He snuck a chunk of carrot from the cutting board and munched it while he studied her face.

"You're really beautiful, you know."

Her hands had been flying over the bowl, but now they stilled as her cheeks began to glow. She smiled, her voice tight. "Now you're sucking up."

"No, I'm not."

She turned her head to look at him, then shook it and went back to work.

His eyes widened. "You don't believe you're beautiful, do you?"

"Cooper." She laughed, incredulous, wishing the cabinets would fall off the wall or the sink would spring a sudden leak, anything to end this awkward conversation.

"Come here." He took her elbow.

"I'm making dinner—"

"Come on. Put that stuff down," he demanded. He pulled her into the hall where there was a large brass mirror in the shape of a sun. "You look at that and tell me you're not gorgeous."

"Cooper, the meat's ready to go on."

"Laney." He held her. "Look at yourself."

She gazed at his reflection in the mirror, her eyes pleading with him, but he shook his head. She looked at herself, resigned. The bruises on her face had started to show the yellow tinge of healing, but she hid it pretty well with makeup. Still, when she measured herself, it was all she saw. She glanced away. "Oh, yeah. A real charmer. Bruises under my eye—"

"Come on, Laney. Look beyond that."

Understanding he would give her no choice, she tried again, but her eyes only stayed on the image for a minute. "My eyes are too big."

Cooper laughed.

"Don't laugh at me!" she yelled and tried to get away from him.

"Wait." He forced her to turn toward him. "Laney. I wasn't laughing at you. I was laughing because that is the most ridiculous thing I've ever heard. Your eyes were what drew me to you, that first night at Phat Jack's." He held her face in his hands, rubbing his thumbs on her cheeks, looking desperate to make her see the things he saw in her. "They're incredibly blue—"

"Stop it." Uncomfortable, she dropped her eyes.

"—and breathtaking. You take my breath away, Laney, every time I look at you."

Her eyes flew to his, her lips parted in mid-protest. She searched his face and saw reflected there the love in his heart, and it terrified her. She turned her head to lay it on his chest. "Please, Cooper." She squeezed her eyes shut, trying to block out the image of his face. "Can we finish making dinner?"

"If that's what you want." He kissed her forehead and pulled her in for one last squeeze before returning with her to the kitchen. "I'll go put the meat on."

WHEN HE CAME BACK, struggling with the door against the wind, he found her wine glass empty. "Do you want me to fill you up?"

"You wouldn't be trying to ply me with wine, would you officer?" she smiled at him, seeming much more relaxed.

"Damn straight, I am." *Is it working?*

"So, Cooper Sullivan," she said, her voice more fluid than usual, "tell me about your family."

"Well, I have an older brother, Ben...he owns a construction company, married, three kids...three great kids," he said with a smile. Laney stopped what she was doing for a moment to listen to him. "Then there's Bree—Brianna. She works for a record company, and does all right for herself. She handles parties for various celebrities, record launches, organizes tour buses and trucks for equipment... I'm not sure what all she does, but I know she's good at it and she has access to concert tickets and has gotten me in to see groups I would have never gotten to see on my own."

She leaned against the counter, halfway through her second glass of wine. "Like who?"

"The Who, for one, and The Red Hot Chili Peppers—"

"You saw The Red Hot Chili Peppers? I'd kill to see The Red Hot Chili Peppers."

"Okay, not exactly what you should say to a cop, but, yes, I partied with Anthony, Flea, and the guys."

"You are kidding. Oh, my gosh. I am so jealous. Could she get me in?"

"I'll see what I can do."

"That would be awesome." She jumped into his arms and planted an ardent kiss on him. Her lips were warm and tasted pleasant, like the wine. But, as quickly as it started, it was over. "I need to go change for dinner."

He stood there, still stunned by the kiss. After several seconds his mind rolled around to, *Should I be changing for dinner?* But he decided instead to go check on the chicken. He was afraid the strong winds might blow out the flames. When he came back, he took his bag to a small bathroom he had seen and changed into a white shirt that buttoned up the front and khaki pants. As he sat on the couch, she entered the room. The clothes she changed into were simple enough, but on her, they had a certain VA-VAVOOM effect. Sexy black heels with long-legged jeans, dark in places, and faded in others, a stop-sign red camisole, which conversely, seemed to be screaming "Go. Go. Go!" and over that, a sheer, long sleeved black blouse lending an air of mystery and raciness to the whole ensemble.

"Ouch," he muttered under his breath, his mind traveling to dark places where she was moaning his name. "Hey. Hey. You're back," he said cheerily, although his voice sounded strained in his dry throat.

"Yes, I am." She poured herself another glass of wine.

He thought about telling her to slow down, but she began searching through the drawers for an apron, making a lot of noise. She found a black one and put it on, starting the fettuccine she had chosen to accompany the chicken. He watched her cook and chatted with her, occasionally letting his eyes slide up and down the lean lines of her body and mouthing, "Wow," to no one in particular. Dinner was fantastic and he poured the last bit of wine into their glasses as they moved to the couch.

"You know, most of my mom's places have this kind of cold, rigid feel to them, but I kind of like this place. It seemed so huge before, more like a museum than a home, but the lamplight seems to draw everything together in its glow, making it homier."

"I agree." She was sitting with her legs curled to one side, her wine glass in hand, and he thought he would agree to about anything she said right now.

"But did you see the elevator?"

"Yeah, it said there are four floors."

"I rode it up and down. There is a sort of freight entry at the top, this floor, the pool/deck area, and then it goes all the way down to the beach."

"Pretty cool."

"Yeah," she said sarcastically, rolling her eyes. She took a sip of her wine and began again. "Okay, so there's Ben and Bree, and you—anyone else?"

"McKenzie. Remember? You saw her at the police station."

"Oh, yeah," she said, her face coloring. "I remember. What does she do?"

Cooper laughed. "About anything she wants. She's the baby, so she's spoiled. She floats around from job to job like a butterfly to flowers. We ended up in the same grade, I was this side of the cut-off line, she was the other—we're eleven months apart—and I was constantly having to get her out of trouble. But it was never much of a bother really. She has such a bubbly, outgoing personality, sometimes guys took it the wrong way, and I ended up having to...explain it to them. She wasn't coming on to them, that's just how she was. For instance, one time when we were in college, she was at a crowded bar with a group of people. There was this guy behind her, and she reached back to help him through the crowd so they could all stay together. He took it as a come-on, but she would have done it if it was you, or my mom, or my grandma. It wouldn't have mattered who it was."

"So you had to explain it to him."

"Yeah," Cooper said with a frown. "And he didn't take it too well." He pulled the hair that fell down over his forehead up and revealed a ragged scar. "That's how I got this. Broken beer bottle."

"Oh," Laney cried, bringing a finger up to trace the scar. Her touch sent a tingle through him. "You're a good big brother."

"I try," he said lightly, playing with her hair.

"I wish I had a brother like you. But Sydney was kind of like a big brother to me, she defended me..." She stopped speaking.

Cooper thought about how it would feel to lose Ben, Bree, or McKenzie, and he couldn't fathom it. "I'm sorry, Laney." His voice was soft. "I'm sorry you lost her." He found his heart in his throat, as he so often did with her around. His eyes roamed over her face, and without even thinking, he heard himself saying, "I'd like to do that for you, defend you, protect you, from whatever might hurt you."

Her eyes searched his, and then she began to move forward. He closed his eyes as their lips met. Her fingers came to the side of his face, tentative at first. She pulled away, but her eyes remained on his lips. She ran a thumb over them, her face a study of concentration, then, she moved forward again, pressing her lips to his hungrily until it felt like their heat was searing him. His hands slid to the back of her neck, under her hair, pulling her closer. She changed positions until she was lying across his lap, her back on the thick arm of the couch. His hands traveled down the length of her arm and touched her leg, rubbing the ultra-soft fabric of her jeans along the side of her thigh, then sliding under her more intimately. She pulled away, standing up alongside of the couch.

An apology was ready on his lips. He had gone too far, put too much pressure on her, and then she was reaching for his hand. "Let's go to bed."

At first, his brain didn't register her intent, but reflex had him sticking his hand in hers and following. But as his mind caught up, he cried out, "Wait. Wait!"

She stopped, turning to him with a curious expression.

He brought his hand again behind her neck, caressing as he asked her, "Are you sure, Laney? Are you really sure?" She nodded, and with a rush he pressed her against the wall. Their hearts knocked in their chests, their breath coming raggedly. He kissed her once, hard, on the lips. "You're sure?" She nodded, desperate, as his lips sought hers again and again. Her leg circled behind his as his hands stroked along her sides, untucking her tank top and finding the desired warmth of her flesh. "Where's the bedroom?" Instead of answering, she took his hand again and started to hurry down the hallway.

After what seemed like an eternity, she opened a door to a bedroom the size of Cooper's entire apartment. The bed itself was the size of Aidan's room, which was the master bedroom, something he had lost to a coin toss the day they moved in. The bedspread was antique white with gold swirls, covering matching satin sheets and heaped with gold pillows of every shape and size. He kissed her again, then picked her up and moved to the bed, plopping her on it and falling on top.

Their kisses were feverish now, a tangle of tongues and lips, heat and moisture, and racing need. He shifted his weight to the side and again pulled up on her tank to reveal her stomach, and his hands explored. They touched her stomach, both soft and hard, the indention of her waist, the curve of her hips where her low-slung jeans allowed him to feel the beginnings of those fabulous hips before his hands hit soft denim again. She drew her right leg up as if by reflex, bending it at the knee to plant the tip of her heel against the edge of the bed, enabling him to reach all of her leg. He pulled away and rubbed his hand up and down her leg, alternately watching what his hands were appreciating, and gazing into her face, relishing the effect his touch had on her. He slid his hand under her heel and pulled her shoe off, caressing her foot before releasing it and bending to kiss her once more. She wrapped her legs around him in such an erotic way he thought he was going to lose it, but she used her bare foot to kick off her other heel and then brought them back on either side of him. He reveled for a minute in thoughts about how strong and flexible she was and what it could do to him.

His hands wandered under the tight spandex of her tank and he attempted to remove her strapless bra. She shifted and arched her back, again showing him how limber she was, allowing him access to the hooks. He unhooked and removed the bra, tossing it somewhere on the enormous bed. He brought both hands to her sides to encircle her waist, prolonging the anticipation as he brought them up, inch by inch, to cup her breasts. They both groaned as he touched her, and then the need to be pressed together, flesh to flesh, was overwhelming.

Laney had worked his buttons open and he pulled back so she could take his shirt off. Her hands trembled as they returned to his skin. Her eyes followed her hands as they touched his chest and then his arms. Mimicking hers, he brought his hands to her upper chest, watching as they parted the fabric of her shirt and then he lowered his head and began to kiss her there. "Oh, Cooper...mmm...oh, that feels so good."

The sound of her cries, coming from deep within her, honed his desire and he pulled at the fabric to expose more skin. He unintentionally pulled too hard and popped the top button. The sudden give of the fabric before it strained against the next button was exciting and he began to pull with recklessness, popping button-by-button until the sides of her shirt were free. He yanked it off her shoulder and brought his mouth down to sink his teeth into her flesh for a minute. And then she reached down to pull his head back up until her mouth found his again in a frantic rush of pure lust and he knew if he didn't slow things down, it would all be over too soon.

Showing more restraint than he thought possible, he pulled away, gazing down into her flushed face. The rush of blood had made her lips ruby red, her hair was fanned out around her like a peacock's tail, and as he watched her chest rise and fall with each gasping breath, he thought he had never seen anything more beautiful. No sunset over the beach, no mountaintop could compare to her, and the words came out as if pulled from him. "Laney, I love you."

He could not read what was in her eyes. He only knew what had been misted with passion, now cleared and became serious. Without a word, she pushed against his chest, squirmed out from under him, and ran out of the room.

CHAPTER TWENTY-TWO

Back in the bedroom, Cooper was chastising himself. *I should have never pushed her so hard. Slow and steady, remember, Cooper. Ugh. What was I thinking? It's her first time and I start ripping her clothes off.* He got up and followed her. He reached the elevator as the doors closed and got the briefest glimpse of her anguished face as she hugged herself, trying to draw together her ripped blouse.

"Dammit!" He pounded on the door, and punched at the button. The Roman numerals on the dial above showed she had descended to the bottom level. He glanced around for a staircase, but seeing none, waited for the elevator, which was returning relatively quickly, leaning his forearm against the wall. He squeezed in as the doors parted. He had pulled his shirt back on, but not bothered to button it back up. He rode the elevator down, and when the doors opened, the wind rushed in and seemed to suck the breath right out of his lungs. He saw her ahead in the sand, stumbling toward the beach. "Laney, wait." She turned and he rushed forward until he was five or so feet away and stopped dead in his tracks by the look of utter misery creasing her face.

"I'm sorry," he blurted out.

"Sorry? Sorry?" she screamed over the howling wind, her hair whipping around her face in a frenzy. "Wasn't I the one who led you to the bedroom, then ran out on you? Or was it all some bizarre nightmare?"

He was caught up short by the anguish lacing her voice, coupled with anger. "Please, Laney, can't we go inside to talk?"

"I don't know what the hell I'm doing anymore," she cried out, more to herself than to him. She pulled her hair back roughly from her forehead, holding it on the top of her head.

Seeing her torment and knowing he had been the one to cause it was killing him. "Laney," he pleaded, "won't you come back?" He held out his hand to her and she stared at it without moving. He took a step forward and she took a step back. She turned her back to him, but before he could make another move, she whipped around.

"I'm afraid, Cooper!" she screamed.

"I know. I'm sorry. This was your first time. I should have taken it slow."

"No." She stepped forward. "Ugh." And then she did something he didn't expect, she pushed against his chest. "It's not that for God's sake. I'm not afraid of that."

He put his hands on her arms, happy at least to have reestablished some physical contact with her. "Y-you're not scared of me? Because Laney, I'd never hurt you. I got a little out of hand, but—"

"No. It's not that. I wanted you up there. I wanted you." Her voice caught. "And that's what frightens me," she finished weakly, the wind almost taking her words. She turned away from him. "I'm sorry."

Cooper stood there, trying to make sense of her words and then noticed her back was shaking. He stepped forward and locked his arms around her. "It's not your fault."

"Yes it is!" she yelled, but she turned in his arms to wrap her arms around him. "Yes, it is." One fist came down to hit him in the chest and then sobs began to wrack her body.

"Come on, babe," Cooper said desperately. "Won't you come inside with me?"

She pulled her head from his chest, looking up at him as the wind continued to buffet them both. "I can't keep doing this to you. I can't keep doing it to myself. Can't you see?" Tears streamed down her face and the lights from the cliff turned them to silver.

He tried to soothe her. "Come with me."

She allowed him to lead her back to the elevator. Once inside the doors, he breathed a sigh of relief. At least she had come this far. She leaned on him on the way up and he stroked her arm without saying anything. When they got to the main floor, he decided the couch was safer than the bedroom and so he took her there. He sat in a corner, and she sat, leaning her back against him while he draped an arm over her shoulder. They were quiet for some time, the only sounds, the wind beating against the windows, and his hand trailing up and down her arm. She was so still, he thought for a moment, she had fallen asleep until she released a shuddering breath.

He hesitated. "Do you want to talk?"

She sighed. "I guess it would be the grownup thing to do."

"I've heard being a grownup is overrated."

He saw her cheek rise and knew she was smiling. That was a good thing; at least she still had her sense of humor. "Believe me, it is." He shifted so she could sit up, but she said, "Can we just stay like this? I don't think I can look you in the face right now. I'm too embarrassed. I guess I'm not that grownup."

It was his turn to smile now. "There's no reason to be embarrassed, but if that's what you want." He settled back down.

"First of all, I'm sorry about hitting you."

"Yeah," he said, rubbing his chest. "You pack quite a wallop. You ever think about going into police work? Skills like those might come in handy."

"They come in pretty handy as a teacher, too."

"At Walter Davis, I guess so."

She chuckled quietly. After a brief pause, she started in with her explanation. "What was about to happen in the bedroom...what was going to happen...I wanted it to happen."

"Still, I shouldn't have pressured you."

She leaned back across his lap so she could look him in the face. "As I recall, I was putting some pressure on, too."

He smiled, remembering every kiss, every touch.

"And you responded, which was wonderful. I thought I could handle it," she murmured, looking down.

"But I pushed things too far."

She pressed a painted fingernail to his lips. "Shh. Nothing happened inside that room I didn't want to happen, I hadn't dreamed of happening." Her face colored at this revelation. "It's just... How can I explain what I don't even understand myself?"

He played with her hair without speaking, then, wet his lips. "Please try, Laney. I want to understand what you're going through."

"It makes it so much harder when you're nice," she complained.

He laughed. "Did you want me to be mean?"

"No, no." She toyed with a button on his shirt. "Okay, let me try this again. What we were going to do, I wanted to do it mindlessly. I wanted to be with you, but not feel anything, but I couldn't do it."

His confusion registered on his face. "I don't understand."

"It's easy for you guys. You could be with any number of women—"

"Wait one minute here," Cooper interrupted. "Don't you think you're assuming something there?"

"B-but..."

"I have only been with one woman—girl, really—and that was a mistake. But I thought I was in love. I wasn't just...jumping her bones."

"I-I'm sorry. I just assumed."

"Do you think I'm the kind of guy who would do...that...lightly?" He let his ire go, tracing a hand along the side of her face. "I told you, Laney Essex," he murmured, tapping her on the lips. "I couldn't have meaningless sex with you." He saw the flash of pain in her eyes, but didn't understand it.

"Don't you see? That makes it worse."

"Laney. You are the most confusing woman I know," he muttered, exasperated. For some reason, this seemed to amuse her. "Oh, you think that's funny, do you?"

"No. I'm sorry." She brought herself back under control. "Oh, Cooper," she sighed. "You don't know how sorry I am—"

"No, that I get. It's the rest that's fuzzy."

"I don't let many people in. I think it has to do with my mother somehow. If you don't let people close, then they can't be disappointed in you."

"But I would never be disappointed in you."

"So you say now." She looked down at her hands. "And it's not just that...when I do care for people, like my father, and Sydney..."

"You end up losing them."

"Yes." She looked him in the eyes. "I don't think I could stand that. I know it's stupid. I know I'm disturbed. I don't blame you for being mad at me."

"So...you wanted to have meaningless sex with me—and I can't believe I am questioning this—but, why? Why would you want that?"

"Well, for obvious reasons. You're hot."

"Good to know," he said, but his face became hot.

"And...I wanted to please you."

This answer made him less happy. He frowned. "Like you've always tried to please your mom?"

She nodded, seeming unnerved by his stern expression.

"Laney, if there is one thing I will not stand for, it's you doing things only to please me. I want you as you are. Whatever you want to give to me, nothing more."

She reached up and stroked his face, unable to speak, and then kissed him.

"So why did you end up running out on me?" he asked carefully. "Was it because I ripped your clothes off?"

"No." She smiled. "I liked that."

He was quiet, and serious for several seconds and Laney squirmed in his lap.

"Is it because I told you I loved you?"

She looked up at him, biting her lip.

"No choosing your words now," he warned. "I want the truth. I think I deserve that."

She swallowed and her eyes filled up with tears. She nodded her head vigorously up and down. "I'm sorry. I'm sorry."

"Shh. Shh. It's okay." He lifted her wet face. "Laney, it's okay. You weren't ready to hear that yet, I shouldn't have said it." He paused. "But I will say it again someday, so you better get used to the fact." She smiled at him but shivered. "Are you cold?"

"A little."

"The temperature dropped a lot out there. I saw some cocoa in the kitchen. Do you want me to make you some?"

"I'll get it."

"No, no. I know where it is. You sit here for a minute. I'll get us some."

Cooper headed into the kitchen and filled two coffee cups with milk. While he waited for them to warm in the microwave, he leaned against the counter and sorted through everything that happened. He idly buttoned up his shirt, all the while thinking about how her hands had unbuttoned it.

When he reentered the living room, she was leaning her head on her arms, which were crossed on the side of the couch; her legs curled to one side as she lay fast asleep. He set the mugs on the table in front of the couch, and bent to look at her quiet face. He skimmed his hand over her hair. "Laney Essex, you are a quandary. But I have all the time in the world to figure you out, darling." He kissed her forehead, beyond the bandage, and then sat to sip his hot chocolate as he watched her sleep.

CHAPTER TWENTY-THREE

Laney woke up at two in the dark. Cooper had found a blanket and draped it over her.

Propped up on her cold glass of cocoa was a small piece of paper, which read: If you need anything, I'm in the bedroom. She got up to look out the window. The winds had died down, though the deck was wet from rain, and the ocean was coming in much more calmly now. She stood with her arms crossed, staring out at the water, for some time. How could she have attempted to have meaningless sex with him? She was already too far gone.

At three, she shook Cooper awake. "I need something," she whispered. She stepped back and took her blouse off. Reaching down, she pulled her tank top off over her head, revealing her bare breasts. Cooper sat but didn't speak. She unzipped her jeans and peeled them off, then rid herself of the skimpy underwear underneath. She walked over to the bed. He swung his feet over the side and watched her. She placed her hands on his shoulders and he rested his on her naked hips. She started to push him backward, but he resisted.

His choked voice broke through the darkness. "Are you going to have meaningless sex with me? Not that I've ruled that out entirely," he added quickly, "but I'm not sure if I can."

She laid a finger on his lips. "That's why I stopped before, I couldn't have meaningless sex with you either, because I love you, too, Cooper."

She could see his broad smile in the moonlight filtering through the edges of the drapes, which didn't quite meet. "Okay, then. Take me, I'm yours." He fell backward and she fell with him, laughing.

And when his lips were on hers, she simply felt...wonderful. It was as if he were breathing life back into her, life and light, warmth and comfort. The deeper he took the kiss, the more willing she became to surrender to him, to give up the pain and fear and anger, and float away on the dizzying power of his kiss.

They made love slowly, sensually, she rising above him in the hint of moonlight like some goddess, her hips driving him wild with each subtle movement until they fell together in a heap of ecstasy, their bodies shaking with wave after wave of pleasure. After a minute, she fell off to lay at his side.

"Whoo," he breathed. He turned his head to look at her, smiling, on the pillow beside him, her body looking so relaxed it flowed over the sheets like she had been poured out. "Are you sure you haven't done this before?" She laughed, shaking her head. "Well, lady—" He rose up on his elbow to give her a kiss. "—you're a natural." She laughed, throwing her arms around him and pulling him back down on top of her. They lay together, letting their breathing come back to normal. He fell on to the mattress again and she curled up along his side. "Man." Cooper was still astounded by the depth of pleasure she had evoked. He looked at her again. "Any regrets?"

She giggled. "Not having done this sooner." When he raised an eyebrow, she added, laughing. "With you I mean, only with you."

He pulled her close, and then turned on his side so they were face-to-face. "You know, after this you have no chance of ever getting rid of me."

She giggled. "Shut up, you goof."

"No, I mean it. I want you to come to dinner at my mom's house tomorrow."

"Wh-what?" she answered, sounding startled.

"I want you to meet my family, and more importantly, I want them to meet you."

She flipped over and he pulled her in against his body. She was quiet. Too quiet. "Are you going to try to run away again?"

"No." She paused. "What if they don't like me?"

"What are you talking about? They're going to love you." He gave her a big, smacking kiss on the head. She relaxed and snuggled closer to him. They lay in wordless contentment for several minutes. "Lane?"

"Hmm...?" she answered, sleepily.

"I love you," he whispered in her ear.

"I love you, too, Cooper Sullivan."

They fell into a deep slumber until five a.m. when Cooper felt a nibble on his ear, followed by a voice urging him, "Cooper, you know...as a teacher, I believe practice makes perfect."

He smiled, and threw her onto her back on the mattress, rising over her. "Well, who am I to stand in the way of higher education?"

They got up later and made scrambled eggs and bacon and brought them back to bed.

"My mother would kill me if she knew I was eating in her bed."

"I think your mother would have more of a problem with some of the other things we did in her bed."

She giggled. "Nah. She loves you."

"Yeah, right." He snorted. "Give me your plate." He added it to his and set it on the floor. He crawled over to her. "Are you rejuvenated?"

"Yeah," she said slyly, linking her hands behind his neck. "Are you?"

WHEN COOPER LEFT THE room, he looked back at the door to see Laney sprawled across the bed, half-covered by the sheet, bare limbs everywhere, and his heart swelled with love.

I've got to get this guy.

He went into the living room to log onto the server at headquarters from his laptop. He looked over his files again and reread the autopsy report. His eyes focused in on the line, which began with "murder weapon."

Murder weapon- woven material, about a quarter-inch thick, two and a half inches wide, like a drapery tie, or maybe a narrow tie, like men wore in the eighties.

He read, and reread the description. "Or like a karate belt," he said out loud. He picked up his cell phone and made a few calls.

"HEY," AIDAN CALLED as Cooper jogged up the stairs of the courthouse, waiting for his friend to catch up. They shook hands. "How was your night?" he said, raising his eyebrows to make his real question clear.

Cooper smiled, keeping his lips pressed together.

"Oh, come on. I turned Laney down when she invited us to her mom's plush place in Malibu, I think you owe me some details." They continued up the stairs and into the building.

"Okay. She offered me cheap, meaningless sex..."

"You dog."

"And then ran out on me." He pushed the button for the elevator.

"Ouch."

"But then we made up."

"Yes?"

"And she fell asleep on me."

"Does this have a happy ending?"

"Then I woke up to find her in my room undressing."

"Hold on, let me visualize this."

"Don't you dare," Cooper snapped, jabbing him in the ribs.

"Oof!" Aidan rubbed his side, laughing. "So...how was it?"

The elevator arrived. Cooper turned and looked him straight in the eye. "Which time?" He stepped into the elevator, and turned to see Aidan still standing outside, with his mouth hanging open. Cooper reached out and grabbed him by the shirtfront and pulled him in as the doors began to close.

A few minutes later, they stood in front of Judge Amos Parker. The heavyset man, whose graying hair was leaving him just shy of bald, read the file with his reading glasses on the tip of his bumpy nose. He finished reading and looked up at them curiously. "So, Officers Sullivan and McConnahy, you are here for a search warrant, but I don't see enough evidence here to justify it."

"But sir, the suspect is a karate instructor. The description of the murder weapon is consistent with the size and shape of a karate belt."

"It's not enough."

"I believe there is tracking equipment in his house. We found evidence of it in Ms. Essex's cell phone."

"I'm sorry, I'm still not convinced."

"Please, Judge Parker. I've got to get in there."

"Why is this so important to you, son?" he asked, squinting up at Cooper.

He sighed, putting his hands on his hips under his suit coat. "Because I'm in love with the woman he's trying to kill."

Aidan's jaw dropped again.

The judge snorted. "Hmpf." Parker looked back at the file, but stole a quick look at Cooper, rubbing his eyes. His defeated posture must have done the trick. "You say he's got access to her condo?"

Cooper looked up quickly, hope stirring in his chest. "Yes, sir."

"And you think he's got the hots for your girl?"

"Yes, sir."

He slammed the file down on his desk. "You've got your warrant, son."

"I could kiss you, sir."

"Save it for your girlfriend," he stated, signing the warrant with flourish.

"Thank you, sir." Cooper beamed as he accepted the signed warrant.

Judge Parker gave him a wink. "Go get him. And make the case stick."

CHAPTER TWENTY-FOUR

C ooper stood in front of the open doors of Steve Bertrand's bedroom closet. The entire back of the closet was filled with surveillance equipment, on top of which sat a framed picture of Laney. Aidan still held the evidence bag containing the black belt they had retrieved from the Gi hanging from the rod. Cooper stepped back and opened the door to the balcony. He kicked off his loafers and hopped up on the convenient thick ledge surrounding the balcony.

"What are you doing?"

"Hold on." He lifted himself up onto the roof with little effort. Looking over the edge uneasily, he inched over on his rear to Laney's balcony and hopped down, giving Aidan an exaggerated bow.

"You comin' back the same way?" Aidan asked with feigned boredom.

"Hell, no." Cooper grinned, opening the doors to Laney's condo and disappearing within. When he came out her front door, he noticed a spilled bag of groceries on Steve's door step. "Shit!" He searched the parking lot as he ran toward the neighboring condo.

He yelled in the open doorway, "Wasn't anyone watching the parking lot? Call in an A.P.B. on Steve Bertrand. Make sure the airport is covered as well as the train depot and bus station."

Aidan walked up. "What's wrong?"

"He's on to us."

"IS THAT WHAT YOU'RE wearing?"

Laney looked down at her peach sundress. "You don't like it?"

"No, it's pretty. It's just...I'm wearing blue jean shorts. My brother and I will probably shoot some hoops on the driveway." He shrugged with a smile.

"I'm overdressed," she said, disgusted with herself. "I'm going to change." She turned and Cooper grabbed her hand.

"Wait. You're fine. I shouldn't have said anything."

"No, no. I'm glad you did. I want to look right."

"Lane, you'd look right in anything you'd wear."

"It's just...dinner with my mom is a formal occasion, and my choice of attire is always a subject she loves to upbraid me for, so I was expecting... I'll only take a minute."

When she returned wearing khaki shorts and a black, sleeveless sweater, he had his arms stretched along the back of the couch, but he rose when she entered.

"Better?"

He captured her in a huge lip-lock. "You look fantastic."

She looked down at her shorts. "You're just saying that."

He grabbed her chin and forced her eyes to his, kissing her again. "You look fantastic. Relax. They're going to love you. I know. I'm one of them."

She laughed. "Okay. Let's get going or we'll be late."

As Cooper wound his way through several one-way streets, the neighborhood began to look familiar to Laney. When they pulled up in front of the little brick-front house his parents owned, she drummed her fingers on the Tupperware containing the appetizer she had brought. "Maybe this was a bad idea..."

"Laney Cassandra Essex, you're not getting out of this. So you might as well buck up and face it." He got out of the car.

"How did you know my middle name?" she asked, closing her car door and coming around to cross the quiet street with him.

"Your mother used it."

"Figures," she said dryly. "And you remembered?"

"I remember everything about you, lover," he teased, goosing her on his parents' front door step.

"Cooper. Stop!" She yelped as a gray-haired, barrel-chested man opened the door, towering over them.

"Is my son misbehaving?" His voice was gruff.

"Uh, no...well, yes, but..."

"Well, which is it?" he scowled at her, his lined face stern, despite the twinkle in his blue eyes. He wore a navy blue t-shirt with the L.A.P.D. insignia in the upper-left corner with faded blue jeans. His huge arms were crossed, and a large, blue anchor tattoo was visible where his fingers looped over his upper arms. He was an impressive figure. "Pops, quit giving her a hard time," Cooper said, brushing past his father and pulling Laney in behind him.

The older man broke into a wide, familiar smile as she passed. She recognized it as the same one she'd seen on Cooper's face before.

"Hello. Hello." a short, round, salt-and-pepper-haired lady bubbled as she scurried up to them.

Cooper's dad bowed slightly and extended his arm in her direction. "My wife, Liv." She smiled at him, then returned her gaze to the newcomer. "Welcome to our home. Laney, isn't it?"

"Yes, ma'am."

Olivia Sullivan pulled her into a hug, surprising her. "Oh, no." the older woman laughed. "Not ma'am. You can call me Mom. All of Cooper's friends do."

"I told you they'd love you," he whispered.

Two tall blondes came out of a swinging door, which presumably led to the kitchen. "These are Cooper's sisters," Mrs. Sullivan said, waving a dish-towel in their direction. "Cinderella and Sleeping Beauty," she added, snapping the towel at them as they passed.

They skillfully sidestepped the towel. "Oh, hi."

Laney took the offered hand.

"I'm McKenzie, and this is Bree."

"Nice to meet you." Her stomach dropped and her palms began to sweat. She knew it would be these two who would be her toughest critics. Moms, other than her mom, of course, were programmed to be polite and accepting. Sisters could be lethal. "Cooper tells me you're a teacher," McKenzie opened.

"Yes. I teach English at Walter Davis—"

She was interrupted by a couple falling, laughing, through the swinging door.

The young woman commented, "That means you better watch your grammar, Benjamin."

"Huh? My grammar ain't got no problems."

Cooper snatched an apple from the dining room table and chomped on it. "This here is my brother, Benny." He captured his red-headed sibling in a headlock with his free hand. "Cooper. Don't talk with your mouth full." Mrs. Sullivan looked at Laney apologetically. "You try to teach them manners, but, I swear—" She raised her voice. "—the minute they walk in here they all revert to the fools they were in high school."

The brunette who walked out with Ben skirted the two wrestling brothers and introduced herself. "Hi, I'm Veronica. Fool # 1 belongs to...me," she said, as Ben grabbed the back of Cooper's shorts and tried to give him a wedgie. "I'm so proud," she added.

"Stop it. Stop it, you two knuckleheads." Cooper's mother began beating the pair with her towel. "You're going to break something, and Laney's going to get a bad first impression."

"No. No. Not at all." Laney laughed, despite herself. It was hard not to get caught up in the warm camaraderie and she found she was becoming relaxed. How strange to feel at home in someone else's family, especially since she'd only just arrived. But somehow she sensed she was with kindred spirits. Sure, their backgrounds were vastly different, but there was something here she understood, even though she had never had it herself, loving acceptance.

Cooper bent and gave his mother a peck on the cheek. "Sorry, Momma. I'll behave." Behind her back, he thwacked Ben's head. Ben stepped out of her eye shot and raised his fists at Cooper and danced around threateningly, until his mom turned in his direction and he had to act like he was pushing down some stray hairs and smile at her, the picture of innocence.

"Oh, you two idiots. Go outside and play basketball with your nephews."

"But Mom, I wanted to stay with Laney."

"She'll be fine with us," Bree said as she and McKenzie looped their arms through the newcomer's. "We're going to show her pictures of you."

"You wouldn't dare." He took a step forward, but his mom's hand came out to block his path. "Outside," she demanded with a furious stare.

Ben was already pulling him back through the swinging door where it seemed like a half-dozen, while in fact it was only three, boys started shrieking, "Uncle Cooper! Uncle Cooper!"

"Hey, munchkins," he said, and she saw him bend to hoist one up on his hip with a bright smile before the door swung back, blocking her view.

"We've got some great stuff on Cooper," McKenzie said conspiratorially. "Before he learned how to use styling products." She and Bree laughed.

"Come on into the kitchen," Mrs. Sullivan called over her shoulder. "Everybody ends up there anyway."

CHAPTER TWENTY-FIVE

C ooper's sisters dragged Laney through the door, which seemed to be some sort of magical porthole to the home's heart. The kitchen was unusual, long and skinny with a lengthy, oval-shaped island, which was only wide enough to hold a plate. The walls were covered with glass-fronted cabinets on one side, and a couple of windows and a door on the other, which Cooper was stepping through as she entered, being careful to duck low so the nephew riding on his shoulders wouldn't get knocked off. He glanced up at her with an apologetic grin, and was gone. McKenzie pulled out three thick photo albums from a recessed alcove in the island and slammed them on top as she boosted herself up onto one of the red barstools surrounding the counter.

"This is an interesting kitchen," Laney commented. "You cooked for your whole crew in here?"

"Yes," Olivia Sullivan responded warily, and Laney realized her statement might have sounded pretentious.

"I love all the counter space on this long island, and the cabinetry is beautiful. Lots of space. Who did it for you?"

Cooper's mom's face seemed to relax. "My Thaddy did." She gave her husband a proud hug.

"I have a lot of time on my hands now that I'm off the job," he commented with a rueful smile as his wife patted his spare tire. "I'm putting on weight, too," he said, frowning at her.

She smiled up at him. "Oh, you're perfect just the way you are, you old coot."

McKenzie burst out in raucous laughter. "Ha! Look at this one."

Bree peered over her sister's shoulder. She hooted along with McKenzie. "Oh, my gosh. Is that all hair? It can't be."

Laney's hand went to her mouth to conceal her smile. "Is that Cooper?"

"Uh huh." McKenzie watched her reaction.

"Let me see," Laney cried out, pulling it closer. "He was so skinny."

"We all were back then," McKenzie said mournfully.

"How old was he here?"

"I don't know. Mom, how old would Cooper have been when we went to Colorado?"

"Hmm...let me see..." She laid a finger against her chin. "Seventh or eighth grade. Seventh, I think.'

"He's so adorable."

"Ooh." The sisters voiced their disgust at the same time.

"Look, Bree. Your senior picture."

"Ugh. I hated that sweater. Mom made me wear it."

"No, I did not."

"Yes, you did. You said it brought out my eye color."

Mrs. Sullivan came around the counter, still holding a spatula. She took a quick look at the picture. "I was right."

"So, you admit it."

"Ohh." She laughed dismissively. "Talk about hair."

"We all wore it like that," Laney commented. "In fact, my senior picture is almost identical, down to the sweater."

"Where did you go to school?"

"Our Lady of Lourdes." Laney named the prestigious private school casually. All three Sullivan women exchanged a glance. She pretended not to notice, looking down again at the photo album. "I'm well aware people call it 'Our Lady of Whores.' And, to be truthful, there were several loose cannons when I went there. But, I'm happy to say, I wasn't one of them. I was one of the good girls," she said with exaggerated primness. She looked up and winked at McKenzie.

McKenzie put her arm around Laney. "I think you're going to fit in here just fine."

Cooper and his rowdy crew burst in the door as she said it. "Where are the spoils for the winner? I'm starving." He pulled the lid off of Laney's Tupperware and brought out some sort of chicken dish on toast.

His mom slapped his hands. "Your hands are dirty."

Cooper gave her a sheepish grin and Laney laughed.

"I'd hardly call P-I-G a fair game. I only missed three shots after all," Ben said, stuffing one of the appetizers in his mouth.

"Spoken by the Pig, himself."

"Mmm...this is good. She's pretty and she can cook." Ben winked at Laney. "Why'd you hook up with this loser?"

Laney shrugged. "Error in judgment?" she said sweetly.

"Ooh," the siblings all chorused. Cooper strutted toward her and Bree stepped in front of her new friend to defend her. But when he came astride his older sister, he turned back toward Ben. "On second thought, I think I've found my spoils...*here*." He dodged Bree and put his hands around Laney's waist, pulling her off the stool. McKenzie reached out to keep the stool from toppling over as he yanked her up and wrestled her over his shoulder.

"Cooper." She laughed helplessly. "This is very undignified." She beat on his back. "Put me down, you jackass," she said just loud enough for his sisters to hear. They roared with laughter, McKenzie almost falling off her stool.

"Put her down!" his father bellowed, his voice reverberating off the cabinetry. He swung her down, and she straightened her clothes.

"Thank you," she said to Mr. Sullivan, giving Cooper the eye. She glanced around as everything had become eerily quiet, all of the faces looking on as if expecting something. "What?" she asked nervously.

"If you're going to pick up a woman, son, you do it like this." Before she knew what was happening, the big arms of Thaddeus Sullivan had swung her up off the floor, cradling her as she instinctively threw her arms around his stout neck. "That's how you do it."

Everyone broke out into hysterical laughter, except for Mrs. Sullivan, who threw up her hands. "I give up. Dinner time." The ex-police officer moved to set Laney down on her feet. "The least you can do is carry our guest into dinner, Thad."

"All right," he responded, his voice booming, and he swept her off her feet again like she was a play toy.

"Me next, Grandpa!" one of the nephews begged, tugging at his sleeve.

"Okay, you next, Nathan," the great bear of a man said amicably.

Ben snagged four more pieces of toast from Laney's tray and stuffed a couple more in his mouth. Bree grabbed one from him, ignoring his mumbled complaint, coming, as it was, from a mouth full of food, as they all headed toward the door. "Don't hog them all," she hissed.

When they were all seated, Cooper squeezed Laney's hand under the table and she grinned at him. The sisters didn't fail to catch the exchange and nudged each other and smiled.

"So," Thad addressed his guest. "Laney is an unusual name. Is it a family name?"

She nodded. "My mom's sister was named Laney."

"I thought your mom said your dad named you?" Cooper interrupted.

"He did. My mom and my Aunt Laney never got along. They were twins, actually, and my grandma said they even fought in the womb. My name was kind of a lifelong jab my father took at my mother." She took a bite, and then added, "She wanted to name me FiFi."

Kenzie laughed. "Fi-Fi?"

At the same time Cooper said, "Fi-Fi" with a corny French accent. He chuckled like a dirty old man and started kissing Laney on the neck.

"Cooper," she admonished, laughing, but pushing him away. McKenzie and Bree exchanged glances again.

Toward the end of the meal, Laney disappeared into the kitchen and when Olivia and Bree entered later, she had already made a pretty good dent in the pots and pans.

"Oh, no," Cooper's mom fussed. "You get away from there."

"Oh, no, please," Laney protested. "It's the least I can do. It's been such a nice evening."

"She does seem to be in a groove, Mom."

"All right," Olivia consented. "I'll dry. Bree, you go and get some more dishes." Bree backed out of the kitchen but mouthed, "Good luck," to Laney.

Before she had much of an opportunity to make heads or tails of that, Cooper's mom asked her, "So, you're a teacher. Did your mom teach, too?"

Laney laughed. "I'm sorry. It's just, the thought of my mom teaching is so funny. She...doesn't do well with children." *Even her own.* "My mom grew up in the South in a family where the women didn't work, they married well." She continued conversationally as she rinsed off a platter. "My mother met my father at a cotillion. He was starting his business then, and didn't really have a dime to his name. She wouldn't give him the time of day, at first, as the story goes. But he was handsome, and persistent, and after a bit she married him, against her family's wishes. Lucky for her—" Laney drained the dirty dish water. "—my dad was very good at what he did. And before long, he had a successful business."

Olivia Sullivan listened politely, but her face was tense. Her hands stopped drying the platter she held as she asked, "My son seems to be quite smitten with you—"

Laney wasn't sure how to respond to the obvious probing which was under way, but she was saved from having to respond by Bree sticking her head into the room. "Dad wants both of you," she announced.

Laney set down her dish towel. She smiled at Olivia, but as she walked out of the kitchen past Bree, she gave Cooper's sister a grateful look.

Thaddeus Sullivan sat on a piano bench in front of a mini, upright piano. The other family members were gathered in a semicircle behind him. Cooper waved her over, placing his hands on her shoulders. He bent to whisper in her ear. "Did I tell you about the Sullivan family sing-alongs?"

"No, you most certainly didn't," she whispered back, panicked.

"You are never, ever to speak of this in front of anyone from the job. And most especially, never, ever in Aidan's presence. Capisce?"

She nodded but was distracted by the question Cooper's father threw at her. "Do you play, Laney?"

"Oh...only classical."

"Well, I'm pretty certain the notes are the same. Sit." He patted the bench next to him, and since he hadn't made it seem optional, she sat beside him. He opened a well-worn song book, so worn, in fact, a page fell to the floor. She bent to retrieve it and placed it on the music stand on the piano. Thaddeus had opened the book to a Beatles song. "Do you know this one?"

"Well, yes, I've heard it before, but—"

"Good. Then jump in wherever you want. Do you want a belt first?" The big man indicated a bottle of Jameson's on top of the piano and three used shot glasses.

"Well, I could probably use one, but, no thank you. I don't do whiskey."

"How about Irish cream?"

Laney turned her head to see McKenzie, Veronica, and Bree holding up glasses as if to toast her while Olivia was pouring a fourth. "Sure, why not? Sounds good."

"Here," Olivia handed her one. "I'll get myself another glass. Go ahead and start without me."

Thad began to plunk the keys and soon everyone was belting out lyrics, loud and surprisingly well. Laney played hesitantly at first, but soon it was as if she and Cooper's dad had been playing together all their lives. Ben and Cooper sang "When I'm Sixty-Four" together, as must have been a tradition as no one tried to cut into the rollicking duet. Several shots later, the Beatles song book was put away and an Irish folk tunes book was brought out. The Sullivans were all very impressed with Laney's knowledge of Irish music, as she knew most of the tunes they played. She explained that her grandmother on her father's side had been from Skibbereen. At the end, Thad began playing a lively version of "Goodbye Mick and Goodbye Pat". With each verse, he became faster until he and Laney's fingers were flying over the keys; she kept up until the end when everyone was laughing and howling and slapping her on the back, which seemed to surprise and impress her playing partner.

"That's quite a gal you got there, Coop." Thaddeus' brogue came on thick, as it always did after a batch of good old Irish folk songs. "Now, woman," he called out to his wife. "Where's me pie?"

"On its way, me lad, on its way," Olivia responded gaily. Everyone filed back to the table, catching their breath from the laughter, but Laney followed her hostess into the kitchen.

"Can I help you carry things out?"

"That would be delightful, dear. Where did you learn to play so well?"

"Oh, it was something my mother insisted on. But if she knew I had played anything other than classical—anything which held the faintest whiff of fun—I'm certain she would disapprove." She smiled. "Not that I'm not grateful to her for the lessons. If I hadn't learned classical, your husband would have had no one to show off with."

Olivia chuckled, handing her two pies. "He is a horrible ham, isn't he?"

"Yes. And quite charming, too. You're a lucky woman." Laney turned at the door, as she was about to back her way through. "And, by the way, I'm quite smitten with Cooper, too." She gave Olivia a glowing smile, and entered the dining room to a round of applause supplied by those waiting for pie.

About halfway through dessert, Thaddeus hailed Laney again.

"So dear, Cooper never told me, how did you two meet?"

"Well, he was working on my sister's murder case," she said quietly.

She looked up to catch Cooper wincing, and noticed the other forks around the table paused in mid-air. Quick, alarmed glances were exchanged. Why was it that she kept feeling a beat behind? She looked around at each face, hoping to find some clue as to what she did wrong.

Thad choked down the rest of his bite. "He was working on your sister's murder case?" His gaze flicked to Cooper's.

"Dad..." Cooper murmured.

Thad turned from him and reached across the table, giving her hand a squeeze. "I'm sorry about your sister," he said sincerely, but then he spun back and his voice changed to steel. "Cooper Andrew Sullivan. In the kitchen."

Their eyes a matching liquid fire of blue, both men threw their napkins on the table and pushed away, their chairs scraping on the hardwood.

Olivia bustled in with a second batch of whipped cream as they rushed past. "What?" She glanced at the watchful faces.

"Dad found out Cooper and Laney met on the job," Bree said glumly.

"Oh," Mrs. Sullivan exhaled, the bowl seeming to become heavy in her hands. She sank into her chair, putting an elbow on the table and her chin on her fist.

The shouting was quick and explosive and Laney recoiled in her high-backed chair.

"Should I do something?" she asked Olivia, but the older woman only shook her head.

"It wouldn't do any good."

She looked around the table, but everyone was avoiding eye contact. Except for McKenzie, who looked back at her sympathetically. Her stomach turned to knots. The shouting continued, and increased in intensity, though Laney would have thought it impossible.

"What have I told you about acting responsibly on the job? Dammit, Cooper, you not only represent yourself there, you represent the whole Sullivan family."

Cooper snorted. "I've done nothing to embarrass the family—"

"The hell you haven't. Taking up with a woman whose case you're working? What got into that thick head of yours, son? Are you sleeping with her?"

"Dammit, Dad, that's none of your business and you know it."

"Don't you try to tell me what is my business and what's not. And you bring her into my home—"

Laney couldn't stand to listen to another word. "I'm sorry," she mumbled. "I need to get some air." Before anyone could stop her, she was out the door.

COOPER AND HIS DAD were going at it when his mom barreled through the swinging door like a linebacker.

"What are you two idiots carrying on for? I swear, you are both enough to turn an old woman's hair gray. As for you, Thaddeus Martin Sullivan, I will not have you being a hypocrite under my roof. And you, Cooper, that pretty, young thing you brought here this afternoon just took a hike, so if you have an ounce of brain left in your head, I suggest you get out of here and find her." The poor woman ended her tirade with a fit of coughing, brought on by straining her vocal chords.

Without another word to his father, Cooper stormed through the swinging door, to catch his siblings all leaning back toward the table as if they hadn't been listening in on the entire shouting match. "You get yourself an earful? I'm glad I could entertain you all." He continued out the front door without a backward glance, but McKenzie bravely followed him through the door.

"Coop, she's gone. I should have followed her. There's no telling where she went now."

"I know where she went," Cooper said with a sigh. "I'm sorry I barked at you all," he said without turning. "I would have been listening in, too." He pulled out his keys and started for his car. "Do you want any help?"

"Nah."

"Are you sure? I really like her, Coop," she blurted out.

Cooper turned around with a wry smile, "I knew you wouldn't be the problem." He glanced back up at the house to see his dad through the storm door, staring at him with his hands in his pockets and his jaw still tense. Without another word, he got into the Corvette and sped down the street.

CHAPTER TWENTY-SIX

He pulled the car alongside the curb, but he could see Laney wasn't at Sidney's grave site. An instant of sheer panic filled him.

He threw the car into reverse, squealing as he spun the car around to leave, and that's when he saw her, up a hill on a bench. He parked the car and began to climb. As he drew nearer, he could hear the gentle murmur of her talking to a lone goose. The wind had picked up, carrying the noise to him, and, at the same time, muffling his footsteps so she didn't seem to hear him coming at all. The goose strutted up to her, honking conversationally.

"Well, Mr. Goose, I really messed things up this time. And everything seemed to be going so well, too. You know what I mean? I should have known it wouldn't be easy." She sighed and the goose came closer, honking consolingly. Cooper crested the hill and the goose took notice, his mood turning hostile. Laney swiveled and saw him, but spun back around.

The closer Cooper got, the more aggressive the goose became, striding around to the side of the bench and sticking out his chest as if to bar the way.

"Hey there, fella," Cooper said in as soothing a voice as he could muster. "I guess you are a fella," he added. "I'm not gonna hurt her. I only want to talk to her." She turned her head and their eyes locked. He was hit with a wave of emotion born from his love for her, a feeling that had become as familiar as his own heartbeat. The moment was broken by the goose charging. Cooper stepped back, throwing his arms out in front of him, and nearly toppling down the hill. Laney laughed, and he smiled, but then shifted his gaze back to the goose. "A little help here, Lane?" he asked nervously.

"Hey, Charlie."

"You named him?"

"Do you want help or not?"

He looked back at the goose, which had begun hissing at him and flapping its enormous wings. The embattled policeman kept his mouth shut.

"Charlie, it's okay. He's all right. He won't hurt us." The goose turned to look at her. "Come on, pretty boy. It's okay."

The goose folded its wings back in place with dignity and turned from him to waddle back around to Laney.

Cooper made a move to advance from the other side of the bench, but the goose paused to give him the evil eye once more. "Keep talking to him, Lane. It's working."

She cooed to the goose until Cooper was at last able to sit on the bench next to her, although her web-footed companion did not let him out of his sight for a second. "Hey you stupid Feather Mattress," Cooper quipped in a relaxed tone, stretching his arm carefully over Laney's shoulders. "Back off. She's my girl. Aren't you?" Cooper turned to her, his gaze searching, and she melted into his side.

"Oh, Cooper." She sighed. "What are we going to do? Your dad hates me now."

"He doesn't hate you."

"And I can't stand the idea of the two of you fighting about me."

"People fight, Lane. Believe me, it's what we Sullivans do best. Did I ever tell you my uncle was a boxer in the Navy?"

She smiled a little. "I believe you're trying to change the subject."

"Yeah," he said, kissing her temple. "How am I doing?"

She reached up to turn his head toward her and pressed her warm lips to his as the breeze beat against them. Within seconds, she had his heart pounding in his chest and a sweet thrill riding through him in waves. As her tongue sought, and teased, and probed all sense left his head in a rush and he drowned in that certain pleasure only they could create together. When they parted, he rested his forehead on hers, eyes closed. "Oh, man, Laney. The things you do to me."

She laughed, and drew him in again, pulling her legs up and stretching them across his lap. Their lips found comfort again with their mingled breath, until Cooper felt a jab in his stomach. He opened his eyes to find himself face-to-face with an angry goose. "Geez!" he cried, scrambling up on the bench and pushing the feathered beast away with his foot. Charlie responded by honking boisterously and spreading his wings again, which Cooper was alarmed to see were every bit as long as the bench. He reached down and helped Laney to her feet as the goose rushed them with a whoosh of air that rivaled a helicopter's. With a shout of distress coupled with hysterical laughter, they climbed on the back of the bench and hopped down, running pell-mell down the hill. At first, they didn't notice the small crowd assembled at the bottom of the hill, waiting for them with more than a little amusement. Hands were ready to stop their momentum as they barreled down, the goose clamoring in their wake, until they all ended up in a heap of arms and legs and laughter.

"What are you all doing here?"

"We heard there was a cage match between Cooper Sullivan and Elmer the Angry Goose," Benjamin quipped, pulling grass from Laney's hair.

"Charlie," Laney and Cooper answered at once.

"You named him?" Benjamin asked, incredulous. They exchanged a glance, laughing.

Bree spoke up. "We wanted to make sure the two of you made up. Which we could see, you did," she added suggestively.

Laney swatted Bree with good humor even as her face turned red. Olivia stepped forward, saving her further embarrassment. She stared at her group of dirty, laughing children. "I swear you've all got your Uncle Ollie's crazy genes. Let's go home. It's getting cold out here."

Cooper noted the obvious hole in the group, which was his father's size. "Thanks, Mom," he replied, standing and wiping his hands on his shorts before offering McKenzie a hand up. "But I think Laney and I had better head home."

His mom tried to make her smile mask her disappointment, but it wasn't hard to miss behind her tired eyes. "Okay, Cooper. If that's what you want."

Benjamin helped Laney to her feet but the smile she was wearing dissolved with the exchange between mother and son. "Maybe we could go back for a little while," she suggested lightly.

"No. I think we need to head back. Malibu's a bit of a drive." Even the pleading look in Laney's eyes wouldn't sway him.

"Well, never mind." Olivia seemed to be aware Laney was feeling awful about the whole tiff. "I'm certain we'll get to see each other soon." She gave

Laney a hug. "They're both stubborn fools," Cooper overheard his mother whisper in her ear. "But they'll come around eventually." She gave Laney a smile as she pulled away. "It was so very nice to meet you, and it was a delight to have you as our guest today."

"Thank you so much, Mrs. Sullivan, for everything. The food was delicious and the singing was great, and..." She faltered, perhaps remembering what had happened next. "Well, thank you for welcoming me into your home, all of you," she added, glancing around at the assembled group. "I had a wonderful time."

"Nice meeting you, Laney." Ben was the first to step forward and kiss her cheek. "I hope you'll be by again soon. Take care of this buffoon," he said, taking a few imaginary shots at his brother before hugging him, too.

Goodbyes were exchanged all around and the group started trudging up the block together. Mrs. Sullivan hovered in the wings until the last of the group was gone. Laney seemed to sense she had something more to say to Cooper. "I'll be waiting in the car. Take your time."

Cooper's jaw became set. "Now, Cooper," his mother began, laughing, "you know that look never phased me."

He glanced over her shoulder at his siblings walking down the street, catching Kenzie kicking Bree in the derrière for some comment, and then he peered down at his mom, placing his hands on her shoulders. His voice was tight. "He was out of line, Mom. I pulled myself off the case when I realized I was developing feelings for Laney."

"But you know how he is, Cooper. He just...wants so much for you."

"The best thing for me is sitting right down there in that car, Mom."

"I'm glad you see that, too. She's a great girl. You do what you have to do to make this thing work out for both of you."

He hugged her, a little choked up. "You're the best."

She pulled away and pinched his cheek. "And don't you forget it." She glanced down for a minute at her feet, but then looked him in the eye. "I swore I'd never tell anybody this, but I'm tired of carrying it around." She took a deep breath and Cooper was suddenly nervous.

"The reason this upsets your dad so much is because he lived it himself. Your father always says we met at a dance, and we did. What he doesn't say is he was responding to an assault charge at the time. A boy tried to get fresh with me, and I decked him." Cooper laughed at the image, and Olivia joined in for a minute. "Believe me, it wasn't funny at the time. The boy wanted to file assault charges against me, but by the time your father was through with him, not only did he not want to press charges, he was begging me not to. You see, after your dad found out why I had punched the S.O.B.—excuse my French—he was so mad he gave the guy a lecture on how gentlemen behave, and, I think, threatened him. In any case, your father and I both kind of had the eye for each other from that point on. I brought cookies to him at the precinct house to thank him for his help the next day. But he didn't ask me out right away, because of having met me in a professional capacity. Things were much stricter then. To tell you the truth, he was kind of embarrassed by our whole relationship at first." She smiled. "But he got over it. He still never talks about it, though. So I never have either." She paused, gazing at him earnestly. "Please, don't stay mad too long."

He smiled. "You know I never do."

"You're right. You're a good boy, Cooper." She gave him another quick squeeze, then turned to go.

"You want a ride, Momma?"

"No, the exercise will do me good. But Cooper, can I ask you a question?" He nodded. "Kenzie said the man who killed Laney's sister is after her, too. Is that true?"

"Yes. But I served a search warrant on his place today and I have enough evidence to arrest him. There's an all-points bulletin out on him, so I'm sure they'll be bringing him in any time now."

Mrs. Sullivan's eyes drifted down to the car. "You take care of her," and then they returned to his face, gazing on it lovingly, "and yourself, too."

"Yes, ma'am." He gave her a mock salute, and a final kiss goodbye. "Thanks for telling me about you and Dad."

She gave him one last hug, then, turned to traipse after the others.

CHAPTER TWENTY-SEVEN

The sun set like a broken yolk on the horizon, spilling its yellow-orange glow into the ocean. Cooper and Laney sat out on the deck drinking wine and watching as the tide came in and the fading light turned the sand to sparkling glass. Each was reflecting silently about their day, having discussed the ups and downs on the ride home.

Cooper set his glass on the porch rail. He took Laney's hands in his. "I have something to tell you, and it's kind of one of those good thing/bad thing types of discussions."

"Okay. I could tell that something was bugging you. What is it?" Her voice quivered but he plunged ahead.

"The good thing is, babe...we have the guy who was after you. He fled to Buenos Aires, but he's in custody now."

"You're kidding. That's fantastic." Her smile faded as she watched his face. "So why are you not happy?"

"Oh, I am. Believe me, I am. It's just...the reason I know all this is because...this morning when I left, I went to ask a judge for a search warrant...for Steve Bertrand's condo."

"Steve? But I told you he couldn't—"

"We found surveillance equipment in his closet."

She stared at him for a moment, then countered with, "Of course you did. Steve works for a security company. He—"

"There was a picture of you on top of the equipment."

She seemed shaken, but doggedly refused to believe Steve would be capable of such things. She got up and walked to the porch rail. "I might have given him one at some time."

"Laney," Cooper rose and crossed to her. "You know you didn't. This was a picture...a very candid picture—"

172

"I don't want to hear this." She started to walk away, but he grabbed her arm.

"Laney, I'm sorry, honey, but you have to know this. He took a picture of you while you were sleeping." She shuddered, but didn't speak. "Guido confirmed the equipment that was in the closet worked with the tracking device we found in your phone. I think Steve's been jumping from his balcony to the roof and then down on your balcony. I did it myself. It was very easy—"

"Cooper, no." She shook her head weakly and tears formed in her eyes.

"Laney, he murdered your sister."

"No!" she shrieked, her body beginning to shake.

"I'm sorry, honey. I know this hurts, but you need to know. You need to know what he is capable of."

"But why?" she shouted. "Why would he do that to Sydney? It makes no sense. It makes no sense." At the end, she sounded like she was pleading with him.

"I'm not sure about that, but I have an idea. I think—maybe, of course, I would have no way of confirming this until I talk to the scumbag—but I think it's possible Sydney caught him at it—caught him in your room—and she was going to tell you about it. In fact," an idea occurred to him as he was speaking, "maybe that is one of the things she was coming to tell you that night at Phat Jack's." Cooper continued to speculate, thinking out loud. "He followed her there, and strangled her with a karate belt, maybe he even had his Gi on at the time..."

"With his belt?" Laney reached down to feel for her seat before sinking into it. He sat beside her, watching her. She put her face into her hands. "Oh, my God, maybe you're right." She sobbed. "Syd...oh, no!"

"What is it?"

He could barely make out what she was saying through her gasps, her voice muffled by arms as her head sank lower. "Sh-she was going to g-go t-to my house that day. Sh-she wanted to borrow— Oh, this is all wrong." She lifted her face, shouting in anger and pain. "He killed her because of me. Because of me." The realization seemed to rip through her like a machete. The sister she adored had been killed because her neighbor was obsessed with her. The look on her face pained him.

"I wish I could have spared you this. I wish I could do something to help you."

Her face became savage. "You say they have him? The police have him?"

"Yes. In Buenos Aries."

"I want him to pay for this. For what he did to Sydney. I want him to pay."

"He'll pay. I'll make him pay. You can be assured of that." That, at least, seemed to offer her some measure of reassurance.

Cooper held her that night, knowing she was fragile, and it was many hours before either of them could sleep.

"Cooper?" she murmured in the darkness.

"Mmm?"

"Thank you. Thank you for figuring it out."

"It's okay, baby," he mumbled, flipping over on his side so he could hold her better. "You don't have to thank me. Sleep now, honey. You have to be tired."

"I am." She sighed. After a few minutes she said, "I'm glad you're here."

"Me, too, baby. Me, too."

Mercifully, the night claimed them both, and they drifted off to sleep.

IN THE MORNING, HE awoke to the sound of the shower running.

"You're up," he said, surprised, when she stepped into the room wrapped in a towel, a second one turbaned on her head.

"Yes, I'm going to work." She sat on the end of the bed, and bent her head to free it from its towel. She rubbed her hair with it while he watched a few drops of water wander down the middle of her back and become absorbed in the other towel. Her skin looked so fresh and dewy, and she smelled incredible.

He sat and chased another droplet of water down her back. "Why don't you come back to bed?" he asked, his implication clear.

She leaned back into his arms and pulled his head down to kiss him. Just when he thought she had decided to take him up on his offer, she sat up. "I can't."

"And why not?" he asked, pretending to be hurt.

"I've got to go to work."

"Work?"

"Yes."

He thought about this. Since Steve was behind bars, maybe it would be okay for her to go in for a while. Maybe it would take her mind off things.

"Well, in that case," he said, pulling back the sheets, "I guess I'd better get going, too."

When he finished his shower, a warm plate of French toast and bacon was waiting for him. She was quiet over breakfast, until she laid her fork down abruptly and commented, as if the discussion from last night had been ongoing, "What I don't understand is...Steve is so..." She seemed to search for the words to describe him. "One time he hit a squirrel," she explained, "just ran over him in his truck on accident. The squirrel zipped in front of him, and he swerved—but you know how kamikaze those squirrels can be—and Steve was upset for weeks about it. How does a guy like that do...the things he's done?"

Cooper reached across the table to take her hand. "I wish I could help you make sense of it all, but sometimes it doesn't make sense."

Laney frowned, clearly not satisfied by the answer.

Minutes after, Cooper had gone into the laundry room to iron his shirt, and there was a knock on the door.

"Mr. Sullivan." Laney stood dumbfounded as the big man shuffled his feet on her doorstep, his hands behind his back.

"Uhh...hi." The pair stood looking at each other for a few seconds, but then Laney threw her arms around him.

"I'm so glad you're here." She beamed. "Come in, come in." She stepped back to clear his way. "I'm sorry...I was just so surprised and happy to see you."

"Really? I was afraid you might not be."

"Nonsense. Cooper's in the—"

Thad's face lit up when he saw the amazing interior of the house and he whistled. "Nice place. Oh," he said, refocusing. "I'm not here to see Cooper." The warm glow inside her dimmed. "Not yet anyway. I wanted to talk to you." He took her hands in his large, weathered ones, and seemed to speak from the heart. "I want to apologize for the way I acted yesterday. You see, we

Irish do everything with passion. We love with passion. We fight with passion. We sing with passion. Hell, we even drink with passion. But having said that, it's still no excuse for my behavior yesterday. I was a lout, as my dear Livvy would say, and I only hope you'll forgive me."

Laney didn't hesitate. She stood on her tiptoes to kiss his leathery cheek. "Done. And I'm sorry I ran out yesterday. We British aren't very good at handling our emotions. We're tight-lipped, and annoyingly stoic."

"That's not how I see you."

"I'm glad. But we are nonetheless. We may stay cool on the surface, but we burn just as hot underneath. So, I understand your reaction completely."

As she talked to the retired police officer, she saw him shift his attention to the living room below, where Cooper had stepped out into the hall, still tucking in his shirt.

"What are you doing here?" he said, his voice cool.

"I came to apologize," his father responded in his rough way.

"What? What was that?" Cooper put his hand to his ear in an exaggerated manner to indicate he couldn't believe what he was hearing.

Thad grinned, and whispered loudly to Laney as he traipsed down the steps behind her. "He gets his wise-acreness from his mother."

She laughed. "Yeah, right." The two men stood at a distance from one another uncertainly. "I'll finish gathering my stuff and let you two gentlemen have a talk." As she passed Cooper, she caught his hand. "Be good," she said in a low voice.

He brought her hand to his lips and kissed it. "Always am," he said with a sexy little wink that sent shivers up her spine.

The men were silent, eying each other until they heard the soft click of the bedroom door shutting. Cooper knew for a fact Laney had nothing to gather in the bedroom, but he appreciated the privacy she had given them.

"You were saying?" He raised an eyebrow and folded his arms across his chest.

"Boy. You never make this easy, do you?"

He unfolded his arms, holding them out, palms up. "This? I don't believe this has ever happened before. So excuse me if I enjoy it a little."

Thad gave him a crooked grin. "You sure are some piece of work, you know that, Cooper Sullivan?"

"Yeah. I heard I take after my old man."

Thad grunted. He studied Cooper and then took a deep breath. "Okay, okay. I'm sorry, okay?" He spit it out, like a dog spitting out its chew toy after fighting over it, with great reluctance. "I just don't want you to make the same mistakes that I made."

"Man. You even know how to make an apology insulting."

"Insulting? Insulting?" he yelled. "What the hell did I do now?"

"Are you calling Mom a mistake?" Cooper enjoyed his look of surprise. "Mom told me how you and she met." He walked over behind a sofa table, running his hand over a piece of statuary there. "All these years and you never told me you met on the job? And then you call it a mistake?"

"Now, son, you know I love your ma, and she's, without a doubt, the best thing in my life...and for some strange reason, she's been under the delusion for the past forty some odd years that she loves me. You know I understand how lucky I am to have her."

Cooper turned back to him. "Yeah. I know all that. I was just trying to give you a hard time."

"Oh, you were, were ya? You know, Cooper, I may be old, but I can still whoop your ass."

"Oh, you can?" He grinned, folding his arms again and lifting his chin. He walked back over to stand in front of Thad. "I'd like to see that."

"Oh, yeah?"

Cooper feinted to the right, but his dad anticipated his move and the older man grabbed him in a headlock and proceeded to grind his knuckles into the younger man's head. Cooper howled as Laney stepped out into the hall.

"Oh, no. Mr. Sullivan, don't."

Both men looked up in surprise, then realizing what it looked like, backed off, and explained at the same time.

"I was showing him I could still whip his butt, if I had to."

"We're just goofing around, honey."

They were both panting from their roughhousing.

"Ugh." She put a hand over her heart. Then her face colored. "You, two...idiots!" She stared at them both, hands on her hips.

"Ooh. She sounded just like your ma there," Thad said to Cooper. Then he turned to her. "Good job." He punched her shoulder lightly. "We'll get some Irish brewin' in you yet."

She frowned at him. Then rolled her eyes. "I give up." She turned and walked back to the bedroom.

"Whoops. Just when we had made up."

"Don't worry, Pops," Cooper said, catching his breath still. "I think she's nervous about returning to school today. To tell you the truth, so am I. We have her sister's murderer in custody in Buenos Aires, but I'd feel better if we had him on U.S. soil."

"Do you want me to walk by there today? Keep an eye on her?"

Cooper thought about this. "No. I'll talk to the security there and stop by myself at lunch. She'll be fine. I'm being a little...overprotective, I guess."

"If the guy put those bruises on her, I would be, too."

"Oh, you noticed those, huh?"

"Once a cop, always a cop." He headed toward the door. "Well, call me if you change your mind. I've got nothing else going on today."

Cooper followed him. "Okay, I'll do that, Pops. Thanks for coming by."

"Sure thing." He gave his son a bear hug before leaving. "Don't forget...I can still kick your butt."

"Yeah, right." Cooper leaned forward, to whisper exaggeratedly, "Rematch?"

"Anytime, kid," he answered with a grin. "Anytime."

CHAPTER TWENTY-EIGHT

At first, Laney's chest was tight and she jumped at the slightest noise. But by third hour, she was back into the swing of things. During lunch, she decided to eat at her desk in order to catch up on some neglected lesson planning, and, if she was honest with herself, to avoid the questions and sympathetic statements of colleagues. She wanted to pretend it was a normal day. It felt good being back.

As she sat leafing through her planner a huge apple came down and was placed in front of her. She looked up. Cooper was leaning on her desk with a grin. The bright, blue shirt he had picked out earlier in the morning was giving his eyes an even more devastating gleam than usual. The corners of her lips turned up a little, but she raised an eyebrow at him. "Do you have a pass, young man?"

"Ooh," he responded, leaning in to press his lips to hers. "I love it when you get all teachery with me." He took the kiss deeper and she found her heartbeat beginning to race. She pulled back, aflutter, feeling the heat rise in her face and chest.

"Why do I suddenly feel like this is the Apple of Temptation?" she asked, pushing back in her rolling chair to put some distance between them.

Cooper lifted it and tossed it up and down. Watching the apple, Laney didn't realize how close he had gotten until he snatched the apple out of the air, and laid it back on her desk, bringing him within inches of her. "You can call it anything you want," he said with a wicked smile. She tried to move away again and rammed her back into a tall, metal filing cabinet. Without warning, he burst into Van Halen's "Hot for Teacher" and air-guitared away from her, hopping on one leg.

Now that she was able to breathe, his proximity making it difficult before, she laughed. "Don't give up your day job, Sullivan." She sat back down and pretended to be engrossed in adding grades to her grade book, running her finger down columns and marking in it.

He strode smoothly back over to her desk. "S-o-o-o," he said, running the back of his finger down the side of her face as he leaned against her desk. "You're telling me you're not in the least bit turned on right now?" His voice was almost a low purr.

She trembled, and looked up. "Okay. Maybe a little by the visitor's badge."

He chuckled and cupped his hand under her chin, lifting her head and bringing his mouth down on hers savagely. He was in the process of kissing her breathless, when someone clear their throat.

A tall, rail-thin, dark-skinned student in baggy clothing and a baseball cap sauntered in, laughing in a falsetto voice. "Ooh. You go, Ms. E.!"

Laney pulled away and straightened her clothes, though Cooper hadn't even touched them, she'd only wanted him to. "Oh, Truman. I didn't see you there."

He raised his brows, his eyes laughing. "That's 'cause you were too busy—"

"Uh-uh-uh. I do not want to hear whatever colorful phrase is about to come out of your mouth—"

"—doin' the tonsil tango with Mr. G. Q. here."

"And there you have it," she said, resigned. "Truman, this is Cooper. Cooper, this is Truman Trueheart, and yes, that is his real name."

"My momma's funny."

Cooper couldn't help but hear the George Thorogood lyric running through his head, "Now you funny, too," but he kept it to himself, offering his hand to the young man. "Nice to meet you."

Truman clasped Cooper's hand with his right, then, slapped the back of it with his left.

"Way to go, man. Ms. E.'s one hottie, ya know what I mean?" He pretended it was only for Cooper's ears but said it loud enough for Laney to hear and blush.

"Yes, she is." Cooper pulled the kid in closer. "But she's my hottie, got it?" he said as a pseudo-threat.

"Yeah, man, I got it. You look like you work out," he added. "You a cop or somethin'?"

Laney laughed, but then pretended to cough when Cooper shot her a look. "I'll let you get back to 'work,'" he said, hanging invisible quotation marks in the air. "What time you want me to pick you up today?"

"Can we make it late? I've got a lot of catching up to do. I'll take you out to dinner before we head back to Malibu."

Truman pretended to be perusing his textbook, which would have been more convincing if it looked like the spine had ever been tested. She knew he was listening to every word, no doubt ready to start the rumor wheel next hour.

"Sure. I've got some paperwork of my own to catch up with, down at the precinct house." He made his statement especially loud

Truman made a show of waving him off and turning his back on them as if still engrossed in the book, which she noticed now was upside down. Before she could protest, Cooper bent in and gave her one last quick, but heart-pounding kiss and left her feeling slightly dazed.

"Ooh, Ms. E. You got it bad," Truman said with a whistle. Laney reached back and whipped an eraser at him. "And you've got bad aim, too," he teased.

COOPER WORKED LATE, logging in entries from his notebook he had neglected to put in his file lately. When he got up to leave, turning off the lamp on his desk, he saw Aidan exiting the locker room. "Hey, bud. You eat yet?"

"Nah. Thought I'd grab something now. You?"

"I was going to pick Laney up and go out for something. You want to join us?"

"I don't know, man. Isn't three a crowd?"

"Not when it's you. Besides, we could pick up Jenna if you want to."

"No. She's working an ambulance shift tonight to pick up some extra coin, but I'll join you. If you're sure?"

"I'm sure." They walked out together and hopped in Aidan's sedan, since the Vette was too small. Night had fallen when they had been under the false daylight-like glow of fluorescent lights inside. Minutes later, a call came over his radio. "Aidan, you know where Cooper is?"

"I'm right here, Captain. What do you need?"

"Coop, I got a call from a Sgt. Escovar in Buenos Aries. He wanted me to make sure to tell you they have the wrong man. The man they have in custody admitted he's not Steve Bertrand. Bertrand gave him a grand to take a flight to Buenos Aries and handed him his passport and license. According to them, he's a dead-ringer for Bertrand, but when he showed them his real I.D. they finally bought his story."

Cooper looked over but Aidan was already pulling lights out to stick on top of his car. "Where is she?" he said with a scowl.

"Walter Davis." Cooper could feel the blood drain from his face as he thought of Laney all alone in the school building.

Aidan pealed out onto a main artery from a side street, taking off with blinding speed.

"Call her."

LANEY WORKED ON A LESSON for next week on the beginning chapters of Charles Portis's True Grit. Every once in a while, her mind wandered back to Cooper's antics at lunch and she chuckled, shook her head, and returned to her work. The lines of the text were beginning to blur together when she heard a noise in the hall.

"Ricky?" she called out, hoping the janitor's friendly voice would return her call, but she heard nothing. Maybe the heat, or the air conditioning was clicking on, hard to tell which because it was perpetually the wrong temperature in the building. Or maybe the clocks, the clocks always seemed to be ticking too loudly when she was one of the last teachers left in the building. A couple of minutes later, she heard a similar metal click, and she got up to reassure herself there weren't any large creatures of the rodent-nature in the hallway. She picked up a thick text book, ready to wing it at the first sound of scurrying if need be, and approached the door to the hallway. She reached out to flip on the switch, hoping to scare the little beast away, but she heard only the click without the accompanying, soothing light.

"Damn." She looked to her right and saw nothing, but when her head swung to the left, she froze in sheer terror. She couldn't see his face, but the light was shining around a figure from the next hallway down, and she could tell from the silhouette it was Steve. Without pausing to review her options, she took off running to the right, dropping the book as she ran. She could see at the end of the hall the bullet-proof glass doors were closed, something that only happened, as far as she knew, when the school was on lockdown. When she reached it, she pushed the metal bar in frantically but the door wouldn't give. She glanced back over her shoulder, and saw her pursuer was ambling down, as if in no hurry at all.

"Laney. Long time no see." Could that be Steve? It was the same icy voice she had heard in the shower room on the beach, but it sounded nothing like him.

She searched around for a fire extinguisher or something she could throw through the glass, but saw nothing. He was coming steadily closer and she could feel the sweat seeping out of every pore. When he stepped into the light she could see it was Steve, only it wasn't Steve at all. The face was...thinner? The cheekbones, more prominent. The eyes had a flat, dead, cruel look to them. She knew she should do something to try to get away, but she was mesmerized by the eyes that were, yes, the color and shape of Steve's, but so weren't his.

"Steve?" she couldn't help but ask.

"Oh, no. Come on, Laney. You don't think that pussy is capable of locking you in here for his own amusement." With the last words he grabbed her by the back of the hair and began to haul her toward her classroom. "Steve," he chuckled joylessly. "All he can do is watch you sleep, and write pretty poems to you he is too weak to even send. I, on the other hand—" He pushed her back up against the lockers outside her door. "—when I see what I want—" His eyes slid over her, coming to rest on her bosom. "—I take it." He reached for her blouse and tore it down to the top of the curved neckline of her sweater. He bunched the sweater up in his fist, pushing against her so it felt like a heavy iron weight was lying on her chest. He put his face near hers, his teeth gleaming in the darkness. "You know what I mean, Laney?" He was breathing heavily, his jaw clenched and she could almost feel the anger radiating from him. "Huh?" he shouted, banging her head into the locker. "I asked you a question. Do you know what I mean?"

He bit off each word and she shouted, "Yes. Yes! I know what you mean." In her sheer terror, she had forgotten what the statement even was she was agreeing to. Her mind raced. There must be somebody left in the building. The night janitor? Or Mrs. Camarino, the young, single Spanish teacher? Hadn't she seen her a half-hour ago in the hall? "Help! Someone help!"

"Oh God, Laney. How I love that. The way your little helpless voice bounces off these here lockers is really turning me on." He brought his hands to her breasts, kneading roughly. He made grunting noises as he rammed his pelvis into her. "Do you like it, Laney? Do you?"

She gazed into his eyes so like a crazed animal's. It was the face of Steve, but so contorted with rage and violence it looked like a whole different person. It was Steve's voice, but not distinguishable as his. And then it clicked. Could he be suffering from Multiple Personality Disorder? She knew very little about schizophrenia, other than the Hollywood version.

The voice became softer, pleading with her, the hands fondling her gently now. "Do you, Laney? Do you like the way I'm touching you?" Her mind reeled. It was Steve's voice now. "Steve?"

"Yeah, Laney, honey. It's me."

"Oh, Steve, Steve." She was happy to see her friend back, to feel a sizable lowering of tension in his body.

"I'm sorry. Ed can get out of hand."

"Ed?"

"Yeah, Ed. But I love you, Laney. I do."

"I u-understand that now, Steve."

"Do you?" His eyes searched hers. "And you love me, too?"

Laney knew her life depended on how she answered his questions, and she found it was easy to lie, because there was part of her who did love part of Steve, as the good friend he had been to her for many years. Slowly, so as not to alarm him, she brought her hands up to his face and placed them on either side. "Yes, Steve, I love you."

His hands stilled on her breasts and he leaned forward to kiss her. She pulled back, just a fraction, involuntarily, but she let him kiss her, and it was warm and soft at first. But all at once she felt the iron grip of his hands again and his tongue forced its way down her throat, choking her. She felt his facial features morph under her fingertips and he was back again, Ed. She wrenched her mouth from his, coughing.

He grabbed her chin, squeezing without mercy. "Oh, Steve," he mocked. "I love you.

Do you think I'm going to fall for that crap? That loser might, but I know you're a whore, just like all the rest of them." His fingernails dug into her face, and the pain forced tears from her eyes. "Yeah. You cry, Laney." He jerked her head around, banging it into the lockers. "I like it when they cry. Now, we've got about ten hours or so for us to have us some fun, before anyone is supposed to show up. Mmm, yeah." He ground his pelvis into her again. "But if we're going to have us a party, we need to have your old cop-boyfriend over. So you're going to give him a call." He gripped her elbow and steered her toward the classroom.

She shook her head. "No. I won't do it."

He froze. "What did you say?"

Her voice caught in her throat, fear choking her. He whipped her around, wrenching her arm behind her back and slamming her against the bullet-proof glass window of her classroom door. She hit it with her shoulder and face, feeling the warm familiar ooze as the skin of her forehead which had just started to heal tore open again, spilling blood across her face and down the window. A short scream ripped from her, but she bit down on it, refusing to give him the pleasure.

"You'll call him."

"I won't," she said through gritted teeth. And then, trilling brightly from her purse, which sat on the edge of her desk, her cell phone rang. Cooper. It had to be Cooper. He was calling to see if she was finished yet. She prayed Steve hadn't heard it, but when she slid her eyes from the purse to his face, inches from her as he pressed her into the door, she saw the glint of recognition in his cold eyes.

"Well, no need to call him then. He's calling us. How considerate." Ed pulled her back from the door, slipping an arm across her chest and jerking the door open with his other hand. He pushed her into the classroom and across the floor, forcing her down on her own desk, twisting her arm behind her as he rifled with the free hand through her purse. He flipped the phone open, watching her face as he talked.

"Well hello there, Cooper the Copper."

"Bertrand!"

A grin split Steve's face. "Ah. I hear the lovely sound of your sirens going. You comin' to see me?"

"Is that what you want?" Cooper asked.

"Yeah. We want him to come join our party, don't we?"

"No. Cooper, don't come!"

Steve jerked on Laney's arm, grinding the shoulder he had slammed into the door down against the wood of the old, scarred desk. She couldn't help but cry out.

Cooper heard her anguish over the phone. He squeezed his eyes shut. *I'm coming, Laney. Hold on.*

"I'm on my way, Bertrand."

"By yourself."

Cooper looked at Aidan, who could hear the entire conversation over the speaker phone. "You're calling the shots. There's no need to hurt her anymore. I'm on my way."

"I'm not making any promises." The phone emitted scuffling noises and then a grunt and Bertrand's exclamation of surprise. "You're gonna pay for that, girlie." His words were tight, as if given through gritted teeth. She had managed to hurt him, Cooper surmised. The phone fell to the floor in the struggle but Cooper could still hear the sound of a blow and her sharp cry of pain. He heard an animal-like snarl and what sounded like desks being turned over.

"Please!" she screamed. "Steve, don't do this."

And that was the last thing he heard as they hit the parking lot of the school and he threw his phone down and hopped out of the car as it screeched to a stop.

Cooper rushed headlong into the building, making his way to Laney's room, remembering how to get there from his earlier visit. His stomach turned as he saw the long streak of blood on the glass of the door and an even longer one as he peeked into the classroom. Desks were slung everywhere,

THE HEART TEACHES BEST 187

some sitting precariously on top of each other. He spotted the cell phone, open on the floor by the desk but the room was vacant.

"Laney!" he called into the dark hallway, his voice echoing in the emptiness. After the last echo faded, he heard a faint whimper down the hall. "Lane?" He hurried in the direction of the noise. When he passed a doorway, he noticed blood dripping down the white cinderblock wall. They must have been hiding there when he walked by. He had walked right past her.

He doubled back to the atrium where he entered, which was a wide open area, with several halls leading off of it in a half dozen directions. A loud thud sounded to his right. His head snapped around and there she was, behind a closed door, her face smashed up against the glass. Her arm had flown up defensively as Steve swung her around and it was flung, bent, over her head, her eyes squeezed shut. A section of her hair was matted and blood flowed from the cut above her eye, which had been reopened. Blood also dripped down the arm held above her where her elbow was cut. When she opened her eyes and saw him on the other side of the glass, he saw despair wash over her. She had actually hoped he wouldn't come, he realized. That he would leave her to this...animal. She was breathing hard and he could tell by the way her shoulders slumped, she was exhausted. Steve also had a cut open above his eye and scratches up and down his arms. So she had inflicted her own damage. *Good for you, Lane.* But looking at her again, it became obvious she had paid the price. Without even realizing he was doing it, he walked toward them, stopping only a few feet from the door.

"Welcome," Steve called merrily. He held a gun in his hand. "You've been missing out on a lot of fun, hasn't he Laney?" He pushed his forearm against her back harder and she grunted. Cooper could tell by the gleam in his eye the monster was really getting off on her pain. When Steve looked up at him he saw something else in those eyes. This was all for Cooper's benefit. The psychopath was hurting her to get back at him.

"Why?" he cried out, needing to hear it from Bertrand himself. "Why are you doing this to her?" As he watched her labored breathing, his emotional pain was now as raw and searing as her physical pain.

Steve shrugged. "He saw you. Steve saw you kissing her."

He was talking about himself in the third person...did he have some sort of splintered personality?

"The sniveling wimp was broken up about it, and even though it pains me to do anything to help him, it's sort of like my job. Besides," he grinned evilly. "I enjoy it, so it's sort of a win/win situation."

Cooper looked at Laney. Her eyes were shut and her breathing was still coming jaggedly through her cut lips. He banged on the glass panel that ran along the side of the door frame in frustration. "Let her go, dammit! Let her go. Come out here and face me like a man."

"Be glad to," he sneered, and Cooper could see now that his whole facial structure looked different from the man he had met on the porch steps...could it have really been less than a week ago? "Get your sorry ass back from the door."

He stepped back. Bertrand typed into a keypad on the wall with his free hand, bringing the gun to Laney's head, and the door hissed open. He shuffled through the door with Laney, using her as a shield. Cooper continued to back up, his hands held out in surrender, though still holding his gun. Her eyes were open now, and she gazed at him with such sorrow he felt like he was being torn in two.

"If you're such a man—" Bertrand taunted, "—then, slide your gun over here."

Cooper complied, bending to set it on the floor. He kicked the forty-five over and it stopped near Steve's feet.

He smirked sadistically and knocked the back of Laney's legs hard, sending her crashing to her knees while he still gripped her hair. "That's where you belong, Laney," he jeered. "On your knees." He jerked her head into his crotch and held it there, while still keeping the gun trained on her. She shut her eyes, appearing ashamed of her own weakness. Cooper took an angry step forward. Sensing the motion, Steve glanced up and tugged Laney's hair around so she faced him and he could see the agony in her eyes.

"Leave her alone, you bastard!" Cooper cried out.

"Oh, no way. We're not finished with her yet. We got a lot of good times ahead." He crouched next to her and stroked her face suggestively, running the muzzle of the gun down her neck and along her collarbone while still yanking on her hair and straining her neck back. "Get the damn gun, Laney," he barked. Her trembling, bloodied hands felt around on the floor. She couldn't see because he purposefully held her head up and tears blinded her, forced from her by the sharp pain he inflicted as he tore her hair out by the roots. Cooper watched, seething inside with both a white-hot fire, which was his hatred for the man before him and a gnawing ache for the woman he loved. Finally, her fingertips found the gun and as she brought it up, something made Steve whirl around, knocking the gun, which flew from her hands.

Aidan had located them, and was aiming his gun at him, inside the double doors of the school. Steve loosened his grip on Laney as he brought his gun up and she broke free, crawling to Cooper. He helped her to her feet, and they both spun at the sound of gunfire. Aidan flew backward through a glass door with an earth-shattering crash. Laney's piercing scream caused Steve to turn back and raise the gun again to take aim at the helpless pair.

"Come on." Cooper pressed on her head and they ran, crouching low, down a wide set of stairs that was behind them. Shots zinged off railings and imbedded themselves in glass. They hit the landing and turned to descend farther before Steve could reach the top. Running down the hall with Laney, Cooper picked a room at random to enter.

"Cooper. Cooper." Laney sobbed as soon as they were behind the door. "Aidan...!"

He grabbed both sides of her face in his hands and brought her head up. "It's okay, Lane. He had on Kevlar. He signaled me. He's fine. Are you okay?" He searched her face.

She nodded, looking too tired and scared to speak.

They heard Steve's voice echoing along the corridor outside the door. "You two might as well come on out—" he drawled, "—'cause you can't get out. You're a pair of mice in a mighty large trap. I've got nine plus hours to find you, so you're going to lose out in the end. Might as well quit prolonging the inevitable."

Cooper took Laney's hand and led her through the large, barren room, broken up by lines of posts to support the low-slung ceiling. He could tell it had once been a cafeteria by the few posters of the food pyramid that still clung, crookedly to the wall. Telltale crumbling, small, multi-colored tiles behind the posters hinted of food fights and made him think of sour milk cartons. They slid through a door in the back as quietly as possible. It was a long, wide open room with tarps draped over dark, bulging objects of odd shapes and sizes. "Do you know where we are?" he whispered.

She nodded. "This is the old kitchen. They don't use it anymore since they built the new one. Just as storage."

He nodded. "Is there any way out of here besides the way we came in?"

Laney nodded. "Yes. I like to talk to the lunch ladies sometimes and they've shown me around." Now she led the way. They were headed back in the direction they had come when they had run down the dark hallway leading to the cafeteria. They left the large, overhead fluorescent lights off and worked their way through the room using only the small amount of light filtering in from the narrow windows above, which must have pretty much been at ground level outside.

In a matter of seconds, they came to a narrow passageway running along an inside wall. The area offered no light at all, but she raced through the inky blackness—which somehow still smelled of French fries and sloppy joes—until they emerged on the other side, in an abandoned dish room. Even here things were stored— from broken desks to metallic gold, furry garland and laminated Santas with lopsided smiles, to box after box of furnace filters, enough, it would seem, to maintain an entire stadium. They made their way to the back of the room, to another wall of furnace filters. "I'm sure it's here."

Despite her words, she sounded uncertain. "It's somewhere behind all these boxes."

Cooper nodded and started moving things to the side. She reached to take boxes from him and soon they uncovered an odd-shaped door, slanted at the top.

"This is it." She opened the door, and dove into the dark interior. He heard a click and the small room was filled with light. The ceiling slanted almost to the floor to their left, and rose a few feet above their heads where it met the wall on their immediate right. He surmised they must be under a staircase. The walls were not dry-walled and between the framing, spider webs crisscrossed. A similar slanted door stood a yard or so beyond them, presumably where the stairwell ended. She started to move forward again.

"Wait," he called. When she turned back, he reached up to touch her face, examining her new wounds. An overwhelming wave of guilt hit him. "Laney, I'm so sorry. I told you I wouldn't let him hurt you again."

She shook her head. "No. You can't blame yourself for this. You thought he was in custody—"

"They had the wrong guy," he explained. "Bertrand paid the guy to pose as him, gave him his passport and license." As he spoke, he stroked her matted hair, his face contorted with worry and remorse. "I should have stayed with you."

"No, Cooper." She slid her arms around his waist and laid her head on his chest for a minute. "It's okay. I'm okay."

He closed his eyes and let himself breathe in her warmth for a minute. Then he pushed back. "You didn't want me to come for you."

"I didn't want him to hurt you."

"You'd rather he hurt you?" His words came out angry.

"To tell you the truth, I'd rather have had some other option altogether."

He couldn't help but chuckle. He inclined his head to the far door. "Where is this going to take us?"

She looked in that direction. "We'll end up in a stairwell that comes out in the hall where my room is."

"Do you know where the main control pad is for the security system?"

She nodded. Something flickered through her eyes before she dropped them and murmured, "He took me there."

He didn't want to imagine what had gone on with the two of them in this building all alone. He could see her shirt was ripped and noticed her flinching when he touched her shoulder, from some yet-undisclosed injury. Though she smiled, he sensed a hollow spot in her smile where the pain her sister's killer had caused had taken up residence, perhaps permanently. The thought stirred a deep ache inside.

"Laney." He spoke her name softly and she lifted her eyes. He feathered a kiss over the corner of her swollen lip, giving her a faltering smile. "Let's get out of here."

She reached up and brushed the hair back out of his eyes with a thoughtful expression on her face, making his heart skip a beat. "Take me home, Cooper."

She said it with such childlike earnestness his voice broke as he responded. "I will, baby, I will." He took her fingers and brought them to his lips before turning to lead her.

Now he knew where they were going.

CHAPTER TWENTY-NINE

Aidan knew he bought Cooper and Laney some time when he distracted Bertrand. When he fell backward onto, ironically, the school's welcome mat, he smacked his head pretty good and had to shake it to clear it, but he raised his hand subtly to give Cooper the high sign. When he sat up and saw Bertrand gunning for Cooper and Laney, he searched for his gun, which flew out of his hands when he was shot. But it was too close to Bertrand to be of any help to him. He scurried backward out of the front door of the building.

Bertrand turned and ambled toward him, as casual as if he were out on a Sunday stroll. Aidan stared at him, his mouth hanging open, knowing Kevlar could only do so much at close range. But his pursuer stopped at the door, reaching over to type into an electronic key pad. He heard the sharp sound of a bolt being drawn, sounding like its own gunfire, and knew he was locked out. Steve smirked at him and sauntered back to pick up Aidan's gun.

"Thanks for the additional ammo," he yelled, his voice penetrating eerily through the glass door that separated the two men. He tilted the gun, holding it up to the light to admire it, then he peered into Aidan's face. "It will be nice to have more bullets to rip them up with. See ya, cop." Steve waved at him with a sarcastic grin, then turned and rambled away.

Aidan's jaw clenched. He would find a way into the school, even if he had to drive his car through the front entrance. As he stood there, weighing his options, he heard the sound of a siren approaching.

WHEN AIDAN HAD SENT in his call for backup before going in after Cooper when they had first arrived, three things had happened simultaneously. Thaddeus Martin Sullivan made a lame excuse to his wife and left the house, having picked up the call on his scanner. Jenna Richardson, who was out trolling for emergencies in an ambulance, heard the call and asked her partner to respond. And Police Chief Eddy Royanovich, who was already scandalously late to his wife's dinner party with the mayor and his wife, heard the call and turned his car back around. All three individuals arrived at Walter Davis within minutes of each other.

When the ambulance arrived, Aidan decided to wait and warn the EMTs the building was not yet secure, but when it rolled to a stop, Jenna jumped out of the back and ran up to him.

"Aidan!" She threw her arms around him and he cringed. She pulled back and her eyes landed the hole in his shirt. "You're hurt."

"No. No," he reassured her. "I have Kevlar on."

Her face turned white. "We both know that isn't total protection. Let me look at it."

"Not now. I need to go in after Cooper."

"You can go in and risk your life after I'm through checking you out."

"That makes no sense."

She didn't respond but yanked on his shirt as her partner, Ty Reed, came around the side of the ambulance with his kit. The big, dark-skinned man recognized Aidan and joked, "Geez, Richardson, can't you wait until after shift?"

"Shut up," she said, her voice pitching too high, giving away her concern. "He's hurt."

"Jen, I'm okay."

"I don't care. I'm going to look at it."

Figuring it would save time to give in to her, Aidan helped her pull off the vest. As she did so, the trio heard a car approach and turned as an old Ford roared into the parking lot.

Thad hopped out, firing questions at them before the engine had even shut off. "Where is he? Where's my boy?"

Before anyone could answer, a black town car pulled in behind him.

"Eddy? What are you doing here?" Thad demanded when the chief got out from behind the wheel.

"I heard the call. The real question is, what are you doing here?"

"That's my boy in there," his former partner growled.

"And that's my partner," Aidan said, snatching the Kevlar vest from Jenna.

"Yes. And Cooper's one of my men, too. And none of us is going in there until backup arrives."

Aidan and Thad began to argue with him at the same time.

"You can't keep me out of there, Eddy."

"Sir, I should be in there with Cooper right now."

Jenna chimed in with, "Aidan, you're in no shape to—"

The chief held up his hands. "I'm not going to listen to any arguments. The two of you are staying out, for now." He jogged back to his car. Thad and Aidan took one look at each other, and then strode with determination, side by side toward the building. Aidan heard the chief on his radio, checking with dispatch on the arrival time of the first responding cars.

A few seconds later he heard him yell, "Hey. Hey, you two idiots, get back here!"

They ignored him. "He's a security expert. Got the whole place locked up tighter than a penitentiary," Aidan was saying to Thad when Eddy caught up to them.

"Get the principal on the horn," Thad said over his shoulder to Eddy. "Tell him to get his ass down here with the blueprints for the building and any information he has on the security layout."

Eddy raised a hand and appeared ready to argue, but, perhaps seeing the logic in the suggestion, he hurried back to his car.

"You saw Cooper?"

"Yeah, Sully, he was all right. Jackass went in without Kevlar, though."

Thad grunted. "That's Cooper. And Laney?"

"Bastard whacked her around worse than when we were at the beach. Had more time, I guess," Aidan spat.

Thad rubbed his chin. "Son-of-a-bitch."

Eddy returned from his car. "Sully, I want you oughta here. I know he's your son, but, dammit... I hate to say it, but you know and I know you're not the man you used to be."

"That two-bit thug who shot me didn't shoot me in the head, Eddy. I can still help from out here."

The chief paused, appearing torn. "You have always had an innate feel for how the perpetrator thinks, what his next move would be," he thought out loud. "But on the other hand, you're not much for taking orders. And you are way too personally involved in this case. On the other hand, you had my back for more years than I can count. You got me out of more sticky situations than I care to recall. And, you took a bullet aimed at me. All right. Fine. But McConnahy—" He turned to Aidan. "—as soon as backup arrives, you're on the bus getting the glass taken out of you. Hell, I can see a piece sticking out of your leg right now."

Aidan looked down, unperturbed, and pulled a long shard of glass out of his calf. "I'm fine."

"He's right," Thad said quietly. "If you're hurt, you're no good to Cooper."

Aidan threw the traitor a look, but Thad ignored him. "Besides, you know better than to take a hit just because you're wearing Kevlar." Aidan blinked in surprise. How did he know? "I've seen way too many good men wearing Kevlar to their funeral." The chief nodded, both of them remembering a fellow officer who had his heart stopped by the direct impact of a bullet, though it hadn't breached the protection of his Kevlar. "It doesn't make you no Superman, son." He turned to his former partner, while Aidan chewed on his frustration. "Did you get hold of the principal?"

He nodded. "He said he'd be here in five minutes. Told me a night janitor and one security man should be in there, too."

"And—"

"The S.W.A.T. team is two minutes out."

"Good."

The chief shook his head, regret plain on his face. "I had a bad feeling about all of this when Cooper asked me to be taken off the case."

"He did what? When?"

"He didn't tell you? He came into my office day before yesterday and asked to be taken off the case because he'd developed feelings for Laney Essex. I almost spit out my gum laughing because it reminded me so much of you and Olivia. You know, how you had qualms about dating her after meeting her on the job? After all this time, you told him the story?"

"Nah. Livvy did, though. Yesterday." Thad smiled, clearly proud of his son. "Cooper never said anything about it." He was silent for a moment, but then said with resolve, "All right, Eddy. Let's find a way to get my son and his girl out of there."

CHAPTER THIRTY

Laney and Cooper came to the bottom of a dark and musty staircase. When he glanced back, he could see she had one hand clutching her chest. She was struggling to breathe.

"You all right, Lane?"

She nodded, but then coughed and groaned, hugging herself tighter. "I'm just sore. I can't seem to catch my breath."

"I think you may have some broken ribs," he said, concerned.

She nodded. She jerked her head toward the stairs. "Keep going."

He climbed the stairs, watching his footfalls more as they were nearing the top, not wanting to alert their attacker. As they reached the top of the steps, they heard his voice over the intercom.

"L-la-a-aney."

They froze. His thin, sing-song voice blasted through the vacant hallways of the school. "I thought maybe our time together had taught you something, sweetheart. You can't get away from me," he taunted.

Cooper watched Laney's face and knew the words were burrowing into her brain, wracked with terror for too long. Her expression was hopeless.

"I'll always find you. And that worthless cop of a boyfriend won't be able to save you." His voice contained a seductive edge. "You're mine, Laney. Now and forever." Cooper grasped her arms, forgetting to be gentle.

"Don't listen to him," he hissed urgently. "We're going to make it out of here."

She gazed up into his eyes and he could see she wanted to believe him, but she was too broken.

"Laney. You don't belong to him, dammit! You belong to me." Cooper knew the words sounded stupid. It wasn't like she was some rubber ball on the playground the two of them were fighting over, but he could see he had

THE HEART TEACHES BEST   199

connected with her. He had reached past her misery and given her hope. He drew Laney into his chest and stroked her hair. "You're mine, and we're going to find a way out of this." She nodded, seeming unable to trust her voice.

Cooper cracked the door a little and looked out. What he saw wasn't good. Bertrand was directly across the hall in a glassed-in office. The main office was empty, but in a sectioned-off area, Bertrand stood with his back to them, arms crossed, watching a series of monitors banked high on the opposite wall. It was a room Cooper had visited that morning when he checked in with the security guard to make certain the guard was on his toes, even though, at the time, he believed Steve Bertrand was in custody in some South American jail. He looked up and saw the security camera begin to swing back in their direction. He pulled the door to. The guard had said it took five seconds for the camera to make a complete circuit, and there was one stationed in every hall. He assured Cooper no one would get by him. No one except the designer of the security system.

Steve's voice filled the air again. "Laney...I've got a friend here who wants to talk to you."

A second voice floated into the stairwell with them. It sounded carefree. "Hi, Miss Laney." She tensed. Cooper gave her a questioning look.

"It's the night janitor, Ricky Balentine. He has...special needs." She shook her head. "He has no idea he's even in trouble."

As if he heard her, Bertrand responded, "That's right, we've got Ricky here, and..."

They heard a low grunt. "And Martin, who is not nearly as cooperative."

"Martin O'Neal, the security guard."

"As you can hear, Martin and Ricky are with me and are just fine. For now." His voice turned steely. "You've got fifteen minutes to drag your ass down to the office—no, ten, ten should be long enough—or things are going to get very unpleasant for our boys in here. You think about that. I know you don't want that hanging over your head." There was a loud click, and Cooper, peering through the thinnest crack in the door, saw Bertrand lay the microphone down on the counter. He still watched the monitors as he leaned against the u-shaped top of the desk that circled the room.

Cooper closed the door again. "Is the control pad in the security room?"

She shook her head. "But it might as well be. It's in the closet right next to it."

He cracked the door again to study the situation. Two or three yards. Two or three yards stood between them and a way out. He would have to time it perfectly. He closed the door.

"We're going to need to wait until the camera swings past and run, without making a sound, to that closet."

She nodded.

They waited, crouched behind the door, for the perfect moment. He watched the sweep of the camera, and Steve's back. At the perfect moment, they crept out of their hiding spot and dashed for the closet. What they didn't count on was Ricky Balentine. Ricky spotted Laney mid-trip and bellowed out, "Miss Laney!"

Steve looked up at the monitors first, then swung around and checked the hall behind him. Seeing nothing, he kicked Ricky, who was sitting on the floor with his hands tied. "Shut up," he growled.

Inside the closet, Laney and Cooper heard the exchange. Cooper slid back the door covering the large, glowing keypad that was the control center for the security system. He worried about two things. One, that Steve would be able to hear the beeping of the buttons while he tried to free up the system; and two, if he was successful in opening the locks, would he hear that, and be on them before they could get out.

But his concern was eradicated by the sound of a voice booming over a megaphone. A voice that was usually booming without need of a megaphone. A voice he knew. "Steve Bertrand. This is the Los Angeles Police Department. We'd like to talk to you, son. The phone will be ringing in a moment. If you could pick it up, we can talk."

"Shit," they heard him say. "Get up, Ricky." Someone, presumably Ricky, shuffled to their feet, and then the phone began to ring.

All of this offered excellent coverage for what they were trying to do. *I love you, Dad.*

He typed away. "Laney, we need a code. What would your boss have put in here?"

The ringing next door stopped, but the conversation Thad was having with Steve drowned out their movements.

"Kent?" She thought. "Try Tammy, his wife's name."

Laney read the red letters over his shoulder. PASSWORD DENIED.

Steve spoke into the phone. "Yeah. Well, Cooper the Copper ain't here right now. You see, he and I are playing a little game of hide and seek—"

"Timmy or Timothy, their firstborn." Again, their attempts were rejected.

"—which you are interrupting. I've got things to do."

Steve's voice came through the p.a. again. "Laney. Your time is running out. You know I'm not a nice man."

Cooper watched Laney's eyes and saw her sliding away. It was obvious to him when her torturer took on a certain, threatening tone, he could easily manipulate her emotions. It had become a learned response, learned from the taunts and the blows and the terror that had been her reality before he arrived.

"We know that, don't we sweetheart?" Bertrand spoke low, with a lazy drawl. But it was as if he could see the reaction he pulled out of her, a hint of satisfaction coloring the words.

Laney rubbed her hands over the goose pimples on her arms, like his words were crawling over her skin. She was remembering the way he touched her. The softer, more intimate touches would have been worse than the punches and kicks because they told her he owned her, he could do anything to her and she wouldn't be able to stop him. She started to shake.

Cooper held her by the shoulders, but he could see when he touched her, she was remembering another man's hands, and it killed him. "Stay with me, babe. Don't go back there." He had to give her something to hold on to. "My dad's out there, you heard him. He's gonna help us get out of here, too. And Aidan." She peered up at him, and he saw a light beginning to return.

"You've got five minutes, Laney," the voice said, and then it was silent.

Cooper held her eyes, the deep blue swimming with tears. He ran his hands gently along her arms, hoping she would know it was his touch. "I have to go out there, Lane."

"No!" she shrieked, but then covered her mouth with her own hand. They stilled, listening for a reaction from the other side of the wall, and then she stepped closer. "No, Cooper, you can't. Please!" She shook her head. "You don't know what he'll do to you."

"I can take care of myself."

"No. I c-can't...please." She sobbed.

"Honey, it's the only way. I'll stall him while you work on the code."

"He'll kill you. He will!" She was hysterical now.

"Laney, shh." He lowered his lips to hers to quiet her and her protests were lost in his kiss. When he moved away, his voice was soft and sad. "I have to go."

He turned toward the door, and she screamed. "Wait! Try Muskrats."

"What? Now you're stalling."

"No." She took him by the shoulders and turned him to where a big bumper sticker splashed at a diagonal across the door.

WALTER DAVIS~MIGHTY MUSKRATS RULE!

Accompanying the words was a ridiculous picture of a muskrat, or what he believed to be a muskrat, wielding a sword. He almost laughed. "It's worth a try," he muttered. She clung to him as he typed in eight letters. To his shock, green letters lit the screen. PASSWORD ACCEPTED. "Well, I'll be damned." He switched the system off. Door bolts snapped back throughout the building.

But with a blast, the closet door was kicked in. Laney screamed and cowered against Cooper.

"Too late, cop." Steve brought his arm down, the gun in his hands inches from Cooper's temple. "I hope you already said your goodbyes, 'cause—"

Before he could finish speaking, Laney flew at him, slamming into him full force. They fell into a jumble of mops, buckets and ladders with a loud crash. She flailed her arms and managed to knock the gun, sliding, into some hidden recess of the room. Steve rolled to the side, pushing her off and scrambling to his feet as Cooper bore down on him. The first punch knocked Steve into an electric box with a clang, but he was ready for the next. Grasping his hands together he brought both elbows down on Cooper's shoulders as Cooper landed a shot to the ribs. They fell off balance, and like a cross between slow-motion ballerinas and hockey players, they fell to the floor, vying for position and space to free themselves and to pull back to land harder blows. They fell near Laney, who was slow to get up, her breathing coming more raggedly than before, one arm limp, the other crossed over her abdomen.

Cooper connected squarely with Bertrand's jaw, snapping his head to one side. As he drew his arm away for a second punch, Steve reached up to grab the sides of his head, and viciously headbutted him in the face. Blood seeped from his nose. Steve reached over and clawed his nails into the soft flesh of Laney's calves, ripping through the skin. She squealed in pain, kicking out, but he held on.

"You son-of-a-bitch! Let go of her!" Cooper raked at Steve's hands to dislodge them, and Steve took the opportunity offered by his moment of distraction to throw him off. Before they could react, he scuttled over Laney and out the door.

"Stop! Police."

"'That's him!"

There were several confused cries at once and feet pounded down the hallway. Cooper rolled onto his forearms and crawled to where Laney lay, leaning on one elbow, panting. Before he had even reached her, she stretched her hand out to touch his face.

"Are you okay?"

"That's what I was coming over to ask you."

"I'm fine."

"It's all over, babe. Let's get out of here."

They helped each other to their feet. Cooper ducked out of the room first to make sure all was clear, but the action was taking place farther down the hall. They walked, his arm over her shoulders, past the office, where they could see officers untying the roughed-up security guard. Ricky had apparently already been escorted out of the building. They exited through the front door and Laney spotted Aidan sitting on the back bumper of the ambulance with Jenna. His shirt was off and Jenna worked with a tweezers to remove shards of glass embedded in his shoulder. Laney broke from Cooper and ran forward. Hearing her cry, Aidan looked up and stood, as she raced into his arms. He hugged her, lowering his head and closing his eyes. Cooper ambled up behind her, smiling broadly despite the streak of blood on his face and hands.

"I'm sorry. I'm sorry!" Laney sobbed.

Aidan drew away, pushing her hair back and then holding her face to peer into her eyes. "What for?" She was trembling from head to toe. "I'm okay, come here." He brought her over to the ambulance and helped her to sit next to Jenna, but she wouldn't let go of him.

Cooper looked at Jenna. "I think she has some broken ribs."

Jenna's partner, who had been standing nearby, interjected. "We need to sedate her and take her to the hospital."

"No." Laney's head snapped up, her eyes wild. "I'm not going until they have him."

Someone gripped Cooper's shoulder. "You all right, son?"

Cooper smiled, clasping his dad's broad hand. "Yes, sir."

Thad grabbed his son up in a bear hug, thumping him on the back. "Good, good." He released him and crossed to crouch in front of Laney, taking her hands. "What about you, honey? You doing all right?"

Laney nodded and sniffed.

Sully looked up at Jenna. "I think we need to let these good people have a look at you, sweetheart." He rubbed her arm, trying to calm and coax her into being more cooperative with the EMTs.

"Okay," she said. "But no drugs and no hospital until they have Steve, okay?"

Thad wouldn't budge. "We'll see what they say after they have examined you."

"Let's get her in the rig so she can have more privacy," Jenna's partner suggested.

"Can Cooper come in?"

The big EMT looked down into her shell-shocked eyes. "Yeah, sure." People moved so she could be helped inside, followed by Cooper.

Jenna gave Aidan a quick kiss, admonishing him sternly. "I'll finish with you when I'm done in here."

"Okay, okay," Aidan laughed.

Once they got her into the ambulance and lying down, it became evident Laney was really struggling to breathe. When Jenna pulled up her shirt and saw the mass of bruising on her left side, she told Cooper, "We've got to get her in. She could have internal injuries."

He nodded. "Okay." He moved up to speak to her. Her eyes were closed now and she moaned as he came closer. Jenna's partner sat across from her, having already hooked up an IV, with a syringe held ready. "Lane?" She didn't respond, only moaned more and moved her head from side to side in an agitated manner. "Lane? We've got to take you into the hospital. I'm sorry, honey." She still didn't react, her eyes remained shut, her face creased with pain. He nodded at the EMT and Ty injected the IV. Seconds later, she became still and silent, her face pale, lips ashen, giving in to her body's cry for rest. He kissed her on the forehead as Jenna strapped her in for the ride.

"I want you and Aidan to be checked out, too. Get someone to bring you over."

Cooper looked reluctantly at Laney, holding her hand. "Will she wake up?"

Jenna shook her head. "And even if she did, chances are she wouldn't even know who you were. Ty gave her some pretty heavy duty stuff. She's going to be okay now, Cooper," Jenna added with a reassuring smile. He nodded and brushed his busted lips over Laney's hand one last time before leaving the vehicle. Jenna climbed out, too. Cooper watched as she turned to Aidan, grabbing him around the waist and kissing him passionately.

"What was that for?" he said, with a goofy, satisfied smile.

"I don't like patching my friends up," she said, her face serious. "And I don't like patching my lovers up. And I certainly don't like patching up the man who has become so much more to me than that."

Aidan couldn't hide his delight and surprise. "Well, you better quit picking up EMT shifts then, because I tend to get banged up a lot."

"Oh!" she screamed, frustrated. She gave him a jab in an uninjured part of his chest.

He brushed her long, dark hair back, becoming solemn. "I love you, too, babe," he said huskily. Cooper knew what a big deal it was for him to say those words.

"Hey!" he yelled. They turned.

"Could you two cut it out? My woman needs a doctor."

"Yeah, yeah," Aidan said as he moved to close the doors of the ambulance. He glanced in. Laney lay on the gurney, pale and beaten. His smile faded as he looked at her. He swallowed as Jenna's partner looked up. "Take care of her, Ty."

"Done deal, Aidan." Ty nodded, and then turned back to his patient.

Aidan closed the door, and escorted Jenna to the front. Cooper walked over and the two stood side-by-side, watching it roll away. "I'm driving," Aidan announced.

"Then get going," Cooper responded as they bolted to the car. He waved at his dad as they drove away. Sully smiled back at his son, and continued to lead the S.W.A.T. team.

CHAPTER THIRTY-ONE

The months rolled past and Laney's ribs healed enough to go skiing over spring break in Aspen with Cooper, and Aidan and Jenna, who were now engaged. The doctor had explained to Cooper, the first day in the hospital, the reason Laney had trouble breathing. Three consecutive ribs had been broken. Those bones support the lungs, he'd told her, and when that big of a section was weakened, the lungs had trouble expanding correctly. There wasn't much to be done about it other than get the rest the body needed to heal.

Laney agreed to take a week off, but spent those first several days restless, as Steve Bertrand had somehow managed to elude the police at the high school and disappear. The S.W.A.T. team wasn't in place when he made his break and he had the advantage of knowing the building better. But, before the week was out, they received a call telling them Steve's body had been found in his car at the beach. He had driven to the water's edge, put a gun to his head and taken his own life. Cooper hadn't had the heart to tell Laney about the blood-splattered note left on the passenger side front seat, which simply read, "I'm sorry, Laney."

All the same, she had fallen into a strange funk, feeling guilty, to Cooper's consternation, for Steve's choosing to commit suicide. It confounded him that the man who still haunted her dreams was able to claim her daylight hours as well. But all the people who had come to love Laney, his parents and brothers and sisters, Aidan and Jenna, all of them took turns looking in on her and trying to keep her mind off the torturous hours she had spent as a victim to Steve's fractured soul.

But, strangely enough, it was returning to the room, the room where she had been held captive and beaten, the room where they had to wipe her blood from the floors and walls, it was there she started to make her recovery by reclaiming herself. Her students were understanding and patient with her when she would sometimes space out in the middle of speaking to them, and take on a stricken look. They would ask her a question to snap her back to the old Ms. Essex, and after a while those moments became few and far between.

Now, as he looked at her upturned face at the top of the ski slope, the sun shining on the beautiful, blond hair projecting out from the bottom of her stocking cap, Cooper knew she had turned a corner. He hadn't seen her blank out all day, it had been nothing but smiles and sunshine, and his heart leapt with the promise of a new beginning for them. She pulled her ski goggles up onto the top of her multi-colored cap and squinted up at him, the snowflakes sticking to her eyelashes as she spoke, her cheeks rosy from the cold. "What are you thinking about?" she asked, grabbing him around the middle clumsily with her huge, gloved hands.

He bent and kissed her. "About how lucky I am."

She sighed. "Thank you for bringing me here."

"It's your mom's 'quaint, little cabin.'"

Laney smiled, perhaps thinking about the expansive lodge snuggled into the side of a mountain they would be returning to later in the afternoon. Cooper was thinking, himself, about how fantastic it would be to take her back to the room they had all dubbed, "The Love Grotto," a hot tub surrounded by rock, stuck in a nook in the wall.

"Yes, but it was you who made me leave all the research papers behind and come up here to spend time together, and I can't ever remember a time when I've felt happier to be freezing my tush off."

Cooper rubbed her rear. "But it's such a nice, frozen tush. Did I tell you I think you make the cutest little snow bunny?"

She smiled. "A couple of times." She looked up now, in the way that always had his heart skipping a beat. "But I was more interested in you showing me."

"Mmm," he murmured, pressing his lips to her impossibly warm ones. "Last one down pours the wine?"

"Hey, you two losers!" Jenna shouted as she whizzed by, the sleek, black shape of Aidan following in her tracks.

"Winner gets 'The Grotto,'" he called.

Cooper did a hop to free his skis from Laney's and planted his poles. "I'll wait for you at the bottom."

Laney laughed, pushing off herself as she pulled her goggles back down. "We'll see about that."

COOPER DECIDED DRESSING in layers was as hot as seeing Laney in something skimpy, even with all that glistening skin to tempt his eyes. As he slid his hands under the thin, ribbed turtleneck sweater clinging to her and felt the silky flesh beneath, he concluded peeling off her clothes to discover the pleasures that lie hidden was just as much of a turn on. Like a boy unwrapping his presents on Christmas morning, he pulled off each piece, dumping them on the floor with little ceremony. He released her breasts from the confines of her lacy black bra, caressing them while he contemplated the perfection that was a woman's body. He let his hands skim down over her flat stomach, around her luscious hips, to slip beneath the back of her jeans and cup her there. She did a hop and wrapped her legs around his waist while he carried her to the bed and then lost himself to her.

When they woke up later, naked, under the thick covers of a white down comforter, a fire still roaring in the small fireplace of their room, they relished the pleasure of making love in the middle of the day without anyone being the wiser. Except maybe Jenna and Aidan, who had seen them coming in before slinking off to "The Love Grotto." And since they were probably doing the same thing, they wouldn't be standing in judgment.

Cooper and Laney got up and cooked a fabulous pasta dinner for all, working in tandem in the enormous kitchen. They spent the evening in front of a huge fire while a storm raged outside, playing cards and laughing into the wee hours, before parting and going to their separate wings of the house, creeping down dark hallways over cold wood floors, to the welcoming warmth of their bedrooms.

The next day, the men dug them out while the women cooked a brunch that would have fed an army. Before they left, they got into the mother of all snowball fights, where Aidan and Laney became a team, discovering a natural fort/bunker offering them advantage over Cooper and Jenna. At one point, as they lay, laughing, behind the shelter of their snow walls, waiting for a sneak attack waged by Cooper and Jenna, Laney looked over and said, "Aidan, you know I love you, right? I mean, not like Jenna loves you, but—"

"Yes, you nut." He lifted her chilly, mittened hands to his lips. "And I love you, too."

"I've never thanked you for everything. For...helping us to get out of that school alive. For being there the first couple of weeks afterward..."

Aidan seemed touched. "You know I'd do anything for you guys."

"I know, and I love you for it. Just thought I should tell you." She smiled at him. "Now, what do you say we take those two losers out?"

He smiled conspiratorially. "I'll follow your lead."

The pair charged out of their cover, surprising Cooper and Jenna, who were trying to erect some form of protection themselves, barreling through their snow walls and tackling their respective lovers, rolling around in the snow until a hot chocolate break was called for.

THEY HAD BEEN BACK from the mountains for a week. Laney sat in bed, reading papers, her red pen poised to either make corrections, or praise good work. Cooper was watching ESPN, rubbing Laney's feet as he lay on his stomach, finding out why a former Trojan football star had been arrested in Mexico.

"You ready to go to sleep, babe?" Laney asked.

"Sure." He hunted up the remote and snapped the TV off while she shuffled papers and returned them to her briefcase. She pulled the chain on the bedside lamp and slid down beneath the covers as he bounced his way to the top of the bed.

He climbed under the sheets and rolled on his side to pull her close, his arms wrapped around her. It felt so good, so right, being next to her. Ever since their trip to the mountains, however, he'd become dissatisfied with their current arrangement. Every night they would go to sleep together, but sometime during the night, one of them would have to leave. They usually wound up over at Cooper's with Aidan and Jenna, so most of the time it was Laney stealing away in the middle of the night to return to her new condo, a pretty place near the school, although Cooper objected to the level of crime in the neighborhood. But having had the pleasure of waking up to her every morning in Aspen, he didn't understand the reasoning behind their current nighttime separation. When pressed, Laney would say something about being a teacher, and setting a good example, but, more and more, Cooper hated waking to an empty bed.

"You're quiet tonight," she said after a while.

"Am I?" he responded noncommittally.

She rolled over in his arms. "Did I do something to make you mad?"

It's not what you did, it's what you're going to do in a few hours. "No, of course not," he responded, kissing her nose, but she seemed to note his hesitation in responding. The two of them were so rarely out of synch, the slightest division felt like a huge chasm to them both.

She returned to her previous position. He loved the way it felt to have his arms around her, offering her safe harbor and warmth. He loved the sound of her breathing next to him in the dark, enjoying that connection even if their legs or hands were barely touching.

After a while, he began to run his hand along her smooth sides in a preamble they both recognized as a precursor to dark pleasures. He glided over her satiny skin, up and down, taking this simple pleasure before demanding more. She stilled in anticipation as he cruised along her hip, his body becoming hard and tense in response. Then he caressed her backside, rubbing and squeezing her flesh alternately, his breathing quickening. He skimmed across her pelvic bone, one finger underneath the waistband of her underwear, his palm traveling across the flatlands of her stomach. And he kept coming, coming, until he slipped beneath the bottom of her bra, feeling the cool, super-soft skin under her full breasts.

Backing out, his exploring rose over the fabric, squeezing her tightly, then, releasing her, coming farther up until he felt silk give way to the mounding flesh. With painstaking slowness, he unbuttoned and removed her denim shirt, which used to be his, but which she had taken to wearing sometimes at night, when grading or watching a movie together. She lifted herself so he could slip it down over her shoulders, kissing them as they were revealed then balling the clothing up to toss it aside.

Cooper touched Laney's chest again as they laid back, sliding down her cleavage until his fingers met, and back up, testing the curves and letting her fill his hands. He outlined the edge of her bra, titillating her, and he felt her tense expectantly. Then, dipping beneath the material, he grazed her nipple. She inhaled sharply and arched, bringing one hand behind his head, running her sharp fingernails over his scalp, becoming tangled in his hair. Cooper jerked down on the apparel to expose her more, circling and squeezing and pinching as she began to moan, pressing into his palm in a movement that told him *more, give me more.* He trailed his lips down her neck and shoulder, the warmth and moisture of his mouth and tongue forcing a moan from her, an exhale of his name saturated with pure need.

Her voice, laced with desire, incited him all the more, and he sunk his teeth into her in a possessive gesture that said, *you're mine now.* Strong and sure, he dropped lower, pulling her pelvis even closer and then pushed her underwear down to the top of her thighs, before diving between her legs. She was almost frantic now, crying out for him and he began to stroke her in lazy, tantalizing circles, before plunging a finger inside. She reached behind her to find him hot and hard as she ran her palm along him.

She turned in his arms and began to kiss hungrily down his torso, as she removed his underwear, her breath warm and moist against his skin, her mouth taking him in, teeth scraping along his flesh, sending his mind hurtling to the brink of his self-control. When she came back up, he rolled with her, rising above so he could tear at her underwear to remove it, enjoying the feel of her calf as he slid the garment down and off her foot. He began to stroke her again, more insistent, pushing into her and watching her face in the glow of the alarm clock as he took her, drove her, over the edge. She shivered, calling out his name as she climaxed, and after, in pleasure, as her body melted back against the sheets.

He kissed her lightly, while she enjoyed her release, rubbing her all over, bending her leg up to feel her feet and calves. He wandered again to her breasts, pulling on the fabric, which had fallen back in place. He brought his mouth down, his tongue beginning to seduce again, flicking, and then suckling, giving her sweet pain with his teeth as she began to moan again and rise with him. When she could take it no longer he drove himself into her, feeling the mini-release as they were at last coupled. He began to move, pulling away to remain teasingly at the periphery, listening to her panting, almost whimpering, wanting more of him. She grabbed his ass, pulling him in and he obliged, plunging into her. He captured her wrists, swinging them over her head, securing them with one hand as he brought his mouth down again to ravage her breast. He sucked and nipped as he brought himself into her again and again, and as they both neared oblivion, he buried his face in her hair.

LANEY COULD HEAR HIS urgency and matched it with her own until he filled her with warmth and light and pleasure, collapsing on top of her, a comforting weight, reminding her of the lead cape worn in the dentist's office to protect patients from harmful rays. He molded to her in similar fashion, her mind filled with the incredible sensations she knew would soon fade away. When he moved to separate from her, she let out a cry of disappointment, but then a hum of pleasure as she caught her breath. She rolled behind him, pressing her breasts against his back, relishing the feel of skin on skin, her arm wrapped beneath his as it crossed over his chest, tucking under his shoulder.

She knew they had melded together when she woke up a few hours later and tearing away from his side was like leaving a part of herself behind. Withdrawing her arm, she rolled over slowly so as not to disturb him. She lifted the sheets a few inches and swung her foot out. Cooper turned over and lunged, grabbing her around the waist and dragging her against him. She laughed as he rose above her, shaking the hair out of his eyes, his chest gorgeous in the moonlight making its way through the slit in the curtains.

His face was solemn. "I don't like you leaving this way."

"Cooper, we've been through this..."

"I don't care. I don't like to feel you pull away from me every time we're together. I don't want to worry about whether or not you got home okay. I want to wake up next to the woman I love with the sun coming in the windows to welcome us to a new day. Dammit, Lane. I want you to marry me."

She laughed in surprise, but then saw he was serious. "Was that supposed to be a marriage proposal?" she said, still laughing a little.

"Yeah, it's supposed to be a marriage proposal. What the hell else would it be?" He sighed, resting his forehead on hers. "Laney, you drive me crazy."

"And that's what you want every day of your life?"

"You know it is. Say you will, Lane." The hint of desperation in his voice undid her.

"I will," she said quietly, smiling up at him.

"You will?"

She nodded, laughter welling up inside.

"Yes!" he hooted, ecstatic.

"Cooper, you'll wake Aidan."

"I don't care," he said, kissing her.

Aidan tore the door open as if there was a fire. He stood in the doorway in his boxers, his hair all over the place. "What the hell's going on?"

"She's going to marry me." Cooper sat and almost pulled the sheets off Laney, who desperately tried to steal them back.

"Cooper!" she yelped.

"No kiddin'?" Aidan said with a sleepy grin.

"Cooper!" Laney continued to yank on the cover, trying to restore some sense of her dignity.

"No kiddin'," Cooper responded.

"Congratulations!"

"Thanks, man."

"Cooper!" Laney shouted.

"Oh, sorry, babe." Cooper shifted to give her more of the sheet. But then he surprised her by jumping on top of her. "So, if you'll excuse us, I'm going to celebrate with my fiancé." He started kissing her.

Laney slapped at him, embarrassed. "Cooper Andrew Sullivan."

"I knew I'd regret telling you my middle name."

Her laughing response was swallowed up in his kiss.

CHAPTER THIRTY-TWO

The next night, they all dined out to celebrate. When they'd finished dinner, they went dancing, reminding Cooper of their first days at Phat Jack's. The couples parted afterward, Jenna and Aidan having taken the next day off work to pack up Jenna's apartment. Her lease was up, so she decided to move in for the few months before their wedding. Cooper chose the scenic route home, pulling over in the hills above L.A. and presenting a bottle of champagne with a flourish.

"What's this?"

"I thought a toast to our future was in order."

"I never knew you were such a romantic," she said, kissing him.

"I guess you just bring it out in me."

Laney laughed with pleasure when he popped the cork. "That was fun. We need to have champagne more often."

That was one of the things he loved about her. She took such pleasure in the simple things in life. She was rich enough to bathe in champagne every night if she wanted to, but she'd told him long ago she liked cheap champagne and cheaper tequila, finding unbroken seashells and board games. Cooper lifted her up onto the hood of the Corvette.

"Ooh." She giggled. "You'll definitely have to drive home, because this stuff will go straight to my head."

"Scoot over," he told her with a smile.

They sat on the hood, lying back against the windshield, the wipers fitting comfortably into the small of their backs. Laney bent an elbow, resting her head in an open palm as she looked up at the stars. She reached up to balance her champagne flute on the roof of the car, and laced fingers through Cooper's. He copied her example, and put his flute up as they enjoyed the still night.

"My gosh. This is so beautiful. This is the one time L.A. looks spectacular, when the night covers all its garishness. It sparkles, mirroring the stars in the sky. There are so many tonight." Cooper turned his head to look at her as she gazed innocently up at the skies.

"There's a shooting star."

Laney, who hadn't even noticed he wasn't even looking at the sky at all as he talked, asked with excitement, "Where, Cooper, where?"

He reached over her, pointing to the western sky. "There." He closed his fist. "Hey, look. I caught one." He opened his hand slowly to show her the ring he had hidden there.

"Oh, my gosh. Cooper. You didn't. I thought you said you didn't have the money right now."

"Well, I sort of lied about that." He slid off the car. "Come here." He positioned her so she was seated with her legs hanging over the side. "I didn't really do this right last night." He kneeled down on one knee. "Laney Cassandra Essex, I love you more than I ever realized I could love anyone. By challenging me to be a better person, you've taught me so many things. You make me laugh. You make me happy. And now it's like my heart beats in time with yours." Cooper took her hand. "There's only one thing that will make what we have together better, and that's if you agree to be with me forever as my wife. I'm giving you a second chance to come to your senses and back out," he added with a nervous laugh. "Will you do me the great honor of becoming my wife?" As he said it, he slid the ring onto her finger. It was simple, but elegant, just like Laney. She jumped off the car and into his arms.

"Yes. A thousand times, yes, Cooper."

She grabbed him and squeezed him so exuberantly he had to laugh. Tears poured down her face.

"I promise, it won't be that bad."

"Oh, you goof," she said, swatting him. "I'm just so happy." She held out her hand to examine her ring in the moonlight. "It's beautiful."

"Jenna, Kenzie and Bree helped me pick it out. It was the only one they all agreed on."

"And the whole star thing...was that your idea? Did you have that all planned out?"

"No. But it was inspired, wasn't it?"

She kissed him. "Totally."

They gazed at the ring on her hand again, imagining it there forever. "We can take it back, though, if it's not what you want..."

"No! No. It's exactly what I dreamed of. It looks like it belongs on the hand of a fairy princess," she bubbled. "Oh, does your mom know?"

"Not yet, I wanted to find some way to break it to her that her favorite son is about to become a married man."

"Let's go tell them now. Oh, wait...it's after eleven. They'll be asleep," she realized with disappointment.

"So? We'll wake them up."

"Are you sure?"

"Sure, I'm sure. It's not every day I get engaged. Come on." He walked her around to her door, but paused before opening it for her. "Laney, we're gonna have a great life together."

"The best," she responded, kissing him once more.

EPILOGUE

Cooper stood in his dress blues at the bar getting his wife a drink. He caught his reflection in the mirror, and it reminded him of his wedding night, almost ten years ago. Except tonight, Laney wasn't wearing white, she was wearing a killer black, floor-length dress and her hair was up in what he heard her call, "a French twist," which he thought sounded like a sexual position he would like to try out later. Not only was the dress incredible, he had personal knowledge underneath that incredible dress Mrs. Sullivan was wearing some very hot garters. She taunted him without mercy at home by waltzing around the bedroom with them on, in her heels, no less, and if he weren't giving a speech tonight, he would have had fun figuring out how those damn things unsnapped. Even now, he was visually undressing his wife in front of a room full of strangers. He looked around. Most of the men were either annoyed with their wives, or oblivious to them. He counted it as a blessing, as he did every night, that he had found such a wonderful woman.

As he waited for their drinks, he recognized the sweet peal of her laughter. He turned to see her standing next to a table where Aidan and Jenna were sitting, one hand on each of their chairs, her head thrown back at something Aidan had said. The diamond earrings he had gotten her for Christmas sparkled in her ears, complementing the diamond shaped of rhinestones in the middle of her dress where it was gathered. She was still as stunning as the day he met her, and they even more happily in love.

A young cadet, fresh out of the academy, approached him. "How are you doing, Lieutenant Sullivan?"

"Good. And you, Nick?"

"I'm not feeling any pain if you know what I mean," he responded, cheerful. He followed his lieutenant's gaze, then leaned against the bar, resting his elbows on top of it. "Your wife is so hot." Cooper turned at the strange comment to give the cadet a look, but the younger man was oblivious. "She's got that whole, cute/sexy thing going, you know what I mean? The whole good girl/bad girl thing's such a turn on." He sighed, and then looked up to catch Cooper's hard stare. "I said too much, didn't I? I mean..." The bartender delivered the drinks and Cooper tipped him and picked up the glasses. The cadet's eyes shifted to Laney again, "It's just...man. When she's around, I find myself stammering and I can't even put a complete sentence together. And that name Laney," he said dreamily. After a beat, he looked over at Cooper again. "Oh, did I say that out loud? My brother says I talk too much."

"Your brother's right," Cooper said dryly, and walked away.

Laney looked up and caught his eye from across the room. She gave him that slow, sweet smile which assured him he would get lucky tonight. In that realm, he was already fortunate. He'd heard the guys talking about getting it once a month from their wives, on a good month. But Laney was the exception to the rule, a woman with a voracious sexual appetite who was always ready to go when he was. In fact, there had been times when he had been thinking of going to sleep, but just the crook of her finger, or a come-hither look in her eyes, and he was like jelly in her hands. This was the duality in Laney that still made him crazy for her. By day, the staid teacher, by night, a wanton hussy, and she was all his. And tonight, with their girls, Chloe and Becca, sleeping over at Grandma and Grandpa's, quite frankly he wasn't even sure why he was still here.

LANEY EYED COOPER SAUNTER across the room, confident he was going to get some action tonight, and if she had any say in the matter, he would. The whole man in uniform thing was really working for him, and, to be truthful, she'd been revved up for him even as she had teased him earlier in the evening, walking around without shame in her stockings and garters with the new bustier which was really, well, boosting. She laughed over her drink, as she brought it up to sip it, thinking about how she had been flirting with him all night. She was a lucky woman, and she knew it. She was the one who was supposed to be the teacher, but Cooper had taught her so much—taught her to love without fear, to stick up for herself, to be comfortable in her own skin. Not only that, but he had also taught her she was a good mother, despite her fears she would turn out like her own. He had taught her how to let go and be a good lover, and how to be a supportive and caring wife. And he had brought her so much happiness, so much happiness.

Cooper brought the drinks to the table. Aidan and Jenna were having an animated discussion about something, but Laney watched him the whole time as he approached. She smiled even bigger when he reached her and handed her a drink. He clinked glasses with her. They both watched each other drink; then, Cooper threw his hand over his wife's shoulder, and pulled her in. He kissed her temple, whispering as he did, "How about making this our last drink, and then I'll take you home, Mrs. Sullivan?"

Laney reached up and straightened a ribbon on his uniform, sliding her long fingernails down his chest in a way that would have his insides singing opera. "I thought you'd never ask." She trailed a fingertip around his lips, while nibbling on her own provocatively.

Cooper raised his glass, and chugged down the rest of his drink. "Well, I'm ready."

"Gee, Officer," she said, still playing with the decorations on his chest, "drinking like that...aren't you afraid if you go home with me your virtue may not remain intact?"

"Lady, you took care of that a long time ago." She laughed low in her throat. "Not that I'm complaining."

"You better not be," she scolded. She turned to give Aidan and Jenna a kiss goodbye. "Good night, guys," she chirped.

"Yeah, good night." Cooper parroted with a goofy grin. He leaned in to Aidan. "I'm getting lucky tonight."

"Congratulations," Aidan said sarcastically.

Jenna leaned forward. "You never know, you play your cards right, and maybe you'll get lucky, too, mister."

"Mmm," he murmured. "You need to hang out with Laney more. She's a good influence on you."

Cooper laughed as Laney gathered her bag.

Jenna hit Aidan on the arm with her clutch. "Finish your drink, sailor, so I can take you home."

He ran his hand up the slit in her dress under the table. "Who's thirsty?" They looked at each other for one intense second, then bolted from the table.

Laney shook her head with a chuckle and slid her hand through Cooper's arm.

They followed their friends out.

NOTE FROM AUTHOR

Thank you for reading THE HEART TEACHES BEST, part of my REAL ROMANCE COLLECTION. I hope you enjoyed it. Now that you've read the book, won't you please consider writing a review? Reviews are one of the best ways readers discover great new books. They don't need to be fancy or long, just a sentence or two honestly describing your opinion of/experience with the book. I would sincerely appreciate it.

Want more from M.J. Schiller?

Page forward for an excerpt from

BETWEEN ROCK AND A HARD PLACE

Rocking Romance Collection

Chapter One

The brass had called Lieutenant Heath McGowan in on the case because it was a splashy, high-profile murder. He knew how to handle VIPs with diplomacy, and still not let them walk all over him. A rare talent, he'd heard, particularly when it was found in one so young. It was a skill he had often been called upon to put into use, as in cases like this one, in which a woman had been murdered in the condominium of the famous rock star, Jasmine Barrett.

The detective flashed his badge at the door of the condo as he crossed the threshold. His partner, rookie detective Adam Cozwell, followed on his heels. Heath was sporting a gray blazer, stretched to the maximum over his upper body, and matching gray pants. Underneath he wore a bright blue shirt with a wide collar that lent his slate-gray eyes a bluish tint, something his brother had teased him about earlier in the evening.

The suit screamed cop so loudly showing his shield at the door had been superfluous, especially since he was acquainted with the uniform posted there. But, regs were regs, and he was trying to set an example for Adam. The opulent condominium was humming with police life, as he'd known it would be. He could feel his pulse begin to beat a little faster with the excitement of a new case. Crime scene technicians were busy doing what they could to record the scene, but had been told to leave things as they were until he arrived. He said a quiet hello to those he knew by name as he passed them and nodded to those he recognized from other crime scenes. The whole time he was taking in details and recording them, an attribute that had earned him the nickname "Hawk" or "Hawkeye." Some guys on the squad would probably be hard-pressed to come up with his given name, but "The Hawk" was known in circles far and wide.

Now his keen eyes took mental note of the plush white carpeting that still had vacuum trails visible in it despite the large amount of traffic that had been in and out. He surveyed and logged in his mind, a list of the expensive looking furniture in neutral colors, along with pricey glass and wrought iron tables. Very few personal items graced the walls and tabletops, though he saw a large black and white print, perhaps an Ansel Adams, hanging on the central wall. It was an interesting shot of bare trees along a walkway lined with empty park benches.

On the large beige couch he spotted her, Jasmine Barrett, or "Jazz," as her fans called her. She did not look at all like her press photos or videos, where she was often clad in scanty clothing with wild, flowing hair and her legendary pouting mouth parted suggestively. Instead, she wore one of those big, fluffy white robes often found in luxury hotels, provided one had the means to stay there. Her hair was not even shoulder length, he was surprised to find. After thinking it over, it made sense she might wear wigs as part of her "image." The color was not a flamboyant blond or red, as he had seen in the past, but instead it showed a rather staid brown color, although it may have still been damp, which probably muted the hue some. In the call she had placed to the precinct, Jasmine Barrett had stated she had been in the shower prior to discovering the body. Some junior officers had chuckled and wolf-whistled at that, for which he felt compelled to chew them out, despite the fact he had some rather steamy fantasies about that famously fabulous body himself on the way over to the scene.

As he watched her, he noticed the slight tremble in her slender hands as she clutched a white coffee cup and then attempted to raise it to her lips. No doubt someone had slipped something in there to calm her down, but her eyes still shone with terror. She alternately glanced around at all the faces surrounding her, and then stared at the empty table in front of her. She lifted her gaze and caught his for a second. Her eyes were an arresting shade of green. And, indeed, he felt like his heart had been cuffed and read its rights for a moment as he peered into them, but then her gaze darted away. He saw anguish and horror and disbelief in her expression, something that never failed to strike him to the core when he met a victim.

"Hawk."

He turned at the sound of the familiar voice.

"Man, am I glad you're here." The speaker slapped Heath on the back, giving Adam a slight nod. Chief of Police Gary Larson was a balding, but physically fit, sixty-three-year-old who had never given up his habitual gum chewing, despite having stopped smoking some years ago. "I'd have handled this myself if it weren't for IAB breathing down my neck on the whole Menendez thing."

Menendez was a fellow policeman who had responded to an incoming call, and discovered his own fiancé being sexually assaulted. He'd killed the suspect with his service revolver. Heath and Adam had been the first arrivals on the scene after shots were fired, and it hadn't been a pretty one. The girl had been found tied to the couples' own bed, badly beaten, her blood splattered everywhere. She had physically recovered from the attack, but now, the pair had decided to put their wedding on hold until the investigation into Menendez's actions played out. Yeah, the chief had his hands full on that one. "Glad to be able to help, Chief."

"Okay, let me bring you up to speed here, Hawk," he said in a rush, obviously wanting to rid himself of the sticky case as soon as possible. "Jasmine Barrett, as you can see." He motioned to the couch, pausing to gaze, with poorly-hidden desire, at the young singer in the robe across the room. Adam caught his eye, raising a brow. The Chief was not being subtle. "She found the vic, a..." he flipped open a worn notebook, "...Patricia Norman, in the back bedroom, Ms. Barrett's room." He gestured in the direction of a hallway. "Scene's a real mess." He sighed, glancing up at the star again. "Poor thing hasn't said but a few words." He shook his head. "Of course with her jackass of an uncle—name's Brody Barrett, by the way—blabbering on and on..."

Heath took in the tall figure to the girl's left, one hand stretched protectively behind the girl. Or, after watching a few minutes, a more accurate assessment might be that the man's arm was stretched possessively around her since he made no move to comfort her in any way. He had a long face with strong lines, dark-gray eyes, and a cleft in his chin. He wore an expensive looking burgundy silk shirt and black, pleated pants, but Heath couldn't help thinking he would look more at home at a horse track. The feeling was so strong he began to wonder if he had seen the guy at one at some point.

"This dude's such a good mouthpiece," the chief was saying now, "he oughta go to law school."

Heath snorted, giving Brody one last, long look as he sat blathering to some uniform. Across from him, seated in a large, cream-colored chair, the officer took down his every word as if trying out for a position in the stenographers' pool.

Police Chief Larson took off down the hallway. "Right this way."

Heath and Adam followed the chief's long strides to the murder scene. The door opened on a wide room that smelled of new paint and blood. A huge round bed was the focal point, with a short, pewter, viny-looking curved footboard, and a much taller headboard made of the same material. In the middle of the bed, the victim's nude body had been posed like some twisted mannequin. The killer had placed her in a seated position, back resting against the headboard, her hands and legs splayed crudely to the sides. Her head was cocked at an angle, held in place by a bright, pink, silk scarf tied around her neck and to one of the rails behind her. Fire engine red lipstick had been smeared around her mouth, and her eyes bulged out of what must have once been a pretty face, but now was a bizarre effigy of sorts. Oddly, her curly blond hair looked immaculate. A white rose, dipped in the blood and dripped over the bedspread, lay at an angle across the bed.

Heath was almost startled when the chief started talking again. "The victim was twenty-six years old. Lived here, down the hall. She was a photographer and personal friend of Ms. Barrett's." Adam made entries in a small notebook he had removed from his pocket. "Ms. Barrett was in the shower. She claims to have heard nothing as does her dipshit of an uncle. There was no sign of forced entry."

The chief broke off as Heath approached the bed, crouching to get a better look at the girl's face. He glanced up and noticed the coroner, a tall, thin dark-skinned woman, standing nearby, jotting her own notes. "Cause of death?" he asked.

"Strangulation." She pointed with her pencil to the victim's chest. "The knife wound happened shortly after death. The blade entered here and then was moved up and down, as if to be certain it hit the heart. But the heart had stopped pumping or the blood splatter would have gone considerably farther. As it is, the blood is focused in one large pool on the mattress. The knife was left on the bed."

Heath noted an area where blood had dripped from the victim onto the lavender comforter in a line, where it appeared the knife had been discarded. It had apparently already been bagged.

"The knife was clean." The coroner stopped and bit the tip of her pencil eraser, eyeing Adam to make sure he was getting everything down. "This was personal. The knife was pushed in so hard the hilt left an impression on her skin."

She waved her pencil in a circle around the wound where he could now make out the marks left by the base of the blade. He stood to gaze at the wall behind the bed, where a set of filmy curtains were draped. The killer had written in blood with large letters at a slant, "JAZZ." The crimson liquid had dripped sickeningly down the wall from the letters.

"After you've gotten everything you need here, pictures, and evidence..." he instructed, not looking away from the gruesome scrawling, "...let's make sure we try to clean this up."

"Yes, sir."

Heath and Adam followed the Chief back out to the front room, Adam still scratching in his notebook. This was the upside of having a rookie with him. He could think without having to be concerned about recording everything. He noted the location of the shower as they passed. As he walked toward Jasmine Barrett, he noticed her position hadn't changed. She still sat, with her legs curled to one side, holding onto her cup like a lifeline. For some reason, his gaze was drawn to her feet. They were pretty, slender and well-groomed. Again he was surprised to find no flash of color on her nails, as he might have expected a rock star to have. Instead, he saw a rich woman's pampered feet; no hangnails there, no jagged edges, simply clean and classy. His gaze followed the soft curve of skin visible where her calves showed, ending with the line of fluffy, white fabric. Her gaze flitted to them as they approached.

Heath reminded himself to be patient with her. If there was one thing he hated, it was spoiled brat, prima donnas. But, spoiled or not, this one had just been through hell, and he could spare her some compassion. He would just have to work on it a little.

"Ms. Barrett...I'd like to introduce you to Detectives Heath McGowan and Adam Cozwell. Detective McGowan is the man I told you about who will be in charge of the investigation. He's the best."

The girl swung her feet down in front of her to shake his hand and hastily set her cup down on a side table, spilling it.

"Dammit, Jasmine!" her uncle cried out.

She tried to stop the flow of the liquid onto the carpeting with her hands.

"Here, I'll get it," he snapped, hopping up off of the couch and heading in the direction of the kitchen. Heath pulled a handkerchief out of his pocket, quickly handing it to her to mop up the spill.

"Oh. Thank you." Her hands shook more violently as she struggled with the gush of what he now recognized as hot chocolate, and, almost without volition, he covered them with his own large hands. Jasmine Barrett looked up and he could see the tears she was struggling to hold back in that sea of green in her eyes. Her hands were so soft. It was like cupping a dove. "Let me help you." He crouched beside the table next to her.

Brody Barrett reentered the room. "Oh, detective. Let me get you a towel. Jasmine," he barked. "Get out of the way!" He climbed over her with a stack of towels, and she shrunk back. Seeing the soaked handkerchief she held, he snatched it with a huff, handing her a towel for her hands. "Let me get you a new handkerchief, detective."

"No. That's not necessary, really." Heath straightened, but then shifted to sit on the corner of the coffee table in front of the couch. He sat in an open, relaxed stance, one knee pointed in Jasmine's direction, one slung carelessly over the other side of the table, facing a chair. He glanced over at Adam who stood posed with pen and notebook. "Ms. Barrett, I'd like to ask you a few questions if you feel like you're up to it and—"

"My niece has been through a horrible ordeal," Brody Barrett interrupted, sounding like a sound bite for the eleven o'clock news. "Besides, she has already answered all of this officer's questions."

"Actually," Heath responded, injecting a hint of coolness, "it seemed as if you were providing many of the answers. I assure you, I will be reading Officer Davis' report, but I have a few questions of my own."

"Uncle Brody," the singer's voice rang out, startling all the men present. "If I can help them catch whoever did this to Trish..."

"As you wish." He arched his eyebrows, staring at her icily before returning to his seat next to her. Jasmine dropped her gaze, looking at her hands as they fidgeted with the ends of her belt, then seemed to purposefully still them, folding them carefully over each other.

"Could you tell me what happened?" Anticipating Brody's interruption, Heath stopped him with a look and added, "In your own words?"

She smoothed out invisible wrinkles in her robe for several seconds before speaking. "I was taking a shower—I had just finished working out—Tr-Trish and I were going to watch a movie—" Her voice caught and Heath watched as her fists clenched in her lap. "I came out...t-to change. I took an extra-long shower. I had a sore neck from a show...oh, my God!" She lifted her face and he could see her come to some sort of epiphany. "If I had come out earlier, maybe I could have stopped him. Maybe I could have fought him off...or called the police or something." She became nearly hysterical.

"Detective..." Brody placed his arm around his niece, gripping her shoulder. Again Heath saw it more as a restraint than a comfort. "My niece needs to get some sleep."

"Sleep?" she said weakly. "I c-can't sleep. How could I sleep?" She sounded confused.

"We'll get you something to sleep, Jazz."

"I don't want to sleep."

"Detective, as you can see, she really is no help to you in her condition."

"All right," he admitted. "The questions can wait until morning. I'll read Officer Davis' report in the meantime." He reached out to squeeze Jasmine's hand. "I am sorry for your loss, ma'am."

She nodded as he rose to leave, seeming unable to trust her voice. Brody stood, shaking hands with the Chief.

"The crime scene people will probably be here for another couple of hours. I'm sorry for the inconvenience, but some of the evidence taking is very time sensitive—"

Heath tuned the conversation out while sneaking another look at the girl. She sat as if in a daze, oblivious to all the activity around her, wearing that broken look many victims displayed, like all the neurons in her brain were pinging around, unable to connect and make sense of anything. He felt sorry for her. *Hell, her world is usually filled with manicurist appointments and*

Caramel Latte Frappuccino's, or whatever—not friends murdered in her own bed. He half wished she would peer up again and catch his eye so he could give her a reassuring smile, but she didn't. She looked small and lost, set adrift on the ocean of the couch.

"—but if you can't reach Lieutenant McGowan or Cozwell for some reason, feel free to call me. We will keep a uniformed policeman posted until such time as Lieutenant McGowan tells you otherwise."

Heath nodded and all of the men shook hands. He wondered if he should say anything else to Jasmine Barrett, but decided that in her state, she probably wouldn't hear him anyway. The Chief wanted to give the crime scene people some final instructions, so he and Adam walked out on their own. They were halfway down the hall when he heard the door open behind him and the sound of someone running in his direction. He turned to see Jasmine Barrett rushing toward him. She put a hand on his arm.

"You'll find him, won't you?" she asked frantically, grasping at the top of her robe to hold it together. "You'll find whoever did this to Tricia?" She gazed up at him with such stark desperation in her eyes he was speechless for a second.

Her uncle rushed out the door after her. "Jasmine!"

As Heath peered down into her eyes without speaking, he felt an unfamiliar tug on his heart.

"Jasmine! I'm sorry, detective." Brody grabbed her by the shoulders. "You need to leave the man alone," he sniped, but then, seeming to notice the look of disapproval, bordering on anger, in Heath's eyes, he changed his tone. "Come on, darling, now. Let's go back inside." He shuffled her toward the door. At the threshold she peeked back at Heath one more time before disappearing into her condo.

Purchase

BETWEEN ROCK AND A HARD PLACE

at most online retailers.

ALSO FROM M.J. SCHILLER

ROMANTIC REALMS COLLECTION:
TAKEN BY STORM
AN UNCOMMON LOVE
LEAP INTO THE KNIGHT
LADY OF THE KNIGHT
A KNIGHT TO REMEMBER

ROCKING ROMANCE COLLECTION:
TRAPPED UNDER ICE
ABANDON ALL HOPE
BETWEEN ROCK AND A HARD PLACE
ROCK ME, GENTLY
MIDNIGHT MELODY

LOVE AND CHAOS SERIES:
ROCKED BY GRACE
ROCKED BY LOVE
ROCK IT TO THE MOON
ROCK OF SALVATION (Coming soon!)

REAL ROMANCE COLLECTION:
UPON A MIDNIGHT CLEAR
THE HEART TEACHES BEST
DAMAGE DONE
BLACKOUT
HOMETOWN HEARTACHE
TAKE A CHANCE ON ME

DEVILISH DIVAS SERIES:
TO HELL IN A COACH BAG
DAMNED IF I DO
THE DEVIL YOU KNOW
SATAN, LINE ONE
PITCHFORK IN THE ROAD
SIN WORTH THE PENANCE
HELL HATH NO FURY

ABOUT THE AUTHOR

Bestselling author M.J. Schiller is a retired lunch lady/romance-romantic suspense writer. She enjoys writing novels whose characters include rock stars, desert princes, teachers, futuristic Knights, construction workers, cops, and a wide variety of others. In her mind everybody has a romance. She is the mother of a twenty-seven-year-old and three twenty-five-year-olds. That's right, triplets! So having recently taught four children to drive, she likes to escape from life on occasion by pretending to be a rock star at karaoke. However...you won't be seeing her name on any record labels soon.

www.ingramcontent.com/pod-product-compliance
Lightning Source LLC
Chambersburg PA
CBHW071152170626
46809CB00002B/870